obsession

EVA MARKS

A Note from the Author

Obsession is a steamy book, containing explicit, disturbing and graphic scenes and kinks intended for mature audiences only.

Trigger Warnings

Dad's best friend, sexual acts with parts that should have been attached to someone (not performed on the MCs), age gap, stalker, hitman and serial unaliver wearing a mask who's also possessive-obsessive, untouched heroine, red body fluid (a lot of it in various functions), graphic description of people being chopped and subsequently, will no longer breathe, sex next to said nonbreathers, dubcon, Daddy kink, breeding kink, inserting the whole fist into you-know-where, sharp objects play, a very dirty use of a foreign object, bondage, praise and degradation, dirty talking hero, spitting, butt play, self pleasuring, touch her and you'll be torn to little pieces, the heroine and hero lost her parents. HEA guaranteed. No cheating.

To those who whispered, "Yes" to the question "Do you like scary movies?"
Your Ghostface is coming. You just wait.

About the Book

I obsess over her. Protect her. And when she needs me, I'd kill for her. Soon she'll see that. So will her enemies...

My goddaughter is *everything* to me.

I was her dad's best friend, which means I have *no* business wanting her the way I do. She's too sweet, too innocent for someone like me. So, I walked away after her parents died. But I didn't go far.

I stalked her from the shadows, and it's a good thing I did. That's how I found out her so-called friends plan to rob her—of her virginity *and* her inheritance—before killing her. They won't get the chance.
Every one of them is about to face this masked serial killer for the first—and last—time. I'll take them down one by one.

Because no one touches what's mine. And make no mistake...
Darlene Pierce is *mine.*

PROLOGUE

Vaughn

Two and a half years ago

IT'S BEEN TOO long since I've stalked Darlene or turned on my cameras for over a minute to look after her and her well-being.

Two weeks and three days, to be exact.

But work doesn't care about whether you're responsible for your eighteen-year-old goddaughter or not. Whether you're a thirty-six-year-old man in love with her or not.

Even more so, considering my two career choices.

In Fisher & Atkins—the small and mostly unknown criminal law firm that I call my *day job* on top of being my cover for my other operations—I got swamped with a bunch of new and old cases.

There was no one else available, really. Capri, one of the numbered associates working on my team, delivered a month earlier than expected. When her cases dropped on my desk, another two new clients accused of murders were added to my already growing workload.

Then there's my night gig—aka my stress reliever. Killing people for money.

As a hitman, I clear the streets of filth, while also reducing my urge to slaughter on impulse. In return, I'm paid in cryptocurrency I use as my goddaughter's anonymous sponsor.

Since I haven't been able to, nor will I ever, say no to a hit-job—this shit is better than my nonexistent sex life—I have more on my hands than usual.

Yes, I, Vaughn Grimm, am proud to be the one who kills people for money, but only after I make sure they're the bad guys.

I murdered a pedophile the cops couldn't frame. To be the one to end a mobster who killed a little girl to get to her father. I thoroughly enjoyed slashing the throat of the woman who blackmailed one of Chicago's finest with pictures of him being pegged by her "consensually" when, in reality, she drugged and raped him.

I'm not sorry about any of those lowlife assholes. Someone had to make them disappear.

And yes, I don't miss the irony that I might be one of Atkins's clients one of these days if I'm not careful.

I am who I am. I kill the guilty, and I thoroughly enjoy it, along with stalking and shielding Darlene from the outside world.

Usually.

Which brings me to my current predicament.

For the bloody life of me, I haven't been able to stay awake to keep an eye on my eighteen-year-old goddaughter like I should. Because for over two weeks, I've wanted to—no, *needed*—to stalk Darlene and couldn't.

Until now. I delegated a few cases to my associates. Filled my cup concerning my gorier proclivities. I'm done with anything other than my black-haired obsession.

As I lounge in my living room on a Sunday after a full night's sleep, I'm setting up the scene to start watching her. Not in the way her late father Eric asked me to, but still. I look out for her.

Besides, sometime after her eighteenth birthday, my feelings for her changed. I stopped seeing her as my innocent little raven and started looking at her in a whole other light.

A more depraved, lustful light that has my blood running hotter and redder in my veins.

I watch her through one of the many hidden cameras I installed in her apartment—the one I sponsor anonymously. Watching the wide-eyed, sexy-as-sin, curvy young woman who is *mine*.

Even from afar, even when I don't come near her, call, or text her, she's mine.

My girl.

This gorgeous young woman in her black tank top and shorts, who loosens the knot tying her thick, long hair up, is and forever will be mine.

My eyes cast down the length of her body to the outline of her nipples. They tease me across the screen of my tablet, and my dick gets hard in my sweatpants in response.

Her father. I have to remind myself of him. That stops me from fucking my hand while I watch her.

He's the reason why the last time I talked to her was at her parents' funeral after the car crash, why I've restricted myself to guarding her from afar for the past few months.

The hard-ons I have for her can't be hidden; my hunger to conquer her virgin pussy can't be tamed. This attraction for a woman who not long ago I saw as a girl is taboo, one I shouldn't harbor.

That, and the small issue of being close to an assassin. Don't want her to live in my spare bedroom like she hinted.

My job will always get in the way.

One of my clients could drop by without me being home or have her accidentally eavesdrop on a conversation I really, really prefer she'd never listen in on.

I've always known I couldn't have her here. I didn't want her around me even when her parents were alive and loved having me around as a part of their family.

They liked me. They also liked having the buffer my murderous existence provided between their innocent, only child and the world.

And I protected her. I still do by keeping my distance.

She's better off not being subjected to me. For her own good.

4

But in the privacy of my home, where she's not near me and subjected to the toxicity of my life...That's okay. That's safe.

That's...

Oh, fuck, I almost groan out loud, threading a hand through my shoulder-length black hair.

Without warning, while I'm deep in thought, Darlene slumps and starts sobbing on the second-hand loveseat the previous tenant of the apartment left her.

Not this.

It pains me to know I could've refurbished her whole living room. Hell, I could've bought her a new, much bigger apartment than the one I rented her, if not for the need to remain hidden in the shadows.

My identity as her secret sponsor has to remain just that. Any more funding would raise serious red flags.

Generous, random donors opened their hearts and wallets to the orphan, underprivileged students with 4.0 GPAs who scored *very* high on their SATs all the time. They stayed anonymous while providing a random kid with the basics, offering them an equal opportunity at success.

Giving her the luxuries I wanted her to have would've made her wonder. My smart little thing would've found out it was me in a heartbeat.

My clever, sexy, crying little raven.

Her tears cause my frozen heart to clench, and my dick to grow even harder in tandem.

"I know, baby, I feel you," I tell the screen in my hands.

5

My parents' death—my *biological parents* from England—may have been bloodier and happened when I was far younger than her, but it is another tie that connects us.

That, and my hunger to see her cry.

My earlier near-groan becomes a real grunt now, realizing what comes after she starts tearing up for the parents she lost. It always does these days.

The first time I saw her pleasure herself to stop crying three months ago, she talked to herself, like she needed to explain it to herself.

"I'm going to try this, just so maybe I can forget about them for a few seconds," she said to the space around her, before doing what she's doing now.

Watery streaks of black mascara run down her cheeks; her long eyelashes sparkle with tears. With trembling hands, she pushes her top up to reveal her breasts, playing with her nipple that's already pebbled and aroused.

I lick my bottom lip, imagining my teeth clasping around it and making Darlene scream.

She shoves her shorts and panties down, revealing her bare pussy to my camera, unbeknownst to her.

There's nothing noble about me not respecting her privacy the second time. I can't help it, and I'm even less powerless against joining her. Holding the tablet in one hand, I pull my erect cock out of my sweats, stroking it to the rhythm she rubs her clit.

"That's it, little raven," I encourage her from my place on my couch as I watch her gather her arousal and spread it back up. "Pinch that pretty, swollen clit for Daddy."

Right on cue, our invisible connection manifests itself with her doing just what I said. Her fingers clamp on her nub, her free hand twisting her nipple in what seems a painful tug.

A low, agonized moan escapes her parted lips, her tears slowing the heavier her breaths become. What remains of them has my groin on fire, my deviant mind as hungry as I'll ever be, and a drop of precum wets my thumb.

"I bloody love fucking your cunt." My fist pumps faster, squeezing my dick harder. I don't even spit on myself to lube, wanting to experience Darlene's pain alongside her. "So fucking tight and good, darling."

Her curves are a temptation, an invitation to sink my teeth into her, to suck and lick the broken skin. She's always been beautiful, but the way she's grown, the woman she is now, is unlike anything I've ever witnessed.

It's more than her appearance, more than the girl she's always been. She's darker now, or maybe these are just the first few months I'm finally seeing it. Other than her rough masturbation sessions, there's always a serial killer biography book she borrows from the school's library that has nothing to do with the material in her history major.

She's a lot like me, and yet I can't bring myself to taint her fully with my presence.

I can, however, praise her from my home, hoping that somewhere deep down she hears me.

"My good little girl," I encourage her when she slaps her clit and arches her back. "That's it, that's how you do it."

"Mmm, yes," she moans, throwing one foot to the floor.

Bared and open, I'm seeing the inside of her untouched pussy, and it's so fucking gorgeous I almost come. But not before she finishes. Never before she does.

"Yes, Da—" she starts.

"Say it." My command is harsh and demanding. One she doesn't hear.

I want to curl my fingers around her delicate neck and draw the word out of her. Want to force her to scream *Daddy* into space, to imagine she's calling *me* that as I tear through her little virgin cunt for the first time.

Some days, she does. Today, despite her desperate cries and the repeated torture to her tit, she doesn't complete the word, doesn't breathe the name of her invisible owner.

"Say. It."

My second try isn't successful, either. My little raven keeps saying *yes*, her eyes pinched shut, and her hips buckle from the cushion when her orgasm ripples through her.

Filthy words spill from my mouth when I find my own release, spurting cum on my stomach when I wish I could mark her face with it.

The relief I have is short-lived. Darlene's soft sobs return, the sad repetitive tune eating at my ice-cold heart.

"It'll be better, little raven." I use my clean thumb to caress her face on the screen. "Somehow, someday, I'll make fucking sure that everything will be better for you."

Hypnotized, I keep stalking her walking through the house, washing her hands, then brushing her teeth like the good girl she is.

I don't cut our connection until the very final moment, one that even a murderer like me can't stay immune to.

"'Night, Mom. 'Night, Dad," she whispers under the covers.

I switch the volume up, bringing the tablet an inch from my face to listen to her breathy, almost inaudible voice, when she adds, "Good night, Vaughn, wherever you are."

Only when she's fallen asleep do I get up to clean myself, go to bed, and prepare for a new work week.

For a life that I hate. A life that at the moment, I could never share with her.

CHAPTER ONE

Darlene

Today

"AND THEN WAVERLY, out of freaking everyone, had to show up at the party with the dress I chose to wear that night," Caroline complains to her boyfriend, Lincoln, who sits next to her in the driver seat of his dad's Range Rover. "The new one I got. It's like she's following me or something, I swear."

"A catastrophe, no less." Lincoln's sarcastic tone reaches to the backseats of the car. "Exactly the type of shit first-world nightmares are made of."

My heart aches a little for how he waves Caroline's frustrations away. She's one of my best friends, one of the two girls who noticed me in freshman year. Not too many people paid attention to me back then, or if they did, they tended to ignore me.

It wasn't a big deal. I've always been kind of a recluse. But finding a friend after losing my parents and the only other person I loved felt nice.

So nice, in fact, that I don't mind how the rest still more or less ignore me.

Most of the students who attend Cullop College aren't like me. They're not just rich kids, they're wealthy. Old-money kind of rich.

When they look at me—the five-foot-three outcast who likes wearing all-black old clothes—they see nothing but air.

Most of them. Caroline and Elle, however, do see me.

Actually, they've been nothing but sweet to me. Even when I don't make being my friend easy for them. I usually keep to myself, to my books, to my papers.

When I do talk, I don't have much input unless it's school-related conversations.

Much like I do right now as we're headed to our weekend trip in the woods.

Caroline turns back to the four of us. To Elle, her boyfriend Roy, then me and Lane behind them.

"It's the eighth time this year she's done it." My friend blows a long, blond strand of her hair out of her eye in frustration. "It's totally stalking, right?"

"Yes," I agree dutifully, hoping she won't get any madder and enjoy our time off.

"That bitch," she sneers, poison lacing her words.

Unlike me, Elle's response echoes with much more vehemence.

11

That's how they roll. Very outgoing, vocal, and supportive. They have this my-fucks-are-all-gone attitude, a trait I'm jealous of sometimes.

I do have things to say, I am opinionated. It's just...they're so confident that it's easier for me to hide in their extroverted shadows.

For example, throughout their shopping sprees, I tend to keep to myself. I don't know what's hot or not.

I love my black clothes. That's all I know about fashion.

It's not that I *don't* like what they're wearing. I mean what I say. The fashion choices of these two gorgeous women are always a hit, in my opinion.

Elle's ash-blond hair stands out beautifully against the pastel garments she chooses religiously, while Caroline never fails to pick something with blue in it to make her eyes shine.

Which is why my answer to their, "How do I look?" will forever be "Great."

Then—and this is a painful one—is the partying issue. I tag along unless I have papers to write or tests to prepare for.

Even then, I'm not what you'd call the best party partner.

My eyes are usually glued to the floor. My smile attempts are just that...attempts. Alcohol isn't my thing. I haven't kissed yet, haven't hooked up.

I still go, though, because they're my friends, but I slip out early.

They don't seem to care because they already know that school is my number one priority. I can't afford to slack when I'm there on a scholarship. I've been aiming to follow in my father's footsteps. Becoming a lawyer is everything to me.

I received the acceptance letter earlier than I expected during my junior year, and I'm still not taking my foot off the gas.

This weekend is an exception. This trip is my friends' latest attempt to draw me out of my shell.

They asked me to join them on this trip to Lincoln's family's huge cabin in the woods just outside of Chicago. More like they demanded we celebrate my twenty-first birthday coming this Sunday and the last week before our senior year starts.

Their thoughtfulness warmed my heart.

Besides, being outdoors is my favorite thing after reading.

Without exams or papers to hand in, my answer was an immediate yes.

I've missed camping. Which is also why I don't mind having another single boy join us. One I'm not interested in.

Or...I haven't been. Until now.

And as I mentioned, I'm not interested.

"Don't you just hate it when a bitch steals your look?" Lane whispers to my right.

His sardonic tone and out-of-the-blue comment startles me out of my daydreams.

Except it's not just his words; it's his mouth so close—too close—to my ear. I'm not against people, especially men, coming near me. But, I do have my boundaries.

His breath fanning on my skin when I haven't shown signs of being into him pushes that boundary. Hard.

I don't want to seem rude. I don't want to start an intimate conversation with him, either.

Which makes me all the more thankful when Lincoln chooses that moment to turn up the volume. The Red Hot Chili Peppers's "Give it Away" blurs through the speakers, ruining what would have been an embarrassing moment.

"Umm." I shift on the plush leather seat, squeezing toward the window.

That's the best I can do without coming off as condescending. He's not being mean, and I guess other people probably would like the attention.

I've witnessed how other students, male and female alike, ogle him in class or around campus.

I don't blame them. Lane has that classic good look with his clear blue eyes and full short, brown hair. He always manages to appear messily organized, making girls whisper on drowning their fingers in it.

His six-one, broad-shouldered frame he got from being on the swim team doesn't hurt either.

Not to mention, his clean, all-American exterior matches his kind personality.

He's perfect.

For…other people.

As weird as it sounds, he's not my type. For whatever reason, I'm not attracted to him in the slightest. Never have been.

In fact, I haven't been attracted to *any* man except one in my entire almost twenty-one years.

My dad's best friend, Vaughn.

Besides him, there hasn't been a single boy or man who's infiltrated my thoughts. No one who's sneaked into my dirtiest dreams. Not a single man who's gotten my panties wet, and my clit fluttering with need.

Have never met a single person I called Daddy while slapping, pinching, and rubbing my clit to an orgasm.

There's been no other. He left me three years ago when my parents died, yet he's the only man I've ever wanted.

He's the only one for me.

No one will ever measure up to him.

And it hurts like hell knowing he's gone from my life. That he'd seemed to care, in his uniquely somber way, then poof, vanished.

I shake my head, inwardly talking myself out of living in the past.

Lane is here. Being nice.

The least I can do is be a friend to him and reciprocate.

"My look? Uh, I don't think I hate it?"

"Are you asking or saying?" He chuckles, thankfully returning to his side. "Because I sure don't. Half the time Linc and I wear the same polo. Neither of us cares."

He's being his affable-harmless-self again too, by keeping his voice hushed for Caroline's sake.

Lane's not imposing himself on me. He's making a conversation. Trying to make me smile. I'm just overreacting.

"Answering. Definitely answering." I tug at the hem of my black T-shirt, gazing down at how worn out it is. So are my leggings. When my eyes lift to Lane, I say, "I mean, I can't hate every person who wears black."

"Still, I'll make a point of not wearing black around you. It's your look, after all."

Out of nowhere, his blue eyes roam down my body. I shift in my seat as they linger on my opulent breasts. My cheeks heat as they travel lower to my soft belly, my yoga leggings hugging my curvy thighs before they snap back up.

I would've told him to stop, but fuck, it's gonna cause a scene. The last thing I need is to start everyone's weekend on the wrong foot.

I might be imagining all of it, and all he's doing is…looking.

The half-smile Lane sends my way is the one he uses when he tries to charm a girl. "When you're around me, you'll always shine. You'll always be special, lovely Darlene Pierce."

Nope, nope. I can't have it. I don't want it.

What am I supposed to do? I haven't let a man down in the past. I sure wouldn't want to start now. Not with a guy like him, who's so *nice*.

Argh.

Just say something, Darlene. Say something that won't sound like you're responding to him hitting on you. He'll get the hint. Eventually.

"I…uh, I actually…"

In my peripheral vision, I notice Roy eying us. He's eavesdropping on our conversation.

I blush. My face is burning.

Yet it won't stop me from going ahead and speaking my mind. I'll be attending law school soon enough. I can't keep being this shy person.

Dad and Vaughn had never blushed. That's the kind of lawyer I should aspire to be.

"I don't mind blending in." I clear my throat. "I actually like it."

Lane leans into me again, tucking one of my long, black locks behind my ear. I flinch, though it doesn't put a dent in his charming smile.

I guess my friendly approach hasn't sunk in just yet.

"Darlene." He speaks louder now, ignoring how Roy's blatantly eavesdropping on us. Roy's eyes dance between us and his girlfriend, Elle. "You're the kind of woman who was meant to stand out."

What in the what? I have no idea where all this is coming from. For the three years we've seen each other around campus and in classes, he's barely said hi to me once. Why now? It's not that he's shy or whatever.

Then again, no one knows the real me either. I guess we all have our secrets.

In place of judging and questioning his motives, I reach for my tote bag below my feet for my phone. It's rude to sneak a glance at your messages during a conversation for no reason.

I do it nonetheless, incapable of controlling the need to know how much longer I'll have to endure this very forced proximity.

When I look up, he's still smiling. Still so very *nice*.

So, the one thing I can come up with that won't encourage or offend him is, "Thanks?"

My eyes slide from him to the screen, brightening up by some. The time of arrival should be 11:00 a.m., and it's a quarter till now. At home, I was curious about our destination. I checked out the route online, so I know we're close.

"Asking again?"

Overbearing again?

I gaze past him to the outside world. I watch the city's roads change into an old two-way road in the middle of nowhere. Instead of tall buildings, concrete, and glass, we're surrounded by fields with random houses across large acres. By sunshine and greenery.

Soon there'll be more trees bunched up together. The closest town will be way past us, and shortly after that we should arrive at the wooded area. To Lincoln's parents' cabin in the middle of nowhere.

I'll be safe there, engulfed by my two friends. We'll huddle up together. We could go on girls' breaks by walking around by ourselves. It'll be fun.

Hell, even Caroline will appreciate the reprieve. No one would steal her dress here.

And I'd get the chance to get away from the boys. Mainly, to put some space between Lane and me.

"Darlene?" Lane tilts his head to lock his eyes on mine. He's really tenacious. "Asking or telling?"

"I—"

"She's shy around new people." Elle spins toward me. Her eyebrows are raised, her brown eyes trying to tell me something I'm not that interested in hearing. Like *flirt back.* "You two will have the whole weekend to get to know each other. She'll talk then."

I'm aware of Elle's good intentions. Should appreciate them too. Under any other circumstance.

This isn't me being timid; it's me needing space. An extroverted person wouldn't understand it. It's virtually impossible to explain it to her here, as much as I'm itching to beg for her help.

What should I do?

Thankfully, a miracle happens. Her words satisfy Lane.

He relaxes back in his seat, offering me one last grin as he pushes down his sunglasses and looks out the window.

"I'm not worried about that." I hear him mumble. "Not worried about it at all."

CHAPTER TWO
Darlene

FIFTEEN MINUTES LATER, we make it to the cabin. Our home for the coming weekend.

Everyone gets ready to unfold themselves from Lincoln's truck. I, on the other hand, take a moment to appreciate our surroundings.

Caroline wasn't kidding when she said this cabin in the middle of nowhere is monstrous. This isn't some small, two-bedroom shack; it's an actual massive house.

The cabin must be able to accommodate not six people, but six *families*.

I squint my eyes against the blinding sunlight, taking everything in. Polished wood panels and floor-to-ceiling windows decorate the exterior of the house. I estimate the two extensive floors sprawl over two thousand square feet. Copper-colored tiles make for the roof, and bricks decorate the chimney.

It's beautiful.

From the glimpses of the inside, I'm able to catch a view of the interior design. Although I can't see much, I can already tell they've put a lot of money and effort into it. The sofas, the rugs, the way they have placed the floating tables. Everything about this place screams that it should be featured in a magazine.

I'm not jealous or anything, just appreciative. And maybe trying to focus on the interior design rather than on Lane's weirdly undivided attention. Yeah, that's probably it.

After all, I'm no stranger to impressive, luxurious houses. Even though my family never had much, I've seen how other people live.

Elle or Caroline showed me pictures of their own parents' impressive mansions. I've been to Vaughn's family estate, too for Thanksgiving dinners and his parents' birthdays.

Vaughn. I miss him.

An involuntary sigh rushes past my lips at the memory of him. I'm quick to bite my lower lip before anyone—specifically Lane—starts questioning me again. Or worse, thinks the sound is somehow meant for them.

Elle waves a hand to my side, the movement catching my attention. "Hey, you with us?"

I'm too late. They've noticed. Fuck my life.

"Hi." I twist toward my friend, staring straight at her to avoid eye contact with Lane. "Yeah, sure, I'm here."

"Are you coming or what?" She raises an eyebrow. "Unless you prefer to have a shitty sleep in the car."

"Dude, don't insult Dad's Rover." The sound of a backpack's zipper being closed accompanies Lincoln's shout. "I didn't hear anyone complaining when we drove here. They won't complain about sleeping here, either."

"I don't know about sleeping," Caroline purrs, biting her bottom lip and rubbing her boyfriend's bicep. "But yeah, these leather seats are pretty fucking decent. To lie on."

That's another trait of Caroline I'm envious of.

Her sexuality is such a nonissue for her. She got together with Lincoln a year and a half ago, and I haven't stopped hearing about their sex life ever since. It almost sounds like they've been together for years.

Listening to her being so confident about it is incredibly admirable.

My fantasies have always been some of my best-kept secrets. Dreams where I got over myself, picked up the phone, and called *him*.

I've been delirious with how much I've wanted Vaughn for years. Calling him Daddy in my head, letting him be rough and degrade his little girl all he liked.

In these make-believe scenarios, he'd say *Bend over, my little raven.* His slight British accent—the one he adopted for himself in high school, according to Dad's stories—would caress my ear. Sweeter than a lullaby, hotter than the desert's sun.

Then I'd wake up, and it'd be over.

I'm not Caroline or Elle. I haven't been confident enough to even pick up the phone to call Vaughn after he disappeared. He left me behind, practically deserted me.

What am I supposed to expect if I ever asked him to come back?

Anything other than *absolutely no* doesn't feel plausible at the least.

Ugh, this isn't helping. I have to stop thinking about him. It's been nearly three years that he's been away. Not including my crush on him since I was younger, is three years too long to pine for someone who doesn't give a shit about me.

"Exactly, babe. Real fucking decent." Lincoln opens the driver's door, sparing a glance behind his shoulder in my direction. "Spread out some blankets, and you and Lane can see how *decent* they really are."

My cheeks heat instantly. Everyone stops zipping up their bags and casts their eyes on me. They're waiting, expecting a reply I won't give them.

And even though I don't dare turn to Lane, I feel as though his gaze burns the most.

It's what my nightmares are made of all wrapped up into one—telling Lane I'm not interested and talking openly about my nonexistent sex life.

Could this day get any more mortifying?

There's no help from my friends' direction. Elle won't cut in and take the heat off my back, nor will Caroline.

Saving myself is entirely and utterly up to me.

Avoid eye contact.

Yes. That's it. I bend down and away from everyone's prying gazes, pretending I lost something in my bag.

23

Lincoln responds in mutters which I can't hear that blend with Caroline's chuckle and then the thumping of their footsteps on the ground.

The next time I look up, Elle and Roy are out of the car, Lane right behind them.

Crisis averted.

Relief washes over me, cooling the sweat beads forming on my forehead. But it's not a real one. I know now that telling Lane I'm not interested is a topic I can no longer avoid.

If it were just him who'd wanted us to hook up, or date, or whatever, then maybe I could just ignore him. Thing is, everyone's in on it too.

Soon. I'll get to it soon.

As I jump from the car to the driveway, another decision forms in my head. I don't have to deal with how to tell him no nicely by myself. I should discuss it first with my friends, tell them I don't like Lane like that. To ask how I should let him down easy.

Preferably, in a room far from where the boys will be.

With that comforting plan in mind, I gaze around me and find someone was kind enough to take my small carry-on suitcase out of the trunk. I smile to myself, rolling it to where the rest of the group's conversations hum inside the house.

"Calling dibs on the room with the large ass bathtub!" Elle's sneakers thump across the wooden floor of the living room and up the stairs.

Caroline jogs to the bottom of the staircase, grabbing the rail, and tilting her head up. "Not the one with the fireplace, remember?"

"Yeah, yeah." Her voice echoes from upstairs.

Both warmth and nervousness travel through me while watching them. Warmth because it's fun to have them this happy. Anxious since I'm aware the boys will get up there to fill the rooms where their girlfriends are.

Knowing them, they won't waste a second to do it.

I have to talk to them before that happens. But how do I get between them?

Other than Lane, Roy and Lincoln are also a part of the swim team. They've spent most of the past three years practicing, going to the gym, and staying fit for next year. Meaning they haven't had much time for themselves or their girlfriends.

They'll want to have sex, all four of them, not giving me a chance to break them apart, even if it's urgent.

The fact that I'm a virgin doesn't make me blind to the way the world works.

"Warm up that bed for me, Elle." Roy and Lincoln exchange a sly smile. Then the former whispers to the latter, "I'd add, your sweet, round ass too while you're at it, except I brought lube for that."

They laugh and fist-bump each other. Lane doesn't participate in the testosterone party. He heads toward the door that leads to one of the bedrooms on the first floor to our right.

Great, now I can sneak off to the left.

I'm about to. But before I take one step to try to talk to my friends, I notice Caroline stopping halfway up the stairs.

She stands there; only the bottom of her legs is visible to me. My hope is she's about to lay into them about mocking her. Any second now, she'll tell them they can discuss Elle's sex life only as long as she's there and willing to open up about it.

I would've done it if they weren't almost twice my size and far more vocal and aggressive than I'd ever be.

Caroline, though, is able to stand on her own in front of these two. Especially because one of them is her boyfriend.

"Ugh. Boys," she mumbles to herself eventually, rushing up and disappearing from view.

She's right. They *are* boys. Their hormones are on overdrive, forcing them to act just how Mother Nature intended them. They can't help it that they're...crude.

And with Caroline and Elle gone, their attitude might be targeted at me now that the other girls are gone. Staying idle here like a sitting duck is asking them to make me their next target. To continue the icky conversation from the car.

Umm, yeah. Not staying here to find out. No way. They and my friends can go up and have hours of bedroom fun. By themselves.

I bow my head, making myself small and unseen. I traverse past the cozy living room with the wooden furniture, leather armchairs, and fluffy brown-and-gray sectional couches.

My hand hovers above the handle of the only empty room to the left. I'm about to walk in to hide until the campfire we had planned for the evening.

"Hey, Darlene." Lincoln's voice reminds me I'm not as invisible as I hoped to be.

Despite knowing there's no way he's letting me go, I still try. I open the door, hanging on to the handle.

The view of the room soothes me for a few seconds of silence. The entire wall in front of me is one big, paned window overlooking the forest. My eyes wander out there longingly, picturing myself safe after I've closed the door behind me.

It's still morning, and yet it looks dark out there in the woods. The tree trunks and tops of the trees are hunched together, practically concealing the ground, they're so dense. Someone could be hiding there. *I* could be hiding there.

If only.

"Don't run, Darlene." Lincoln's warning reverberates loud, sure, and taunting. "I promise I won't bite."

Like I believe him.

Like I have any other choice.

I spin toward him. His muscles don't scare me. He'll never shove or trip or punch me. At least not while the girls are a shout away.

But there's more to being hurt than just physical pain. His teeth might not bite. His words undoubtedly will.

Unfortunately, I don't have any other choice except to listen to him. Listen and hope Caroline hasn't reached her room yet. That she'll stand up for me in case her boyfriend gets as rude as Roy did toward Elle.

"Yes?" My stomach ties into a million knots, hardening, bracing itself for what's to come.

Roy's glimmering gaze roams over me while he arranges the midnight blue baseball cap over his head, the one that matches his polo shirt. Lincoln takes off his black cap that goes with his black shirt, holding it to the side of his body.

They look like two boys who walked off a magazine. Except they sport an evil glint in their expressions which lowers their appeal significantly.

I wonder how I've missed it all this time.

"We're gonna steal your man here for a while to scour the area." He claps Lane's back, who stepped out of his room to stand next to them. "After that, you'll have him and the backseat of my car all to yourself."

Caroline's laugh rings mockingly down the stairs, pummeling its way through the living room and punching me in the gut.

It feels surreal to have her laughing at *this*. At *me*. We might not be as thick as she and Elle. She might not be the best listener either. She texts most of the time when I try to tell her I miss my parents. And she disappears on me the minute we walk into any college party.

I'm okay with that, it's simply how she is. But I never expected *this*.

I also never, ever, in a million years expected her to add, "Yeah, Dar, you've been clinging onto your virginity for way too long." She peeks from the top of the stairs, her long blond hair hanging down the front of her body. "You don't want to die an old maid surrounded by cats, do you?"

No, she doesn't mean it like that, I convince myself. She hadn't slept well last night, probably still hungover from the party I passed up on.

Then something drags me violently out of the disturbing scene I'm currently stuck in. The embarrassment and need to protect myself take second and third place. The sense of having someone looking at me takes over.

The hairs at the back of my neck prickle. An ominous, looming darkness engulfs me. It's coming from somewhere outside the room, from the direction of the woods. The darkness is cold and menacing, yet it doesn't frighten me.

This *entity*, for lack of a better word, protects me from the pain. It lays a heavy, invisible cloak landing on my shoulders, calling me to join it.

The silenced call baffles me worse than Caroline's behavior. I whip my head toward the window, and my jaw just about drops to the floor.

I'm not hallucinating this.

A shadowy figure looms between two tree trunks several feet away. I'm pretty sure it's a man, a tall one; his figure is wide and looming in the distance. I can't make out his face, but his mere presence sends a blend of ice and fire down my spine nonetheless.

My heart catches in my throat when I realize what he stirs inside me. Whoever's there is the first man after Vaughn who's making my core hot and needy.

29

My nipples tighten, my stomach warms. Arousal dampens my panties.

I'm drawn to him.

Not seeing his face isn't an issue. The possibility of him being a shadow doesn't affect me either. The black metaphorical cloak surrounding him is enough.

He stirs that compelling desire I've only ever had for Vaughn.

How I wish it were him, though. That he's the one stalking me. Loving me.

Maybe it's him coming for me after these three long years.

I want...No. I *need* to go there. I have to.

"Well?" Elle appears out of nowhere on the staircase near Caroline. "Do you? Want to die a virgin?"

"I, uh—" With great difficulty, I tear my eyes from whoever's standing there.

I remember where I am, and with it comes a reckoning. There won't be any explaining to either Caroline or Elle that I'm not into Lane. They and the guys must have shared this plan. One they aim to execute unless I absolutely scream against it.

I'll have to raise my own voice and say no.

Lane, fortunately, doesn't look as eager to either fuck me or taunt me about my virginity anymore. Not at the moment, at least. His hands are stuck deep into his jeans pockets. When I meet his eyes, he gives me a shy smile and shrugs.

He could be faking it to trick me into believing he's after more than sex. But I don't care right now. In fact, I'm not going to overthink it for another minute.

It's been a long drive up here. A long school year, at that.

I could use a few minutes, or maybe even hours, to be by myself.

To be with *him*.

"Have fun outside," I offer them a noncommittal reply, ignoring the "die an old virgin" comment. "See you in the evening."

Before another word is thrown in my direction, I haul my carry-on inside the room behind me, then close and lock the door. I spin and hurry toward the window, hoping to find the creepy, soothing shadow lurking in the woods. To find out if it might be Vaughn.

He's not there.

My lungs deflate as though they've been punctured by a massive needle.

I shake my head at my overactive imagination. I *have* been hallucinating, I'm sure of that now.

This is beyond embarrassing. What a pathetic little girl I must be to still long for and imagine shadows of a man who doesn't give a shit about me.

Hanging my head low, I draw back the curtains and put on my AirPods.

The song "Somewhere I Belong" by Linkin Park is the one that brings me the most comfort, so I play that. With the music in my ears, I slump on the bed and let my eyes drift shut.

Finally, I'm carried to the nap my body's been craving for months.

CHAPTER THREE

Vaughn

THESE PATHETIC, LOWLIFE *scums of the earth.*

Pure and unadulterated hatred courses through my veins, burning fire where ice cold tends to flow.

Flames eat their way through my blood as I slip into the woods on this wretched late morning. They kindle the heat beneath my skin to a lava-hot temperature.

My flesh is seared from them by the time I settle in my campsite. I ignore the need to stab someone with a knife and instead put on my mask. Then I start arranging my gear for this Friday evening.

But the loathing doesn't leave. It lingers there, festering.

I can't stop thinking about how they talked to Darlene. About what they plan on doing to her. How they plan to kill her for something as trivial as her money.

My fury latches on my every pore, poisoning my brain. Making me insanely murderous and hungry for their blood.

They think they're all high and mighty. And proper. Proper my arse.

Maybe they are around their mommies and daddies. At the dinner table. In social settings. Much like the other spoiled brats I've met throughout my childhood and teenage years.

Angels next to their parents, the spawns of Satan everywhere else.

Millions and billions in the bank could buy them fancy cars, diamonds, clothes, and whatnot.

What it can't buy a person, is a conscience.

Decades of education in the top establishments in the country won't teach them right from wrong. That people other than themselves actually matter.

I learned that lesson years ago. At the prep school my adoptive parents sent me to in Chicago after I was taken from Boston.

When I arrived at their home at the age of ten—a year after I moved to the US—I was equipped only with the social skills my hardened biological parents taught me.

The kids here rejected me instantly.

Making matters worse, they were jealous of me for skipping two classes. See, street-smart kids—their words, not mine—were supposed to be cast to the sidelines.

To be nothing and stay nothing, no matter what.

And since I was smaller than most in size back then, they had their go at me. Verbally *and* physically. I didn't care. Every punch, every kick, fueled my homicidal tendencies.

Even with a bleeding nose or bruised ribs, I fought back.

The obscenities they threw my way hadn't bothered me either.

But it had pissed off Eric, my little raven's dad. Had it not been for his intervention, the others would've never stopped bullying me.

He was born into money like them, except he loathed their shitty behavior. He was different. And he was more powerful than they were.

He saw through me. Saw the underlying cruelty in my eyes and my growls.

And as soon as we started getting to know each other, I saw him too. And ironically, I liked his good heart.

Eric and later Darlene's mother, Helena, were the only two people I could stand at school. The only two, in my own way, I *loved*.

Which was a miracle I never believed would happen. Not after my parents were murdered. A soul like mine could not attach itself to someone else.

I'm grateful for my adoptive parents, but I don't love them. And I've tried.

A corrupt soul such as mine possesses zero interest in anything other than feeding its own rotten self. I thrive on the worst this world has to offer, and I'm proud of it.

I'm guessing in retrospect, fate opened my heart to the Pierce family.

My damaged moral compass was meant to intertwine with their kind hearts.

To save Darlene.

It's my rotten soul who recognized the evil in Darlene's so-called friends.

These people, Lane included too, are so fucking obvious. So bloody rotten that their hearts are borderline Satanic.

I caught on to that as soon as they began to plan their little demonic plot. Witnessed it with my bare eyes. I've been tailing their group ever since I started suspecting them.

It took a lot of work. I split my time between my two jobs, watching my goddaughter, and stalking them. But I did it.

Because something hadn't sat well with me.

In my book, no one's worthy to come anywhere near Darlene. Unfortunately, I can't murder any person within a ten-mile radius of her. Can't force her into a lonely existence.

Up until Lincoln came along, Darlene hung mostly with the girls. Nothing they'd done seemed that terrible. The three of them had studied together. They went out to parties Darlene wasn't a fan of. They took her out shopping when she *thought* she couldn't afford it.

Although they'd kept their standoffish exterior, it hadn't threatened her. Typical rich and spoiled kids' attitude. Darlene could and had managed.

I had no proof of any wrongdoing. Still, it felt wise to keep my eye on them.

Then, a year and a half ago, Mr. Lincoln Hopkins arrived. Then Roy tagged along and something shifted in the dynamic of the group.

The guys ignored Darlene for the most part. Yet they had no issues whispering her name when she was out of earshot.

Red flags waved all over the place. They became a risk to the goddaughter I'd sworn to protect with my own life.

That was when I started bugging their apartments.

Then I heard them. I saw crimson fucking red when I heard they wanted her dead. I caught them planning to kill her for her inheritance. She didn't and still has no idea about it. They did, though.

And that made her their target.

One can claim stalking everyone in her *friends'* circle was overkill. I don't.

When you love another person with a blazing fire that consumes you day and night, you do everything for them.

I don't give a fuck whether it sounded intense or obsessive.

My obsessions saved her life.

My first instinct was to kill them all on the spot. After all, it's what I do. This is what God or whoever's up there created me for.

Then I thought it through. Doing that would've returned me to square one. Darlene would've been left alone in this world. Again.

She'd hate me for killing them seemingly without reason.

Regardless of the proof I would provide her with, the story might sound crazy to her. Too crazy.

She could've been angry about the plans they'd made. But from there to believing these friends planned to stick a knife through her and hide her body?

She wouldn't have bought it.

People constantly make plans that end up just that, plans.

A kind, compassionate heart such as Darlene's would've liked to believe they were good like her.

She would've blamed me for senseless killings, for my obsession, for ruining her life.

I hated being away from her. I tolerated it, though, knowing she loved me.

Murdering her *friends* would've surely made her hate me. And that I couldn't fathom.

That's why she has to see it for herself. In the end, she'll be stronger for it. She'll understand for herself and learn what differentiates good people from bad. She'll be able to fend for herself.

Darlene will evolve into the queen I've always thought she was. She's been second-guessing her greatness for too long.

No more. For as long as I have her, she'll be fierce and wiser. She *will* love me after this is all well and done.

So, I bided my time. I'd hated it, regardless of how crucial it'd been.

When they finally started talking about how this false twenty-first birthday celebration would be the perfect opportunity to execute their plan, that was my cue to go.

And I'm here, just in time. Came here even before they had, bugged each and every room in the two-story cabin.

I hid in the woods, ready for them when they came.

Then I saw her. I stood there in the woods, horny with the taste of blood on my tongue, and my heavy balls begging for relief. I would've done something about it then too. Fucked my hand while watching Darlene's figure moving in the room she slept in.

Had it not been for those pricks.

They were bullying her, being verbally violent.

They made it clear they had no intention of being subtle this weekend.

I knew they weren't going to kill her right away. Filthy little monsters these kids are, they aren't idiots.

The conclusion I gathered from listening in on their plans was that they'd be smart about it. They'd work hard to make the sex tape seem believable, to have more leverage on her.

They wouldn't blow the cover they've worked hard to maintain by forcing her. Not unless they had to.

If she looked drugged, drunk, or raped, their threat would be a weak one at best. Because they'd know, as much as Darlene would, that releasing it would incriminate them instead of humiliating her.

They'd rather wait.

I'm sure of it.

Eventually, they'd tire of her. She wouldn't give her virginity to someone like Lane.

She wants her *Daddy*. She cried that name too many times while masturbating. While begging for me.

And that Daddy isn't Lane.

That Daddy is me. Which was why I lingered in the woods, hidden in plain sight. To stalk *her*. To relieve the pressure building inside me for days.

I haven't so much as touched myself for a while now. The physical and emotional pain ripped into my soul.

But that has been the cost I had to pay for going off the grid for a full weekend. I had to make it look believable as if I'd stayed at home and worked the entire time.

For the past week and a half, I labored on my workload. I lied to my boss, saying I hadn't and would be pushing through this weekend at home to get it all done.

On Monday morning, I'd have my work completed. I'll talk to my clients and boss, bill the necessary hours, and have the ultimate alibi for my whereabouts.

For all anyone knows, I've been home working.

Chances are slim that anyone would ever suspect these shits were slaughtered by me. Doesn't matter. I have to be careful.

Because when I kill them, I won't kill them by myself. I'm sure of it.

Until then...

I glance at the branches and twigs I collected about an hour before Darlene's group arrived.

The fire I lit from them was supposed to keep me warm this evening. To provide me with light to sharpen my knives for tomorrow.

It will, later though.

It's time to act. To do anything to protect my goddaughter.

"Sorry, twigs, you're gonna have to wait." I stare at the dried pile at my feet, a slow, malicious smirk tugging at the corner of my mouth. "The hunting game starts tonight."

CHAPTER FOUR

Darlene

"DARLENE!" CAROLINE'S SHOUT reverberates past my door after she slams her hand on it three times like she's about to break through it. "Are you coming out sometime soon or what? You can't sleep, or read, or do whatever it is you do in there all day."

She's right.

With a subtle shake of my head to wake me up, I place my e-reader down on the pillow next to me. I've been reading for the past few hours after my nap, trying to avoid Lane for as long as possible.

I promised myself I'd face him by myself, but when push came to shove, I couldn't.

Another reason why I will never stop being a reader. Time flies when my head is buried in my crime books. Getting lost in a dark world that's both interesting in its psyche and—despite it being nonfiction—is miles away from my reality. There's nothing like it.

It's almost as if I'm being transported to a different planet. The cruelty of it sucks me right in, and I get lost in this meditative state it puts me under.

Especially today while my friends were busy making the beds creak upstairs. They started sometime before I opened my eyes at around 1:00 p.m. and have been going at it for hours.

Which wasn't that bad, really. I'm better now, emotionally and physically.

Napping and reading must be my equivalent of fucking, because I feel like myself again. Refreshed and re-centered and with these emotions comes a new realization—I was just overreacting to Caroline's comments and Elle's giggles.

They weren't being obnoxious or bitchy. They weren't ever that way before. Whatever's happened between the three of us must be some kind of misunderstanding.

All of us were tired, and Caroline was hungover. Everything could be explained, and honestly, there was nothing to it. That's why—even now—I don't make a scene, don't yell at her from behind the door. I forgive them instead of being hurt by someone who didn't mean to hurt me in the first place.

They're my Caroline and Elle. And as proof, Caroline's here, asking me to join them.

I'm safe. I'm loved. I can and should wipe what happened this morning from my memory.

"Be right out." I throw my feet off the bed, unzipping my carry-on and pulling out one of my black hoodies.

"The boys started the fire ten minutes ago." She opens the door, walking right inside with Elle behind her.

Both of them are wearing comfy and expensive-looking monochrome sweatpants and sweatshirt outfits. More importantly, both of them are smiling.

Just like I thought, their typical smiles have returned to their faces. There's no sign of the slightly mean one I saw on Caroline this morning.

Yup, this morning was a one-off mistake. They were just tired and sex-deprived. That was that.

They love me like I love them, the only two people I have in this world to call my own. A tiny misunderstanding will never tear down what we have.

"Oh, you should've told me." The warmth of the hoodie as it slides down my body protects me from the burst of wind the open door lets in. "I could've helped set it up."

"You? I mean, they make it look easy on *Survivor*, I guess." Elle leans on the wall facing me, crossing one ankle over the other with one eyebrow raised in question. "I don't see any of us doing it."

Caroline interjects while twirling a blond lock around her finger. "Yeah, Darlene, since when did you become an expert on lighting fires?"

I bite my lower lip, regretting I said anything. I'm not huge on sharing, even when it comes to my closest friends. Thinking about my parents and Vaughn and the wonderful moments that I'll never get back hurts enough as it is.

Talking and sharing my past equals trudging up painful memories that I do my best to keep sealed shut for my own sanity. My friends never pry or ask me about it either. Which works well for me.

Or it worked, past tense. Caroline and Elle's innocent question lifts the dam on those memories in a heartbeat. And with them the pain I've been able to avoid for the last few hours.

My heart heaves in my chest, my mind is swarmed by flashbacks of our family camping trips.

Then, the one that hurts the most resurfaces in my consciousness. It's from one of the days where I experienced genuine happiness followed by the night I experienced my first orgasm.

From the birthday I'd actually been looking forward to celebrating. The one that was just about perfect until I eavesdropped on the words that shattered my soul into a million pieces.

It hurts, but I remember.

That birthday trip was the last trip my parents and I went on together. The last time we spent a whole day and night together. When me, my parents and Vaughn slept in a tent between the trees and under the stars.

We were celebrating my eighteenth birthday. Really celebrating it, not like the one I'm at now where we're just hanging out.

Mom and Dad were singing "Happy Birthday" in the front seat of our beat-up truck on our way to another adventure together. Our old Chevy wasn't anything close to Lincoln's Rover.

It definitely didn't fit Dad's job title as a lawyer at the small family law firm he worked at. We held on to it throughout the years regardless, since we couldn't afford a newer model.

And we loved it. It belonged to us. It took us on the most wonderful camping trips, through woods and forests around the US since flying was too expensive.

Later, given neither of my parents had any insurance policies and I was broke as fuck, I had to sell it. But I don't want to think about it now.

My memories trail back to Vaughn on that day.

While my parents were singing, Vaughn sat silently next to me in his dark jeans and a black, long-sleeved T-shirt. I low-key wanted to laugh at the picture he painted. How he held the string of balloons Mom was intent on hanging on one of the trees in the camp.

I kept my laugh zipped up.

Because he would've asked why I was laughing. That, in turn, would've made me admit that I thought he looked cute. And knowing Vaughn like I did, I knew he'd hate being called that.

My silence paid off. He didn't get upset at me.

He touched me. Vaughn's strong bicep brushed against mine in the car when Dad took a hard turn. Goosebumps ravaged my skin at the touch.

My heart fluttered in my chest hearing him say, "Sorry about that, darling," with his slight British accent.

Despite being told he was a Chicago native, he stuck to that soft accent. I never minded his unexplained obsession with England.

In fact, I fell head-over-heels for that twang he perfected. Truth was, I fell for Vaughn, period.

"Here." Once we made it to the campsite, he offered me his hand after he climbed out of the car.

Being the man of few words he was, that was all he said, and I was supposed to comply. Which I did.

How could I not? How could I miss out on the opportunity to accept the touch I so desperately ached for?

Not to mention how handsome he looked that day, how he slowly shifted into a man *instead of simply being my godfather. How my years' long admiration toward him evolved into a constant craving.*

I had to have been blind not to see it all these years and even more so on that day.

The strong sun above our heads highlighted Vaughn's corded forearms, blood pumping under his accentuated veins. Wind bristled through his shoulder-length black hair. His pitch-black eyes—incredibly dark, despite the sunlight above us—stared at me directly.

To that day, to that very moment, he'd never looked at me that way. Or maybe I imagined it. Saw in him what I wished would be there.

Deep down, I knew that there'd be nothing between us so long as I'd been underage, but now, now it was finally possible. So, yes, I wished for it. More than anything, I wished for him.

I took his hand.

Time stood still. Fuck, my heart stood still.

"Darlene, honey, Vaughn, are you coming?" my mom called from somewhere in the distance, sounding as joyful as she'd

always been. "I'm lighting the candles on your cake, or like Dad calls it, your birthday breakfast."

Her voice eviscerated the stars that had been blurring my vision. Neither she nor Dad would approve of this. In fact, I was certain it would've broken their hearts, having me date the man they trusted enough to title as my godfather.

Anything more than that, and they—and the world— wouldn't hesitate to call him a predator. They'd blame him for it, and I couldn't have that.

My wishes would have to remain tucked inside my dream world, I realized. There was no chance of Vaughn and me being something, ever.

"Thank you," I whispered, as if I weren't supposed to have any contact with him. Not even to help me step down from the truck.

"No worr—" he started. He couldn't finish the sentence, though.

The sincerity in his voice combined with the touch of his palm hit me like a blizzard. Something in his tone and how his thumb landed on the top of my hand had that effect on me.

Making me forget about every reason why we shouldn't be together.

A swift current of electricity ran through my body. My heart beat as though I just ran a hundred miles. I lost it.

I tumbled. And it wasn't a graceful fall like you see in the movies.

Nope.

My dizziness had me flinging myself right into Vaughn's firm chest.

48

The balloons were released immediately. His strong hands gripped both my arms to steady my fall.

Vaughn glowered briefly. Then his eyebrows un-frowned themselves. His black irises became fathomless pools that reminded me of the darkest, most beautiful, yet sinister night.

He wanted me. I could swear he did. My thrumming heart burst at the change in him. An opportunity that maybe, could it be, I wasn't the only one feeling something.

"Happy birthday, little raven." The hoarse quality of his voice should've sent a tremor through me.

Had it not been for the nickname.

The childhood nickname he gave me.

I masked my disappointment by painting a smile on my face.

The wise thing—the thing I would've usually done— would've been to step away.

But I didn't move. I thought, fuck it. Fuck my childhood nickname. Fuck feeling let down. He was still holding me, still engulfing me in the virile scent of the cologne he was wearing.

I didn't want to be away from him, ever.

He wasn't saying anything, though. We stood in comfortable silence until I remembered my parents were waiting for us.

"Thank you," I managed to say.

Then watched him nod, turn, and walk away in the direction my parents must've taken.

"…that and a butt plug, too." I faintly hear Elle in the background.

"Lincoln doesn't like anything other than his cock fucking me back there," Caroline replies, her eyes dreamy.

"He says he needs my hole tight. I don't think he would've lubed it if I hadn't begged him to."

They're both so engrossed in their sex talk that they don't notice me looking at them back and forth. I'd usually listen in. This time, their conversation fades right into what happened later that evening with Vaughn.

After the candles were blown, more songs were sung and the cake was eaten, Mom, Dad, and I sat by the fire. Vaughn had trailed off earlier as he often did.

I loved being just the three of us. But then my mom leaned against Dad's shoulder and he, in turn, rubbed up and down her arm and kissed the top of her head.

They probably didn't mean to make me feel like a third wheel. I didn't care about being one. That wasn't why I got up. It was Vaughn.

"I need to pee," I lied.

"Be careful not to spray Uncle Vaughn," my mom giggled.

"Helena," Dad scolded her, though there was no reproach in his voice.

My lips quirked up at their playfulness, at the perfect parents they were. It was a mental picture I'd saved in my head years after.

I got up, cleaned my hands on my black jeans, and left to wander the woods.

Meandering in the darkness didn't creep me out. I had my parents to thank for it, combined with my fascination with everything dark, which started in my childhood.

Since I could remember, I'd been reading horror books behind my parents' backs, staying up late to catch slasher movies on TV.

No one knew about my secret hobby or the unsolved mysteries and sleuth accounts I followed on Reddit.

By the time I turned eighteen, what should be scary felt like home to me.

I wandered through the familiar darkness, losing myself until I made it to the river. The ripples of the water and tiny cobblestones scrunched beneath my boots stirred me out of my daydreaming.

I must've been a good forty-five minutes from our camp if I made it that far. There was no sign of Vaughn, so I decided it was a good place to turn around and head back.

Except then I became aware he was there.

We had a few feet separating us, yet I saw him. Beneath the starlight on that night, I witnessed everything as I looked at Vaughn's profile.

Naked head to toe, the silver moonlight caressed his bare skin. It accentuated his toned muscles, his damp longish hair.

He was there on his knees at the edge of the river, supported by one hand alone. The other one fisted his bare dick, stroking it furiously.

I didn't think about why he had to do it just then. I was mesmerized.

Water lapped at his strong calves, licked the backs of his feet, drowning out his hand in the sand.

I'd never wanted to be anything more than I wanted to be those drops of water in my entire life.

He'd been the first man I'd ever seen naked in real life. The first I'd seen jerk off, period. And I couldn't look away.

The man I loved, the man I crushed on for forever, he leaned on the ground the way I ached for him to take me. Pumped his hips to a ferocious rhythm that I craved him to thrust in and out of my pussy.

As he growled while thrashing his honed body back and forth, dirty, filthy fantasies took over me. I stepped back so he wouldn't see me, lowering to my knees on the harsh ground behind a medium-sized shrub where I could still watch Vaughn.

I unbuttoned and unzipped my jeans faster than I ever had, slipping my hand beneath the waistband of my cotton panties. My lips were already swollen. My clit grew hard beneath my finger pads, becoming slippery as I drew my arousal up and down my pussy.

Looking at Vaughn's teeth sinking into his bottom lip, I could almost feel them puncturing my own skin.

I'd never rubbed myself, never explored what turned me on or not. Then Vaughn's brutality brought my sexual need right up to the surface; it was so strong that I couldn't stop if I wanted to.

And I didn't.

I got hotter by the second from observing him. He had the fierce aura of a tiger in the wild, fist stroking his cock, his wet hair swinging back and forth, revealing the hunger in his expression.

Vaughn's rawness had me pinching my clit, twisting my nipple with my other hand. I broke the skin of my breast, turning hotter and hotter by the second.

At this desperate point of my first-ever masturbation session, my mind took over my rampant thoughts. I no longer saw just Vaughn over there by the river, I could actually envision the both *of us there—me beneath him on my hands and knees, him towering on top of me.*

During that very lifelike scene, I could almost feel his powerful hand winding in my hair. The girth of his dick would've stretched my walls wider and wider. My face would've been next to his as he'd bite my earlobe.

The both of us would've been illuminated by the silver moon and our black, twisted love.

A desperate sigh almost slipped past my lips. Logic told me it would be forbidden to get caught, that Vaughn—who came out here for privacy—would be infuriated with me.

It should've woken me up from the lust haze I'd been under. Should've had me rearranging my jeans and running back to my parents.

Should've. But it didn't.

What it did was amp up the fire building in me, driving the flames to scorch the already-heated center of my existence. Though I was physically hiding, I completely rendered myself to Vaughn. Taken and consumed, loved through the pain I prayed he'd inflict.

When I came—and I knew it was an orgasm by how my pussy clenched and unclenched uncontrollably, how I couldn't breathe and yet wanted to scream all at once—I spoke his name.

The name my soul wanted to call him.

"Daddy," I whispered as low as I could.

Mentally drained, I dropped to the ground, supported by one hand like Vaughn had, my long hair cascading down my front.

My eyes remained latched on to Vaughn, eating him up until he reached his own climax seconds after mine. I even licked my lips when he released his cum on the sand when his taut chest heaved in exertion.

Worried that he'd find me now that he snapped out of his trance, I hurried to collect myself, rubbing a flower against my palm to remove my arousal scent and getting out of there.

If I'd realized this would've been the last good moment of my life, maybe I would've lingered around longer. Maybe I would've taken the time to bask in my post-orgasmic bliss, given what happened later that night.

When I pretended to be asleep, I eavesdropped on Dad and Vaughn's conversation. I heard Vaughn urging my father to send me to a college far away from the place I called home, Chicago.

It hurt so bad to have to listen to the man I loved telling Dad, he didn't want me around that my brain shut down and forced me to sleep.

But that wasn't the worst of what life had to offer. Less than a month later, a drunk driver crashed into my parents' car while they were on their way to a date night.

Not only did I lose the two most important people in my world. Vaughn left me too, ran off after the funeral.

After that, I barely scraped up enough money to stay in the apartment I grew up in. I had to sell our memories like the truck and other valuables we had until I made it to college.

All. By. Myself.

"Do you think she's awake?" I find Caroline's blue eyes watching me.

"Never mind," Elle groans, her exasperated tone pulling me from the wave of nostalgia, and I realize neither of them are talking about butt plugs anymore. "Tell us about your fire expertise or don't, I don't care. Let's just get out there already."

They turn on their heels and head out, not caring whether I follow them or not.

My brow furrows at her offending comment, all thoughts of Vaughn and my first orgasm suddenly gone out the window. For the first time in forever, I'm a little pissed. They can't talk to me like that.

Once was forgivable, but this is where I put my foot down.

They can't make a habit out of casually throwing insults at me. I don't plan on spending the weekend forgiving them for being horny, drunk, or tired.

I just won't.

"Wait up," I call instead of putting them in their place, quickening my pace to catch up with them.

If I tell them how I feel right now, when I'm emotional and upset, it'll just blow up into a fight. I need to cool down. Then I'll talk to them.

We'll figure this out. We're friends. We love each other.

I just need to lay out the boundaries. Later.

Until that happens, I might as well go out and enjoy a beer myself.

CHAPTER FIVE

Darlene

THE BOYS DIDN'T need my help starting the fire like Elle suggested.

When I asked how they got it up so fast, Lincoln sneered in my face.

This time, unlike before, Caroline didn't let him be a jerk to me. She nudged him, adding a raised eyebrow to let him know she was upset. Her standing up for me melted my heart, and I decided to forego the talk I planned on.

Neither he nor Roy or Lane shared with us what they'd been doing out in the woods earlier. Honestly, I didn't care. At that point, I was hungry and thirsty since I hadn't put anything in my mouth since earlier that morning.

I didn't ask another question, just sat down around the fire next to my friends for a much-needed dinner.

Since then, three hours have passed.

Things are a little different now.

The six of us are seated in a circle around the crackling flames. Crunched beer cans, and one empty bottle of tequila are thrown all over. And no one's talking or laughing anymore.

There's intensity in the air.

Sex as well.

About six feet to my left, Elle and Roy lie on the red plaid blanket. They're a step away from having sex out here in the open.

He's been lying on top of her for I-don't-know how long, holding her behind her thigh as he's grinding into her. I try not to look, but it's kind of difficult with the sounds they're making.

"Take my dick out," Roy growls just when I shift my eyes to the fire.

I could keep ignoring it if I had someone to talk to.

In another life, maybe.

Because it's obviously not happening in this one.

Chancing a glance behind Lane, further to my right, I see Caroline isn't interested in small talk at the moment. My blond friend has her fingers knotted around her boyfriend's neck. Her mouth is glued to his jaw, kissing, licking, and sucking it.

And he's looking at *me*.

He makes my fucking skin crawl. Lincoln's blue eyes glare directly at me. He doesn't pay any attention to Caroline. Doesn't have a sliver of heat that'd hint he's getting off on what she's doing to him.

He's more of a statue than a living human being, his glare apathetic, uncaring. Thoroughly detached and menacing at once.

Yes, I love anything that thrives in the dark. I obsess over shadows, hidden corners of the worst of mankind's souls. I even have a strong and somewhat unhealthy affinity with spiders. I'm not a stranger to it nor does it frighten me most days.

But soulless eyes and lips that curl into a sneer—that scares the living shit out of me. The nothingness, the emptiness of him, delivers a promise of cruelty Lincoln won't hesitate to inflict on me.

For what and why is anyone's guess. And this uncalled-for hatred, disregard, or both toward me, that probably scares me the most.

So bad that I'm rendered speechless under Lincoln's ensnaring glare, afraid that if I look somewhere else, he'll leap on me and rip me in half.

"Hey, are you okay?" Lane asks, his speech a tad slurred.

He breaks the dangerous connection between me and Lincoln further by leaning forward so I have to look at him.

His eyes—contrary to those of his friends—are somewhat dull and unfocused from the amount of alcohol he's consumed throughout the evening. His breath reeks to the point it overcomes the smell of the smoke coming from the fire.

Unfortunately for me, there's another side effect of drinking where Lane's concerned. He's less of the nice boy who sat next to me in Lincoln's Rover, bolder now as he places his hand firmly on my knee.

"Umm," I start.

In college, I witnessed firsthand how unpredictable drunk people could be. That's why I don't slap Lane's unwelcome hand away. I pat it gently, then lift it, and let it fall to Lane's side.

"I'm fine, Lane. Thank you for asking."

"Lincoln, babe, come on, don't you wanna fuck me?" It sounds like Caroline is trying to come off as seductive. Except her speech is more slurred than Lane's, her words garbled and tumbled, one on top of the other.

"Are you sure about that?" Lane waves the hand I just moved from my knee in front of my face. Demanding my attention once more. "You looked kinda spaced out and…"

The rest of his sentence goes on unheard. I angle my head to see around him in an attempt to check on my friend. I'm still wary about Lincoln and the creepy look he gave me, but I love Caroline and I just have to make sure she's okay.

Something in me doesn't trust her boyfriend to look after my drunk friend like he should.

"Please, baby," she coos in his ear, her slender fingers stroking up and down the crotch of Lincoln's jeans.

He doesn't hit her or shove her off him, which is a good thing, I guess. At least it's not a bad one. On the other hand, he doesn't seem to care for her at all. Same as before, he ignores her completely, focusing on me and Lane. On where Lane's fingers creep up on my knee again.

I shuffle to the side, avoiding his touch as politely as I can.

"I need you," Caroline continues to persuade the disinterested Lincoln.

She moves to kneel between his legs, pushing his knees wider apart. Then she crawls closer until she reaches the button of his jeans.

And he says *nothing*.

Only when she places a hand on his chest to try and push him to lie on the blanket does Lincoln react. He slants his upper body to the side to continue to watch Lane and me.

The longer he stares, I grow accustomed to his emotionless stare. And the less unnerving Lincoln becomes, the more annoyed I get.

I mean, seriously, what's so fucking interesting about me and Lane, whom I'm not into in the slightest? And why does he care about that more than his insanely hot girlfriend?

Wild, disgusting theories to answer these questions run through my head while he and I have this silent face-off.

The one reasonable explanation that sticks is that the three boys placed some kind of bet on how fast Lane could get in my pants. How fast he can fuck one of the last virgins on campus like it's some kind of competition.

My stomach heaves, nausea taking over. I push Lane's hand away a third time, more forcefully now at this sudden realization.

"I said I'm fine," I growl through clenched teeth, squinting my eyes at Lincoln.

Lane's words don't even register anymore, though I'm aware he hasn't stopped talking. It's just white background noise as I watch Caroline fumbling with Lincoln's zipper.

I might be timid. Might do my best to avoid conflicts at all costs. But being some sort of entertainment, a joke to these boys—that I won't do. That and watching one of my closest friends being mistreated.

If we're going to be spending another two days here, I need to learn to stand my ground. Otherwise, I'll spend the rest of the time holed up in my room avoiding everyone.

"Enough." He grabs her shoulders, removing her from him and to the side. He pins her with his ominous stare. "You're pathetic, Caroline. So desperate for my cock, you're willing to humiliate yourself like this?"

His abruptness raises my hackles. I see red, and it's not from the flames licking the air of the night. In my peripheral vision, I notice Lane's stopped talking, but his focus remains on me instead of telling off his friend.

He's useless. It's up to me to save her. I call on every brave bone I have in my body to help me out of the comforts of staying in the non-confrontational zone. Caroline, on her good days, would surely do the same for me.

"Hey." I get up to sit on my knees, twisting away from Lane so Lincoln can see I'm addressing him. "Don't talk to her that way."

"Taking lessons from your friend on how to be an annoying bitch, are we?"

His words smack me right in the chest. All those months they've been dating, they've always been a team, a unit. And he's never done anything to me.

I don't get what's come over him, and I really, really, don't appreciate any of it.

"She's not—"

"That's why you've been staring, haven't you?" He sneers at me, then at Caroline, who—to my relief—already stands on her feet and doesn't beg for his affection anymore. "Want to be like her? To learn how to suck a dick like my little Caroline? She does take it pretty well down her throat on her good days, I'll give her that."

I glance to the other side. Roy dry-humps Elle harder than before, the both of them grunt loudly. They're in their own universe, oblivious to the fact that something's not right around our campfire.

"You're such a jerk sometimes, you know that? To me of all people, the one who brought you…" Caroline trails off, patting down her baby-blue sweater. "Fuck this, I need to get some air."

She storms off into the woods. Her long blond hair glimmers under the moonlight until she disappears into the shadows.

I'll chase her soon, right after I scold Lincoln for what a piece of trash he's being. I might've forgiven Caroline for what she said when she was drunk or tired. Hell, I might've let Lincoln's comment slide if it was only about me.

What I won't accept is how he degrades Caroline. There's no excuse for that, to hurt the girl who's been a family to me for the past almost three years. I won't let him.

Seems like the few beers I had made me somewhat different and a lot braver, too.

But Lane speaks faster than I do. "If that's what you wanted all along—"

"Not now." I'm doing my best not to be obnoxious to him, seeing as I'm still not sure what's his part in any of this is.

I stand up, stepping toward Lincoln with Lane quiet behind me and Elle and Roy still deep in…whatever it is they're doing.

The fire, which no one's attended to in the last hour, emanates less heat than before. Doesn't matter. My blood runs hot enough in my veins to warm me inside out.

"If you have something to say to me." My voice falters when I'm confronted up close with Lincoln's steely blue eyes and raised eyebrow. I clear my throat, starting anew. "Then say it to me. Don't be an asshole to someone who loves you like she does. Caroline has been nothing but good to you, and she doesn't deserve it."

"Pristine Miss Phillips is a lot of things." He stays put. It's not just Caroline he couldn't care less about. It's also me who the ice-cold Lincoln blatantly ignores. "None of them can be qualified as *good*. The deep-throating notwithstanding, of course."

"Of course," I mumble, clenching my fists at my sides as anger pummels through me.

The idea to grab a burning log to throw in his face feels painfully tempting. I fight the urge to wrap my hoodie around my fist, pluck one out, and thrust it at Lincoln. To see how detached he can stay after that.

He'd scream, for sure. Be degraded in far worse ways than what he's been doing to Caroline.

Except I can't do that. Can't allow the things I read to take over my life, to be the reason I end up in jail.

Before I say another word, before I adhere to my dark impulses, I shut my mouth. This weekend is supposed to be fun.

It *will* be fun, dammit. Tomorrow, once everyone's back to their senses.

Or at least, what their senses used to be at home. Not what they morphed into during the hour and a half drive into these woods.

I'll find Caroline, and we'll have a sleepover in my room. Tomorrow will be a new, much better day. I'm sure of it.

"I'm going to get Caroline." I shake my head, not waiting for his answer as I head into the woods.

CHAPTER SIX

Vaughn

MY BLOOD RUNS cold in my veins.

My eyes narrow behind my mask.

Each one of my senses is heightened to the point where I can smell the ground beneath me. See through the darkness of the night. Hear the faintest whistle of the wind.

I recognize these signals my body is sending me. Have known them for years, the intense concentration and life force pummeling through me right before a kill.

Except I'm not about to murder anyone at the moment.

I planned on it, expecting one of these kids to wander into the woods at some point tonight. To take them down with my knife, draw the first drop of blood.

I had every intention of discarding what remained of my would-be rightful murder out there for his friends to see. To instill fear in their hearts. To toy with them is just another form of torment I particularly enjoy.

The opportunity was out there for me to grab using both of my gloved hands.

Caroline made it almost too easy, too. Walking out here by herself.

Gripping my butcher's knife tight in my fist, I fantasized about slicing the she-devil's throat. To have her skin part beneath my blade. To listen to her gurgle as her life source gushed down her throat, coating my fingers.

The murderous, vengeful beast in me relished the vivid images.

I waited in the woods, fantasizing about what I'd do to her.

She would've deserved it, the pain, the terror. Her death in exchange for her sins.

Knowing I could play the part of her executioner satisfied me to no end. She was, after all, the woman that had been lying to my little raven for years.

She and her depraved group of friends, led by her boyfriend, thought they could end the life of my goddaughter. For money, when they already have millions.

They want to break free from their asshole parents and start fresh with her millions. With her inheritance.

They chose the wrong girl to pick on. And they'd pay.

Just not as early as I would've liked.

Because said goddaughter had other plans, apparently.

To make me lose my fucking mind with fury.

I couldn't believe my ears when a minute after Caroline stormed off, my Darlene stood up to Mr. Hopkins and defended that scum's honor.

Couldn't she see them for who they were? If not sometime earlier, then their behavior on this trip should've been an eye-opener for this clever young woman.

Yet she hasn't.

She protected this selfish little twat like she was being a true friend to her.

She was that blind to the signs Caroline's throwing around her freely. Not caring about her. Mocking her. Being careless with her feelings.

All of her cruelty is out there for Darlene to see, yet she realizes none of it. It was as if Darlene wanted so badly to believe their friendship and kindness that she ignored the signs.

They tell her they're spawns of Satan, yet she doesn't listen.

Fury doesn't begin to describe what I'm experiencing.

This is *so* unlike the bright woman I've known her to be.

She's proved how clever she is time and again with brilliant report cards during her school days. I've seen it with my bare eyes as I stalked her while she studied in college and landed one A plus after another.

Throughout the years we'd been a part of each other's lives, I'd learned what an intelligent, intricate mind she possessed. Yes, she'd always been too shy to show it, too humble to flaunt it around others. But around me—more or less a family member—she'd let her inner self shine.

Her soul spoke to me, and I never failed to hear her out.

Behind those black, fathomless eyes of hers, I'd seen how smart she was. Anything her father or I explained to her about our law practice or other world affairs, she soaked up like a sponge.

One doesn't have to blabber nonstop to prove they get what you're saying.

My Darlene, this humble soul, simply understood.

I'd been her biggest admirer for years. Before the first impulse to fuck her had flipped my world on its axis, I adored her.

Something about the multiple layers of her personality—the ones that were out in plain view, and the ones only those who looked hard enough saw—captivated me.

She owned me.

The star that shone relentlessly on my black heart. The brilliant little girl who turned into a wise-beyond-her-years woman.

And therein lies my struggle. Or more accurately, why I'm fuming and rescheduling my plan to rid this world of Caroline.

Nothing takes precedence over the much-needed lesson my little raven needs to learn this evening.

With my mask firmly in place, dressed in black from head to toe, I wait for her deep inside the woods. It makes sense she'll walk on the path leading straight from her camp to look for her clueless little friend.

As I mentioned, my Darlene is clever. Perceptive too. She'll figure out on her own that Caroline doesn't have a clue where and how to walk in the wild. She'll understand the stuck-up city girl will probably trudge forward, not taking any turns that'd get her lost.

Darlene wouldn't have been wrong, either.

That was why I had to trick Caroline. I played a recording of a growling wolf on my phone the instant the blond mane of the cunt came into view, chasing her off in the other direction. Away from my secret campsite.

Away from *us*.

But Darlene doesn't know that. And she's coming my way.

"Caroline?"

I'd heard Darlene's voice over the apps I used to track her. From a distance when I stalked her on those nights she was out late.

This close, though, it soothes and cuts through me violently.

I want to drag her into my embrace, though I'm fully aware I can't. I failed her, left her to fend for herself.

Had I been here earlier, none of this would've happened. I could've shown her how duplicitous and cruel the world is. She could've been my dark queen reigning by my side by now.

Instead, I chose to protect her from myself, and here we fucking are.

With me enraged and tethering on the loss of self-control from the need to administer a lesson I should've given her *years* ago.

And it's not from the lack of love or lust. I still want her. Still ache to fuck her boneless. To call her my little raven while my cock is buried deep inside her.

But the harsh side of my personality overrides the soft spot I have for her now.

It demands to do more than teach her. It urges me to punish her for how she stood up for the girl who wants nothing more than to have her dead.

She *must* be disciplined.

I take a step toward her, leaves crunching beneath my boots as I do.

"Caroline?" Her voice shivers, and I can see her crossing her arms over her torso.

She's familiar with the woods. Knows not to be scared of the dark. And yet something about her tells me that she is.

She senses me, even though she doesn't see or hear me.

My dick has never been harder at the connection we form.

In a deliberate, confident stride, I walk up behind Darlene. I wrap one hand around her mouth, the other around her throat so fast she doesn't have a chance to gasp.

I bring my masked lips near her ear as she struggles in my arms. "Hush now."

Her adorable height of five-foot-three makes cradling her in my large six-four frame an easy task. An enjoyable one.

The soft curves of this good girl melt perfectly into the hard muscles of this killer's body.

The ocean scent of her body mist blends with that of the fire they were huddled around earlier. I nearly tear my mask off to sink my nose into her neck to inhale her skin. To bite her, hard.

To have this moment branded in my memory for life.

She brings me back to the present moment, wriggling in my arms and whimpering into my glove. Her struggles, her fear, turn me on harder than ever.

That's when I decide against revealing my identity to her. For the time being.

"There's no use for that. No one's here to save you, darling," I growl in her ear, my voice muffled by my mask.

She mumbles something. Her lips move without forming words against my leather glove.

My cock jerks in reaction to her. My heart, on the other hand, doesn't soften in the slightest.

I squeeze her tender neck while walking the both of us forward toward the nearest tree bark. She stops trying to talk before she even has a chance to slip a word in when her breasts hit the harsh surface of the bark.

My goddaughter goes limp in my arms when I shove the side of her face against the tree.

Then her eyes blink in terror when I shove my cock forcefully between her supple butt cheeks.

Fuck. I've wanted to do that forever. But nothing could've prepared me for how good it'd be in real life. Especially while I'm slightly cutting off her air supply, while I can sense her desperate attempts to breathe beneath my palm.

"I'm not here to harm you." My lips curl to the side. She can't see it, though she sure as fuck can hear it in my voice. "Well, not to kill you, that is."

Every night Darlene cried in misery is embedded in my brain. Every tear she chased by making herself come for an invisible Daddy is a vivid memory I'll always cherish.

That girl isn't here anymore. While I stand here, expecting her to be a fragile and weeping mess, to be boneless and pitiful, she does exactly the opposite.

There's not a single tear leaking down her cheek. She surprises me with her resilience, in how, all of a sudden, she snaps out of her shock and does her best to wriggle out of my hold.

I turn into a livid animal at her fight.

"I will, however, annihilate the other five in your group unless you obey me."

I grind my erection into her over and over, forcing her clit to rub into the tree as a result, being her bearer of pain and pleasure.

I won't rape her. Thing is, she has to fear me. Has to realize I'm the one dominating her now. That's how she'll learn.

"Do we have an understanding?"

"Don't!" she screams into my palm. The one word comes out as loud as the fight burns in her eyes.

Anyone else that faced me with the horrifying mask I put on had been terrified. The gruesome two Xs for eyes and an inhuman black smile creep people out. The dried blood splatters from the people I've executed make grown men cry.

Darlene is no other man or woman. She's the daughter of the relentless billionaire Eric Pierce.

She hasn't been subjected to that part of him, to the man who secretly ran an international law firm with over thirty offices worldwide.

Despite the goodness of his heart, he knew no fear, from anyone.

And she doesn't either. There's no running from his blood that courses through her veins.

"You don't have a third choice." I push myself further onto her, feeling her jaw almost bruising under my hold. "Yes or no. You have five seconds to answer."

Darlene's black gaze is narrowed, angry, glaring at me. She quits trying to escape, nodding once in agreement.

That fierce little woman. Eric's daughter.

I'm impressed for a moment before my anger gets the best of me again.

Once more, Darlene is protecting these monsters.

The vein in my neck throbs, my pulse skyrocketing through the roof.

I bare my teeth behind the mask separating us, the animal inside me roaring harder than ever.

And the last thought I have before I punish her is, *Fuck, how I wish I could control my temper.*

CHAPTER SEVEN

Darlene

I CAN'T WANT this. *I just can't. It's so…wrong.*

Those three sentences serve as a warning. They blare loudly inside my head on repeat until I hear just them and *his* breath and demands alone.

When I nod in acceptance, they become a living thing, threatening to break through my skull, demanding I take what I said back.

Or at least not run toward it like a reckless little girl.

I'm not. I'm really not that person.

Every sensible part of me begs me not to be turned on by this stranger who threatens to harm me. Who promises to kill my friends. Who pins me to the tree and rocks into me in a way that makes it obvious what he wants in exchange for their safety.

If I could only listen to them.

My love of the dark shouldn't equal being aroused by this violent person who towers over me. His frightening strength and the fact that he could strip me naked and steal my virginity in an instant shouldn't send heat to my core.

Shouldn't make me so wet I just *have* to clench my thighs.

Yet it does all of it. And so. Much. More.

I sense him and this sick need in me everywhere.

There's a sensual tingling in my nipples as they chafe against the harsh, thick tree bark. The cotton bra I'm wearing doesn't protect them from the insistent grazing. It's as if I'm naked while being ground against the rough surface over and over.

With each stroke, the warmth between my legs is ten times more emphasized. The man behind me leans most of his weight on my bottom. His erection presses into my ass while he thrusts my pussy forward, arousing me from both sides simultaneously.

Every moan I suppress makes me want to bury myself. I'm sick to want this violent man with the menacing mask and black hoodie over his head who growls obscenities in my ear.

My fantasies at home revolve around the cold, harsh, and yet familiar Vaughn. I dream about calling him Daddy. About him being as violent with me as he was when he jacked off in the woods on my birthday.

I've never dreamed of another man touching me like that. Nor has it crossed my mind that I'd like anything similar in real life.

Then again, I've never had sex before. And Vaughn did leave me.

Caroline and Elle wouldn't have shamed me for accepting what my body wants. For giving in to his threats to save them.

There's no other choice for me.

I won't waste another minute hating myself for my sacrifice.

As selfish as it might be.

"How agreeable you've become. So fast as well. When you shouldn't." He squeezes his fingers tighter around my jaw, anger slipping into his tone. "You'll live to regret it. I promise you that."

Is that…is that an accent?

Now that I'm at peace with my decision, I think I hear an underlying British accent seeping through his mask.

His cologne, too, that rich scent I remember faintly.

The exact height and girth of the body I've idolized for years.

Maybe it's not some random killer hiding in the woods after all.

Maybe my body and senses are drawn to him with insane intensity for a reason.

Maybe he's the person I've needed like a drug for so, so long.

Maybe he's my Vaughn.

"It'll hurt so bad you'll want to beg me to stop. But you won't do it, little girl, now will you?" He releases some of the pressure from my mouth. "Because when I remove my hand, you're going to stay very quiet. If you disobey me, by the end of the night, these *people's*"—he says, disdain marring his words—"limbs, insides, and even eyeballs will decorate the trees like it's a Halloween party."

Stripped of the ability to use my voice, I simply nod again.

He slides his hand down my body just above my right breast, squeezing himself between the tree and my body. I expect him to grope my breasts, to keep being cruel and menacing. To take my leggings off after that and violate me like his actions have suggested so far.

It's what I agreed to.

My body hums with fear and anticipation combined, laying claim to my emotions.

Because it could be Vaughn. And when he touches me, I'll find out.

I'll probably even love it, no matter how aggressive he'll be.

No air comes in and out of my lungs in the seconds I wait for him to strip me bare; time and life stand still in anticipation for him to make his move.

Which he does.

Just not in the way I thought.

The man behind me yanks my back to his chest, allowing him better access to my breasts. He twists, tugs, and tortures my nipple. A moan escapes my lips. He responds by pinching me harder like he's punishing me instead of repeating his order for me to be silent.

I'm freaked out by his silence. If he doesn't talk, I'll never know his identity.

"Why are you doing this?"

He'll answer, I'm sure he will. Then he'll slip, say something that'll hint toward whether it's my dad's best friend or not. But I have to keep being brave.

"Why would you want to kill my friends?" I breathe out when he doesn't answer me.

Another growl reaches my ears, emanating from somewhere deep within him. It doesn't come off as aroused, though. It sounds like madness. Like he's furious at my question.

As if to emphasize his vexation, he draws back to spank my ass harshly. It stings and it hurts.

It makes me wet and needy, too.

The place where his palm hit me sears me through my leggings, quickly transforming into a million points of desire. My clit flutters, my heart palpitating in my chest.

I sink my teeth into my lower lip, refusing to reveal any sign of weakness or the building lust I'm finding harder and harder to contain. The cry lodged in my throat is that of both pain and pleasure, one I'm too self-conscious to let out.

"I said,"—he backs away again—"be. Quiet."

This time when his hand marks my ass in a bruising slap, I'm driven over the edge. No longer capable of swallowing back my aroused whimper, I surrender and let it push its way out in a choked whimper.

"What do we have here?" He leans in closer, the black marker Xs he has for eyes filling my view, his voice growing more prominent by the second. "This bad little girl likes it rough."

His last words are spoken when his face is inches from mine.

That's all the proof I need.

I was right to assume he'd slip up.

Despite his muffled voice, regardless of this rage, he's never aimed toward me in the past, I know. Everything in my body tells me who the man behind the mask is.

His proximity made it so I heard him better. Including his light accent and the way he pronounces the letter *r*.

Then there are the eyes. Through tiny black holes he punctured into his mask, I can see the startling black irises that are uniquely *his*.

I'm ninety-nine percent sure that the man who currently lays claim to my body is the one who has owned my soul for what seems like ages.

Vaughn. It's him.

I train my eyes to the distance, so he won't see the recognition in them.

I'm afraid that with one word, with a single acknowledgment, he'll dissolve into thin air like he did at my parents' funeral.

But even as I look away, I can't calm down. Confusion attacks me like the freezing winds of a Chicago winter.

What is he doing here? Why is he back and intent on killing my friends? And where has he been all this time?

Although, if I'm being honest with myself, none of these are as vital as the real question: Does this mean he's returned to take me for good?

Shame plunges through me at the thought. So what if he's back for me? That doesn't eliminate the fact that he threatened to kill my friends.

Once again, I hate myself for feeling excited when I should be worried about the five people whom I came here with.

Except this time, this man who I assume is Vaughn doesn't let me wallow for longer than a split second.

"Since you won't answer"—he grabs the waistband of my leggings and cotton panties, yanking them down to expose my ass—"I'll ask your body instead."

A cool breeze brushes across my bare, aching butt when the man pulls back. He nudges his knee against the back of my thigh, pinning me to the tree with it while using his free hand to remove his glove off the right one.

"What are you—?"

"Silence." His gloved hand shuts my mouth up and shoves my profile back into the bark. "You tested my patience enough for one night. Now you're going to shut up, hold up to your end of the bargain, and let me do whatever the fuck it is I want to do to you."

My eyes widen, partly horrified, mostly turned on, as I watch his hand disappear lower and lower. With one touch of his fingers, he'll have the answer he's looking for. He'll find out how wet I am, how desperate.

80

In the past, I haven't given much thought to how I'd tell Vaughn I love him, lust for him, need him. And while candlelit dinners and a bouquet of roses never interested me, this isn't what I had in mind either.

This prying, this *taking*. It'll unravel me, force me into telling him my secret. It's not that I don't want him. I'm terrified.

I don't know how he'll react to knowing how much I want him and just need that sliver of control.

But he doesn't wait for me to say yes. He takes my silence as acceptance to graze his fingers along my crack, down to my dripping hole.

"Oh, my God," I mumble into his palm, pushing back uncontrollably to get more of his touch.

"Yes, innocent, filthy little sex puppet." His fingers part my lips, applying pressure to enter my pussy. Satisfaction mingles with the anger in his tone, and the derogatory name he uses almost sounds affectionate. "So fucking wet for me. How you drip when I punish you."

His hand on my lips blocks me from verbalizing anything. When it slides lower below my navel, I'm already lost to him completely. He flattens his palm on my soft stomach, applying pressure to drag the both of us backward.

My knees wobble, and I rush to grab a hold of the tree as he aligns the top of my body so it's parallel to the ground. "I—"

"Not." He strikes my naked pussy.

"A." My clit flutters with equal amounts of pleasure and pain at the second slap.

The heat pulsing through me brings me shame. The ache in my pussy doing nothing but heightening my ravenous desire.

"Sound." The third one hurts the most as if he's put all his power into it. And the man is the definition of *strong*.

I try to do as he commands, breathing through clenched teeth instead of moaning.

"You're going to take every bit of what I lash at you."

Another slap to my sensitive center thrashes me back to him.

He notices my weakness, gesturing with his head toward the tree. "Hold on tight, my little whore. I'm not nearly done with you yet."

Noises of the night bristle around us, a soft, familiar soundtrack to the roughness Vaughn unleashes on me.

Amid the woods, I bend at the waist, gripping either side of the tree as I follow his demand. Then I twist my head back, looking at his mask and looming, large figure between the strands of my long hair.

"Feeling emboldened, are we?" His fingers pinch my throbbing clit from the front, while the ones in the back drag in and out of my slit. "You've made me mad today, forced my hand to punish you until you want to cry in agony. And I'll take it, I'll swallow your pain. It belongs to me, the only one who truly cares for you. But I won't take your virginity. For now, at least."

He releases my clit, leaving me on the edge of an orgasm.

I want to cry out. Want to beg him to continue punishing me. Fuck, a depraved part of me is about to plead with him to yes, do it, rip my virginity from me.

If anyone should do it, it's Vaughn. Whom I'm positive this man is.

"Your pretty, lush ass, however." Arousal-coated fingers drift up to my pucker, circling it. "That's *mine*."

In a moment of lucidity, I remind myself not to make a sound. Amongst the many things that Vaughn is, I learned long ago one thing—this man is a man of his word.

He said he'd kill my friends if I got too loud. I have no doubt he'll do it.

So, I pull my lips in as the pressure on my sensitive area grows. Then suck them in harder when he plunges one finger inside my tight hole.

It isn't the pain that has me choking on a scream. The sweet, warm sensations of having my ass taken while he returns to massage my clit are much more of a reward than the punishment he intends it to be.

The longer he pounds into me, the easier it becomes for me to release, my muscles giving in to him. He adds a second finger, stretching the sensitive nerves around my rim, and fuck, that's the hottest thing that's ever happened to me.

"That's it," he growls, pummeling in and out of me in the same, quick rhythm that he rubs my clit. "Dripping and tight like the perfect human hole you are. What a perfect little slut you turned out to be."

I'm embarrassed, aroused, and in what remains in between, I'm also confused. I'll need answers.

Once I'm not on the brink of coming in his hands like the sex puppet he told me I am.

The human hole that needs him so badly.

"Vau—" I start in a haze of lust and stop myself just as fast.

"Shut the fuck up. It can get a lot worse for you." The warning is joined by a slap to my clit. To my humiliation, my thighs clench from the heat erupting where he spanked me. "You're so goddamn close, and I have the power to give you what you want or take it away. This isn't about your friends anymore, it's about you and me and how you won't be allowed to come unless you keep your fucking mouth shut."

"Please," I beg.

He's not wrong. I'm hanging in there, hovering an inch above the water, parched and unable to lean in and drink. My nipples ache, and my insides coil with desire. I need to come.

"Please, I'll do anything."

"Good girl. You beg so fucking beautifully." He kicks my legs wider apart, penetrating me with his fingers from the front now too. He curls them inside my pussy, flicking his thumb on my clit repeatedly. "Call me Daddy, and I'll make you come so hard you'll go blind with pleasure."

For a second, I'm horrified and embarrassed, my body going still.

I'm not the one with the upper hand anymore. He knows my secret, too, knows I call him that when I'm alone. I don't care how many people say "Daddy" during sex, this isn't some random coincidence or a matter of sexual preference.

Vaughn has heard me use that name somehow. That's why he's making me call him that now.

He keeps touching me, keeps hypnotizing me through his rough strokes until my sex-hazed brain doesn't allow me to linger on this momentary anxiety.

With him, I only need. I'm only hungry. On my metaphorical knees for him.

A tool for him to use as he will.

"Daddy, please."

"Much better. That's how my good puppet acts to please me. Not to save her *friends* who haven't even come looking for her." He bends low, his mask grazing my ear. "And now you'll come for me. Only for me."

As if he has his finger pressed on the button to make me orgasm, my body responds to his rough command. My world freezes up; my breath is sucked out of my lungs. Then I shudder as I come, riding the endless waves of feelings, pleasure, of this mindless desire I've never felt before.

"Yes. Exactly that." There's no easing of his thrusts and strokes. "Very fucking good, my little puppet."

The onslaught of my climax slowly simmers out. The man behind me, the man who has to be Vaughn, senses it too.

"Don't move, don't even look back," he demands.

He pulls his fingers out of my body. The sound of his zipper lowering slashes the quiet of the night like a knife.

I want to be good for him. But I can't. I have to peek. Out of the corner of my eye, I see his shadow, the sliver of moonlight highlighting the sharp angles of his body. He grips his cock in his hand, stroking it fast while digging his fingers into the flesh of my ass.

His eyes are aimed at my behind where he grabs me, where his dick is aimed.

"Gonna come all over you, my little ra—slut."

Raven.

If I had any doubt about his identity, his final slip-up just put an end to it. This man is my Vaughn. My heart soars, my insides flipping from watching him jack off on me.

We have a long road ahead of us, so many questions I need answered. For now, nothing else matters except having him here.

He grunts loudly as his own orgasm hits, sinking his fingers deeper into my flesh while his cock spurts hot, sticky cum on my naked behind.

"You did so well, my sex puppet." Vaughn smears his seed on my body, massaging it on my lower back and each cheek. "As much as it infuriates me, no one will die. Tonight. But you'll do well to remember that none of them cared where you disappeared to tonight."

And with that final word, he pulls up his jeans, and he's gone.

I'm left bewildered, boneless with questions stacking themselves one on top of the other. Not that I'm nervous.

Somehow, though, I have a feeling none of this is anywhere near over.

CHAPTER EIGHT

Vaughn

I TAKE A DIFFERENT, longer path to my tent to avoid having Darlene follow me.

My rage, endorphins, and killer urges finally simmer down. They don't disappear altogether. Never have, never will. But the violence in me has lessened for the moment.

Teaching Darlene the first of her lessons while marking her ass played a big part in it.

My lips quirk slyly. This was the first lesson. It won't be the last.

I still don't want her to have the full picture. Don't want her to know who I am or what the others have planned for her.

She's not ready for it. Her actions proved as much.

Despite the threats I issued, she cared about them more than herself.

She sacrificed herself. For *them*.

I don't give a damn that she enjoyed it. That she was turned on by the spanking, manhandling, or being manipulated by me.

It doesn't matter that she thought it was me. At least I suspect as much.

The way she looked at me gave her away. Darlene's clever brain worked diligently to figure out who could do that to her.

There's no doubt in my mind that my slight accent tipped her off. Then my frame, my hair.

And yet none of these things can excuse her behavior.

So quick to risk her life, herself, and for what?

They've never been a great bunch to begin with. The boys in particular.

The longer I consider it, the more aggravated I become yet again.

It's going to be a long road for her and me. A harsh one. One which her late kind and gracious father would've frowned upon.

But in the end, it'll all be worth it. She'll come out on top.

I'll make sure of it. One step at a time, she'll learn to see the truth. To understand it for herself.

The hints will be provided by me. My brilliant little raven will be able to use them all on her own.

That's final, then. And right on time. My camouflaged tent appears before me. I navigate through the darkness I'm familiar with, my boots crunching on the brush.

There's no fire to give up my location or any other sign that'd lead anyone out here by any chance.

Only I know the tall rock and the hiding place it provides me.

The zipper of my tent whooshes loudly in the silence of the night as I tug it down, then up again once I'm settled inside.

The food I packed is cold, the perfect temperature for my night hunting activities. And fuck, do I need it now.

I reach blindly for the portable cooler, about to get my food and drink when her scent hits me. My nostrils flare, my blood boils with need.

The relative calm I felt disappears in a flash.

I'm not only famished and parched, I'm hard for her all over again.

It's as though unleashing years of desire opened the floodgates I worked hard to maintain locked. And now, that I've had her, I can't seem to put them back.

More so when I bring my fingers to my nose. The scent of my little raven's arousal is an assault on my senses. Before any food comes to my lips, before I touch anything that'd mask her smell, I bring my fingers to my mouth and suck on them.

A groan rises from somewhere deep inside me.

Her taste reminds me of how Darlene's clit hardened beneath my fingers. How her virgin little pussy dripped like it knew who owned it.

It wasn't for that vicious, inadequate little boy Lane. She didn't let him touch her, regardless of his attempts. I'm willing to bet money she was as dry as the desert no matter the efforts he put into seducing her.

I did it to her.

No one else.

Me.

Her Daddy.

Suddenly, I forget how it bothered me that she gave up her safety for her friends. The one thing my hard cock and heavy balls force me to think about is how my girl came un-fucking-done under my ministrations.

Just how I'd revel in being her first.

Truth is, it makes no difference to me whether she's a virgin or not. If it'd been her choice, I would've wanted her just the same as I always have.

To love her, cherish her. To fuck her brains out as fiercely as I do now.

But I don't need to worry about that anymore. After tonight, I stopped caring about the macabre nature of my work and personality.

No man will touch her. No one will put their hands on what's *mine*.

I'm the first man to make her orgasm, the first to take her ass. And that's only the beginning. I'm not nearly finished with her. Won't ever be done claiming her as my own.

The plethora of ways I'm going to take her with her taste on my tongue gets my imagination going, and desire kicks in.

I part my index and middle finger in my mouth, pressing them against my tongue. A groan escapes me as I close my lips and lick her taste off me.

Darlene and I will have plenty of hours, days, and years in the future. Until then, I'll get off on my fantasies. How my fingers will part her pussy lips and my tongue will lap at her cunt for days.

Behind closed eyes, I imagine how she'll resist me at first. Having someone take care of her, pleasure her, suck on her clit, it'll be too much for her.

I won't care. Won't quit devouring her. I'll fight her on it, will push those soft, thick thighs to the ground and eat her out.

The sweetness of her orgasms will morph into pain. I won't stop, will demand her to come again and again. Her cries of ecstasy will twist into those of torture.

What a beautiful show she'll put on for me while my lips, teeth, and tongue prep her for my cock.

I open the camera app on my phone, connecting via Bluetooth to the cameras I installed around the cabin as I search for her.

She's in her room, dressed. My body doesn't give a fuck that her nakedness is hidden from me.

It's her sweet face that I'm looking at. The hair I'm dying to pull.

This is the visual that makes me push my hand into my briefs and jerk off for the second time today.

After a few quick, powerful tugs—with the taste of her on my fingers and my dick in my hand—I come on my stomach.

"My little raven." I caress the screen, feeling our bond growing by the minute. "I have things to get done. Then you're coming with me. You'll learn what it truly means to be mine."

I put the phone aside for the night, taking out a water bottle and one of the wraps I packed at home from the cooler. The flavors of the avocado and cold cuts of meat blast in my mouth.

A couple of bites into the meal, Darlene's taste dissipates. It's only then that my senses return to me, that my brain retracts to the reason why I'm here.

And why I can't be overly mad at her for being overly trusting. Someone else is to blame for her blind kindness and compassion.

It's my dead best friend. Darlene's dad, Eric.

The argument isn't anything new. In fact, we've had dozens of these while he was alive.

He wanted her sweet, innocent, and humble.

I, on the other hand, wanted her cold and cutthroat. I begged him to roughen her up, so she'd be independent and capable of protecting herself when none of us were around her anymore.

It definitely would've benefited her now. She would've seen her friends' intentions coming a mile away. She would've told the stranger with the mask *Fuck you*.

"You were too honorable, too good for this world, old friend," I murmur into the night.

How I'd wish he'd be here to shield her. To take her on another birthday camping trip. To keep her close to us, so she wouldn't be *here*.

Missing my friends consumes me every single day. Their companionship, how they understood me like no other.

I miss our angry back-and-forths about Darlene's upbringing as well.

He was her father, yet it didn't make me any less her godfather.

The man who was supposed to shield her from this cruel, sadistic world.

The man who loved her.

Who loves her to this day.

I'd never showered her with love and affection. I physically couldn't. But I cared for her. I still do.

I've loved her from the moment she was born. From the second her one-day-old tiny body was put in my strong, killer arms. I'd been eighteen-year-old and mad at the universe, and yet I fell for her.

For many years later until around the time she turned eighteen, I'd felt an innocent type of love. The one of a guardian.

While I admired her parents and cherished our friendship, it wasn't the same. Even as a toddler, Darlene's black eyes and easy smiles were everything to me.

They changed me. I'd become a human shield for her.

I'm the protective, avenging demon I am today solely because of her. Only ever her.

And as this guardian, I fought against her parents' coddling throughout her entire life.

I insisted the warmth they showered her with wasn't helping. Demanded they put an end to the incessant need to have her close, sheltered, and innocent.

For crying out loud, they even steered her toward picking a college within a driving distance from their home.

"She's a sweet girl," Eric would say. *"She doesn't need to be roughened for the sake of it,"* he'd repeat time and again.

"Which is exactly why you need to ship her off," I demanded of him on her eighteenth birthday. *"You're not doing her any favors by keeping her here, using crutches for the rest of her life."*

They hadn't listened to me. Then the accident happened. Then I had to leave because having me there, without Eric and Helena around, was a bomb waiting to detonate.

At the age of eighteen, she wasn't ready to handle the real me.

Leaving her hurt my damaged soul. Sadly, there wasn't any other way to handle the situation.

Since I walked away, she's toughened up some—she showed as much earlier today—but she has ways to go. She's too good, and I need to rip it out of her.

My wrap is long gone by the time I'm settled. I put away the wrapper, hiding the scent from any animal that'd think about barging into my camp, and lie on the blanket I have ready.

I fold my arms behind my neck, getting comfortable.

A week from today, Darlene and I will laugh about this.

Eric, God rest his soul, would've been proud of how I handled things. Of the wings I gave his daughter.

She'll become my fearless queen, and in the process, we will rid the world of unnecessary filth.

Blood of the guilty will paint the woods. Human guts will decorate the treetops soon.

It'll be a sight Darlene will learn to love as much as I do.

Two birds, one stone.

And it's going to be fucking glorious.

CHAPTER NINE
Darlene

"DARLENE?" CAROLINE EMERGES from somewhere behind me in the woods.

"Yes, I'm here." I spin toward her, not before sending a little *thank you* to the stars above me.

A minute earlier, and she would've figured out that something sexual happened here. With me.

I've stayed where Vaughn left me since it's taken me forever to recover and get dressed again.

Yes, I call him Vaughn. I'm so confident it was him, I wouldn't call him by any other name.

And wow, talk about the longest orgasm recovery I've experienced in my life.

The stretch from Vaughn's fingers inside my ass has given me some serious aftershocks. The sting from his slaps and the massages he administered to my pussy have remained until now.

But the physical aspect wasn't the only thing keeping me here.

I have questions. So many unresolved ones. One after the other, they mount inside my already overstimulated brain.

The *why is he doing this to us* is still unclear to me.

Maybe this isn't about my friends. Maybe it's about me.

Maybe he was simply looking to violate me. To release some bottled-up urges by threatening and using me sexually. Of claiming me whether I was willing to give in to him or not.

What bothers me the most, though, is—am I sick to be aroused by it?

The troubling thought had me pull myself back together and dress up before Caroline made it here.

Thank God.

"Why did you come?" she demands.

The hint of sadness and suspicion in her voice barrels a heap of shame into my chest. My selfish joy due to having Vaughn come after me is wrong.

I should be happy that she's alive. I should be relieved that Vaughn upheld his promise. Should be delighted that I'd been able to save her.

For all my timidness, tonight I'd been a fucking warrior.

"I was worried about you."

I step forward, squinting my eyes to see her better in the dark. The moment I do, though, is the moment I regret it.

Because then I see something I wish I hadn't.

Caroline's hands are fastened on either side of her hips, her lips pressed into a tight line. Sadness isn't what she's feeling. She's annoyed. Even my answer doesn't seem to appease her.

The closer I get to her, her aggravation unfolds, revealing itself to me.

"You shouldn't have." She flicks her hair, spins on her heel, and starts heading in the direction of the camp. I follow her there. "You'd be safer with Lane. And anyway, Lincoln would've come for me."

Somehow I doubt the boyfriend of the year would've cared enough to chase her.

Her words hurt. They're a cruel reminder of how she doesn't know me. I'd give up Lane for her in a heartbeat.

Yet she doesn't give a fuck. Sounds like Vaughn wasn't so wrong about them after all. Maybe they aren't my friends. Not over this weekend. Not while they're drunk.

I shake my head to myself, refusing to believe it. I have no clue what could be wrong with them. Furthermore, I have no reason to not trust them after years of friendship when Vaughn hasn't given me any proof to support his loathing.

Until I have one, they're my friends. My only family.

I hurry my pace, falling into step at her side.

"Well, I'm here anyway." The passageway between two trees is too narrow, and I let her walk ahead of me. "I'm glad you're okay."

"Pfft," she huffs.

I don't reply to that. Instead, I tackle the issue that's been bothering me, emboldened by the first sexual experience I had with another human being to know enough to say my piece. "Caroline?"

She doesn't give me her eyes, stalking forward. "Yeah?"

We're side by side again, the smell of beer and tequila poignant in the air between us.

"I'm not interested in Lane like that," I blurt out, my tone, as silent as it is, reaching over the rustling of the leaves. "Could you help me to pass on the message? Because I don't think he gets—"

"Stop being such a baby, Darlene." Her scolding comes out slurred and very much annoyed. "It's sex. Everyone has to do it at some point, and from what other girls told me, Lane is a good fuck. You should be grateful."

Grateful for what? If other girls like him so much, they can have him. I shouldn't be grateful for anyone giving me the time of day, shouldn't throw myself at someone I'm not interested in.

"They're sleeping, these idiots?" Caroline says before I have a chance to object.

Orange lights appear in the darkness ahead of us, and so do four lying-down figures. As we approach, I can tell Roy and Elle aren't grinding on each other anymore. Lane and Lincoln's broad figures rest on the blankets we spread out earlier this evening, slightly snoring from the amounts of alcohol they consumed.

I breathe out a sigh of relief. They might be jerks, but I don't want them to die. And for now, they're breathing and not bleeding from anywhere, just like Caroline is.

"Yup," is all I say in response. I don't have much more in me to deal with Caroline tonight.

Thank fuck Lane's asleep, because I sure can't take any more of him.

Only Vaughn. My heart, body, and soul are immersed in the memories of my godfather. Of how he degraded and praised me. How he threatened and controlled me.

How honest he'd been, fulfilling his side of our deal.

Maybe he just wanted to touch me, to be truly filthy dark as I suspected he'd been all along.

A smile curves my lips up, one I hide by turning away from Caroline.

"I'm leaving these dumb fucks here." I hear Caroline rolling her eyes, although there's no real exasperation there.

Being her friend for the past three and a half years gave me a better insight into her mimics, to the changes in her tone. She's hurt and disappointed Lincoln had no plans of coming for her.

"Works for me." I wrap my arm around Caroline's slender body, pulling her close and turning us to the cabin's front door.

She snapped at me in the woods, but I'm unable to forget the pain I just saw in her eyes. Everyone should be allowed to snap when they're that hurt.

The lessons in compassion my parents taught me won't ever go away. Their family values are ingrained into my

DNA. Without Mom and Dad—and later no Vaughn either, up until now—I don't have any other family than these two girls right here.

They're not perfect, and it's okay. I understand my small childhood circle of Mom, Dad, and Vaughn had been a rare, precious gift the universe had given me.

This new family isn't perfect, but then again, who is? I love them regardless, that was how I was brought up. Nothing will change me.

"Fuck them," she mumbles as we climb the steps.

Elle would've probably agreed and egged her on. She's asleep though. I'm here, and I think that what Caroline could use now is some quiet and a good night's rest.

So do you.

I rub my hand over her shoulder, not saying a word. When we get to the porch, I repeat the motion of backing off so she can go in first.

Once in my room, I decide I don't want to wipe the stickiness—the memory of Vaughn—off my back. I leave my T-shirt on, remove my boots, socks, and leggings, and crash on the comfortable bed in Lincoln's cabin.

I long for a peaceful night. Ache for it, really. And although sleep finds me pretty quickly given the day I had, peace is the farthest thing from it.

All thanks to one of the realest dreams I've ever had.

I'm in the woods again.

The path I choose is similar to the one I walked on tonight.

Same woods, same branches, same silver moonlight filtering through the trees.

Same strong, gloved hands wrapping around my mouth and throat.

Same thrill in my bones when I guess who this person might be.

A delight that multiplies and ripples through me when I come to realize I don't have to guess anymore.

His mask is off in the dream, his mouth coasting along my cheek.

My gaze drifts to the side, and I see him.

It's really him. He's come for me.

Vaughn.

The man I've spent my entire life idolizing and lusting after is here. His full lips trail down my jawline, latching onto my throat.

I gasp from having his teeth sink into my exposed skin. I cry into his palm with a moan that's a mixture of pleasure and pain alike.

"Little raven," he says in the dream, his hot breath fanning on my damp and bruised skin.

His hoarse voice permeates into my body through my pores, landing in the sensitive space between my thighs. All I can do in response is bob my head as much as Vaughn's forceful grip allows me.

There's a general ominous feeling of wrongness in the act. It's different this time around, though. Doesn't involve Vaughn threatening my friends or having anyone else killed.

This one is just about him and me, and our decadent connection. He wants me so badly that he's defiling me in the worst ways, and I'm equally depraved, loving it.

"I'm gonna shove my cock inside that virgin ass of yours," my father's best friend growls. "My fingers were a starter, my whore of a puppet. It's time you let Daddy come inside you."

Vaughn shows me how serious he is by tackling the back of my knee. I follow his lead as he lowers me down to the ground. In his hands, I become a real-life puppet, relinquishing control over my body to him.

He takes and takes, manhandling my body without the slightest remorse.

After releasing my throat, Vaughn arranges me to my hands and knees, pressing his erection firmly to my behind.

"Fuck, you're so responsive." He grinds into me, his thick member parting my ass cheeks wider. "You love doing what I tell you to, such a good fucking girl you are."

"Yes," I whisper into his hand, hoping he can understand me.

Feeling him hard for me, shoving me, controlling me, *threatening* me, it gives me life. Every bit of it lights me up for him. I'm insanely wet and needy. Can't even think straight.

I shouldn't crave him shoving his massive girth back there right away. While I'm still a virgin.

Caroline and Elle both told me their hymens were broken way before they let anyone near their asses. It makes it less painful and scary after you've been having sex for a while—their words.

Except…nothing in me rebels against the idea of Vaughn's dick in my darkest of holes. The trust and love I have for him are stronger than anything else.

There's only him and my visceral desire to take whatever he lashes at me.

"I can already tell how I'll love filling up that tight hole of yours," he groans in my ear, pulling back to shove my leggings down as he does.

"You have my permission to scream this time, to call out for your Daddy however loud you please." In one swift motion, he tears my panties off and relieves the pressure of his hand from my mouth. "I have no doubt you will."

"Vaughn," I murmur his name when his weight lifts off of me again. I miss it, miss his warmth as scary, cruel, and devious as it is. "Please, I…"

I don't know what I'm pleading for. Not that he allows me to consider it a second longer.

"I said *scream*."

His large palm strikes my left butt cheek three times. Just as fast, he changes to strike the right one with equal, merciless intensity.

He leaves me no other choice but to comply. I open my mouth and release my arousal, the embarrassment and ache his actions cause me. The feral crying sounds are hardly as cathartic as I'd want them to be, but the tears come. Boy, do they come.

"Good girl." With his palm laid firmly between my shoulder blades, Vaughn shoves my head to the ground. His other hand grips my hip, tilting it higher to have access to my holes. "You've always been such a good little girl, my raven."

I feel a sliver of tenderness in his voice. His gentleness has me wondering why he told my father he should send me away on my birthday. For a brief moment. Then I let it go.

There's no need for an answer to that question when he praises me like that. When he's being this all-consuming, domineering God I can't help but worship.

"Thank you." The immense love I have for him pours out of me in these two words of gratitude.

Cold, damp spit drips on my ass, and Vaughn rubs it around the hole he intends to penetrate. "Thank you, what?"

His blunt fingers hurt me as two of them are being shoved inside my asshole, twisting within me, opening me up.

"Thank you." I manage to talk around the delicious pain. "Daddy."

"That's better." Vaughn's approval adds to my arousal, and I lean back into him. "That's much fucking better."

The grasp of his hand on my hip tightens, his fingers digging into my flesh. "Get ready to open that beautiful throat of yours and scream for me, my little raven."

"Please." I turn my head back, fastening my gaze on his hungry one.

He removes his fingers from my ass to wind his hand in my hair and tug on it.

I don't close my eyes at the pain of the pull. Nor do I try to squirm out of his hold when he nudges the head of his cock to my ass. I relish the pain, savor it.

What I can't do is scream for him anymore.

Something changed. Something is really, terribly wrong.

Vaughn's face morphs into an angry, raging scowl, and through clenched teeth, he grits out, "What the actual fuck?"

Then he's not Vaughn anymore. I realize it as the dream dissipates, and I'm all by myself, back in the room of Lincoln's cabin.

I try to regain my composure as I wait to see what's real and what's not.

"What the actual fuck is going on here?" A really pissed-off, slightly scared shout comes from outside my room.

It's Roy.

And it's real. So very real.

Oh, fuck. Oh, fuck, fuck, fuck.

Sweat breaks over my forehead, dread gripping my insides.

Could Vaughn have lied to me after all? Has he done something to Elle?

I don't want to find out. I don't want to see one of my best friends hurt, or worse yet, dead.

But being a coward while someone who's practically my family might be in danger isn't an option. This isn't how I was raised.

Though my knees are wobbly, and my insides are heavy with dread, I rip the blanket off me. Next, I leap out of bed and throw on the leggings and boots from last night.

I don't even brush my teeth, just pop a gum into my mouth, and walk out into the early morning light.

CHAPTER TEN

Darlene

THE SUN NEARLY blinds me as I push through the
front door.

I'm breathless, but it has nothing to do with how fast I
walk outside to where Roy's voice came from. It's not
because I just woke up, either.

This is the result of the pure fear that cinches around
my lungs.

I look frantically left and right, scanning the people
around me, counting heads one by one.

Caroline's here in yesterday's clothes, same as me,
rubbing her eyes. I breathe out a sigh of relief as I go to
stand beside her because she's not alone.

Elle is on her other side. Our friend seems the most put-
together of the three of us. Her hair is washed, and she's
holding a cup of what smells like coffee between her hands.

Lincoln, Roy, and Lane circle the Range Rover, sticking their hands into their messy hair. The three of them wear sweats and T-shirts, which, I guess, is what they slept in when they finally peeled themselves off to bed.

I don't care what they look like, though. The five of them could've been donning bandanas to cover their privates and nothing else, as long as they were alive.

No one's injured, no one's hurt.

That's all that matters.

"How the fuck is every tire slashed, in this fucking deserted middle of nowhere?" Lincoln's anger pulls my attention from my friends' faces lower.

My guts twist painfully, a new sense of guilt eating at my insides.

While no one was murdered, damage *had* been caused. And I have a faint idea of who might've been responsible for messing with the car. Because Lincoln is right, who else would've come to this deserted location only to vandalize his car?

Vaughn kept his promise, but still, this is bad.

He could've just taken me home with him instead of disappearing on me and doing *this*. I don't understand it. Don't understand any of it.

"Do you think there might be a bear around here or something?" Elle turns to Caroline and me. Her teeth disturb the corner of her bottom lip while her fingers clench tightly around her mug. "What if they break through one of the windows?"

Seeing her this worried almost makes me tell her *things*. Almost makes me confide my secret meeting with Vaughn with them so she'll know no bear is about to attack her.

My mouth opens for a beat, then clamps shut. I can't tell her. I won't.

First off, it wouldn't matter either way. Yesterday proved that neither of my two friends trust me.

Second, they're in no state to listen to anything I say. They're so scared that they probably won't believe me when I tell them bears paws don't slice through tires this meticulously. Or at all. Why would they?

Last but not least, I'd never give Vaughn up.

There's little I won't do to comfort my friends, for my second family. Other than snitching on Vaughn. He's more family than anyone else has ever been to me.

My love for him has changed and evolved over time. It shifted from looking at him as the uncle who joined our family picnics over the weekends. For a while now, he's been the man I'm pining for in my sleeping and waking hours.

Our lifelong connection trumps anything and anyone. I don't care that he broke my heart. I love him.

I'll never sell him out. Never make him a target of Lincoln's fury.

I'm sure he won't have any trouble fending them off. Vaughn is big and muscular enough to tear through all of these five people by himself. Easily.

Still, I won't betray him. The soreness in my ass, the places where his fingers dented my flesh, they're a firm reminder of the bond we share. He returned to me. It was him behind that mask, and yesterday he finally claimed me as his.

Weirdly, in an *us* kind of way, he locked our bond for good.

The loyalty I have for him stands tall and firm against everything, anything, and anyone else.

Besides—and this is coming from a girl who barely scrapes by—it's just a car. There's a town somewhere nearby. And once we're back home, Lincoln's insurance will cover the damages.

He'll live.

"I wouldn't know." I shrug. "I hope not."

"Don't look at me." Caroline tugs a strand of knotted blond hair behind her ear. "I only watch Discovery Channel or whatever."

In front of us, Lincoln has done his final inspection of the car and is now standing beside the two other boys. They all frown, talking in hushed voices that become louder and louder as their argument intensifies.

"We could rock, paper, scissors on it." Roy leans his hip on the back door of the truck.

"Fuck rock, paper, scissors. This has to be you," Lincoln shoves his finger at Roy's chest. "We have zero reception here, and I'm not about to walk to the nearest town for three or four hours and leave you guys here to do fuck knows what."

It doesn't go unnoticed that Lane's name isn't brought up, despite him being perfectly capable of making the trip too. Both Roy and Lane have a very similar build and stamina, the result of years of being on the swim team. There's no reason the other two couldn't roll the dice on it or something.

Why doesn't Lincoln offer *that*?

Strange.

What's weirder is that Roy doesn't question him, either.

"We're not some kind of animal, Linc." His mouth twists into a snarl, one of his brown curls falling into his eyes. He wipes it away. "It's not fair that I'm the one who's ordered to go."

My gaze shifts to Lane who has his back resting on the door next to Roy. I take note of the dark circles under his eyes that I missed while I was doing a headcount. Of his slouched shoulders, and how he yawns for the tenth time.

Maybe I'm being paranoid. Maybe they just feel bad for him and there isn't some ulterior motive for Lincoln's insistence that it'd be Roy. There may be a shred of humanity somewhere down in Lincoln's terrifying soul. That he isn't all that bad.

At least, I hope so.

"Ugh, Elles, tell him to stop being a baby and go already," Caroline whispers, the annoyance echoing loud and clear in her voice.

Elle makes a low grunting noise and rolls her eyes. "Yeah, you try to talk to Roy when he's pissed. He'll go and do exactly the opposite. Thanks, but no thanks."

"The fuck it's not." Lincoln's no-bullshit tone cuts through the girls' mumbling. He places his hands on his hips, glaring down at Roy. "I'm not leaving my asshole parents' cabin unsupervised. Richmond will have my head on a platter if anything else goes wrong that I can't explain, so yeah, it is fucking fair, and you are fucking going."

I've never met Lincoln's dad. From what Caroline told me, the partner of one of Chicago's biggest estate law firms in Illinois is as ruthless as his son makes him sound.

He spoiled Lincoln by setting him up with a trust fund, a car, and a credit card with no spending limit, yet that's as far as his parenting skills go. The rest of the time, he humiliates him by telling him he doesn't have the drive it requires to be a part of his firm. That even the mail room is too much for his abilities or lack thereof.

Lincoln's right to insist like he does. I wouldn't want to be on his dad's bad side either.

"Jeez, what's wrong with Roy today?" Caroline hisses. "He should be grateful we brought him on board with our pl—" She looks at me, a big smile plastering on her face. "On this *trip*. And just do what Linc tells him to."

I nod, agreeing with her now that I had time to consider it. Not being sexist or anything, but Roy really is the logical choice for the trip.

It can't be Elle and Caroline; they would for sure get lost on the way.

It can't be me either. I mean, I could navigate safely and manage to reach the nearest rest stop to call for help. Then again, who's to say Vaughn would let me get that far?

Goose bumps rake all over my skin.

Vaughn.

He might be still hiding somewhere out there. He might stop me from reaching my destination.

Or…my heart would stop itself once I saw him.

I'm not sure that I'm ready to confront him again this soon. I don't have anything meaningful to say, and I want to say *something*.

The abundance of questions and emotions overpowering me are a big mess at the moment.

I might scream if I see him again on my way to town. I might fall at his feet and humiliate myself.

There's no telling what'll happen. I need to have control over my emotions instead of being this fucked up in the head.

Otherwise, he won't treat me as an adult. He won't tell me what's going on.

He won't let me soothe him long enough to stop his murderous rage.

So I'll stay here.

I'll face Vaughn like a grown-up once I get my thoughts in order and tell him: *Hey, you have kinks, I have kinks, let's be kinky together. No need for tire slashing or killing people.*

All I need is a few more hours by myself.

Yes, it has to be Roy.

"Fine, I'll go," Roy yields, rolling his eyes.

Then he spins to Elle, suddenly remembering that we girls are here too.

The corner of his mouth kicks up, one of his hands playing with his waistband, his annoyance seemingly forgotten. "A blowie for the road?"

"Jesus, why do you have to be such a dick about it?" Elle spits out.

"Stop being a fucking prude, babe." Her boyfriend swaggers in our direction, his hand drifting below his sweats to grab his junk. "Don't tell me you're not hungry for my cock."

My teeth sink into the inside of my cheek to keep down the lecture I'm dying to give him about respecting your partner.

When I was the target of their mocking yesterday, I wasn't this mad. Today, however, my protective instincts are working overtime. Thanks to Vaughn.

Who was much more of a gentleman than Roy. He called me a slut in private. I'm unable to fathom he would do something to purposefully degrade me in public. He'll never poke me when I'll call him out for being an ass like Elle just did with Roy.

It's none of your business, I remind myself, seeing Caroline doesn't intervene either.

I steal a glance at Elle, checking her for any sign of distress. Her agitation from before disappears; she's no longer scowling.

She's...calm.

"Ugh, fine." My friend smiles, causing me to blink a few times to believe what my eyes are witnessing. "Dick for breakfast it is."

Lincoln and Lane are still back there talking while Roy takes his hand out from his boxers. He spanks Elle's behind as she heads into the house, making her squeal and giggle.

I shrug, realizing I was wrong. Apparently, pushing him off is a part of their foreplay or whatever. Cool, then. To each their own.

"I'm going to go back to my room," Caroline tells me. "No one's dead, obviously, and I could use another hour or two of my beauty sleep."

"Yeah." A shiver runs up my spine at her words. "No one's dead, all right."

She spins and starts walking off. Without being invited or another word said, Lincoln stops his conversation with Lane and prowls after her.

He passes by me on the porch, not sparing a look my way, but I see him.

His eyes are dark and intention-filled as he stalks into the house, his steps determined.

Caroline will have to catch up on her beauty sleep another day.

"Looks like we got ourselves some alone time."

While I've been busy analyzing what's happening around me, Lane has snuck up on me. He stands at my side, creeping me out all over again by curling his fingers around my arm.

I scream at the contact, though still too surprised to free myself from him.

"It's just me." He strokes his thumb along my bicep like it's supposed to comfort me. "So about that alone time…"

116

"Yeah." I still struggle to come out of the shock.

His unwelcome touch and the step he takes to crowd my space wake me the hell up. I clasp my hand on top of his, removing his fingers one at a time.

The adorable grin he shoots disarms me by some. Once more, it's the only thing keeping me from being rude by telling him just how badly I'm not interested.

"I kinda need that." I back up into the cool, dark house where sex sounds vibrate through the walls. "For myself. Didn't get much sleep last night. Seems like you need it, too."

"But—"

"See you later." It takes everything in me to curve my lips up to match his smile before turning around and racing to my room.

"See you," he says to my back.

I feel bad slamming the door in his face.

I don't feel bad at all, though, for being left peacefully alone with my books.

For the quiet of my room where I can think about the man I long to touch.

CHAPTER ELEVEN

Vaughn

PLANNING AHEAD ISN'T just important in my profession and way of life in general. I would've called it vital, but even that feels like I'm belittling it.

I'm not sure how many people are aware that even the messiest, bloody act of murdering someone needs to be perfectly set up step by step. They're in no way aware of the agonizing thinking ahead and how thorough a—responsible, at least, like me—killer applies to each detail once they've chosen their mark.

One misplaced action would otherwise get me caught by the authorities' new technologies. That, or another unfavorable scenario would happen; the fantasy I carefully constructed would have been dented.

And that sure has a way of taking all the fun out of butchering someone well-deserving.

My alarm goes off in the middle of the night, hours after I took Darlene. I don't so much as yawn. I don't even hit the snooze button.

I've got business to take care of, and I'm more than eager to get to it.

After a quick check of the cameras around the cabin, I find the campfire area empty. All the drunken idiots who stuck around have crawled back inside the house. Finally.

I would've slashed the tires of their car with them passed out there. But you won't hear me complaining when a mark makes my life a whole lot easier.

Not that I let my guard down for a second as I creep over there. I slither through the woods in my black clothes and mask, sneaking around the burned ashes of their fire, and work on remodeling Mr. Hopkins's squeaky-clean SUV.

Hidden behind my mask, my smile stretches as I fish my butcher's knife out of the sheath attached to my belt. The maniacal and vengeful parts of me relish cutting through the rubber. I'm growing more satisfied as I imagine how it'd feel to cut through Lincoln's flesh.

It'd be quite the sight, watching Lincoln's blue blood drip down my forearm. Marveling at how it'd stick to my shirt, darkening the black fabric.

I can already smell the copper in the air. Hear his screams when he understands that it's not karma coming to get him—it's Darlene's avenging angel who will torture him until he parts from this world with one final breath.

Her angel or…demon. Depends on whom you ask, I guess.

Soon.

Once the great, black Rover collapses a few inches to the ground, I slip back into the woods and start walking out of there.

My plan doesn't stop here. That's why I keep going instead of lingering here to absorb the stench of their fear. I'd have loved to be there when they realize someone fucked with them.

They might not understand that at first. They'd be pissed but through their anger, a sliver of worry would filter in.

The guilty have this incessant tendency to look over their shoulder. And so will they.

The one person who'd have any idea it was me would be my little raven.

She wouldn't get mad. Ruining their property isn't breaking my promise to her. I said I wouldn't kill anyone that night, and I hadn't. I never mentioned potential damage to their mode of transportation while getting under their skin.

The lawyer I am knows better than to trip over his words.

The son I am—the biological son of Edward and Sophia Graham—he dares to hope that one day soon Darlene won't just be okay with his violence. He prays she'll love it.

Her dad might've instilled kindness and compassion in her. I love that side of her like I love everything about her. She, however, is under *my* supervision now and will be *my* partner soon.

It's not that farfetched to wish for her past and future to coexist.

I think about it throughout the four hours of my journey from the cabin to the paved road ahead. That's all I allow myself, then as I reach the nearest rest stop—the only one around here for miles—I refocus on my task at hand.

The little brats would send one of their own to call for a tow service or a change of tires since there's no reception where they are. There's hardly even one bar as it is on my phone, and I'm less than fifteen feet away from the gas station up ahead.

But still, coming up here is their only hope for a phone call. A hope I intend to sever.

Out of everything I've done so far in my life, this one's a walk in the park. I'll cut the landline, steal the clerk's cell phone, and pay him off to disappear for the day.

Whoever of the spoiled bunch comes here will surely be too lazy or inadequate to walk on their own to the nearest town. They'll go back to the cabin, tail between their legs, and that's when I'll strike.

Simple, really.

Unless they send Darlene. An unlikely scenario. Every second she's not around that pathetic excuse of a human, Lane, is a setback to their scheme against her.

Like hell they're letting her out of their sight.

With the metal-cutting scissors stashed in my back pocket, I stand in the shadows. I'm hiding behind the last line of trees separating me and civilization as I assess the rest stop for any surprises.

The brick walls on the small building of the convenience store look like they were put here around the time the Civil War happened. Either that or they've fallen off altogether, leaving holes and making the exterior look like a bad set of dusty teeth.

Paint chips away at the three lonely gas pumps in the front, giving them the appearance as if they're out of order. And yet they're not.

The pearl-white Cadillac parked next to one of them that has fuel pumping into her tank is proof enough.

Its owner is nowhere to be seen, I gauge, as I meander toward it. The mask I wore earlier hangs on the back of my head, hidden under the hoodie I have pulled over my head.

I'm calm and collected. Most of all, I'm plain and ordinary-looking to whoever might see me walk around here.

Just another man passing by on his way from one town to another. A harmless stranger wandering through the woods.

Nothing about me says *murderer.*

I'm unmemorable. Forgettable. John fucking Doe.

The CCTV doesn't worry me either, since deleting the recording is a part of my plan. So is threatening the clerk that if he peeps a word about my identity, it'll be the last word he ever says.

Despite my boring looks, I'd rather not take any unnecessary chances. I slip around the back of the convenience store to lean against the broken-down brick wall and wait.

Surely, the owner of the Cadi will pay for their gas and leave any second now.

The fewer witnesses, the better.

Several quiet seconds tick by.

Then the silence of the rest stop is cut off by a sound I hadn't anticipated hearing.

"No, please." A woman's muffled cry cuts through the air. "Please, stop. You're hurting me!"

She comes off as desperate, miserable, and terrified. I've seen my share of people role-playing sexual fantasies, listening in on the tiniest edge of arousal slipping through their voices.

This is not that.

"Shut the fuck up, bitch," a man roars over her pleas. "I'll do whatever I goddamn please, you pretentious, stuck-up cunt."

He doesn't care he's being obnoxiously loud. Doesn't think anyone would pass through here who'd give a damn about what he's doing.

Doesn't imagine there'd be consequences to his actions.

Except I'm here.

Fuck waiting. Fuck going unnoticed. I won't allow an innocent person to get hurt while I'm around.

Besides, the wanker just made my day a whole lot more interesting. After putting Caroline's death on hold last night, it feels like I've found the perfect mark to take the edge off.

Going for a spontaneous kill isn't something I've done since I was a kid. Then again, with the way this asshole and my body are begging for it, I'm sure I can improvise.

I shove myself off the wall, yanking down my hoodie and fixing the mask on my face. In what takes less than half a second, I have my scissors out of my pocket and in my grip. What cuts through metal will slice through human flesh easily.

A bell chimes above my head as I step inside the convenience store. It announces my arrival as I breathe the stale air of my surroundings. The filthy ones.

There's dust on the shelves, faded candy wrappers, and multiple cracks in the tiled floor.

There's no hiding the scene unfolding before my eyes.

Once again, I realize this man with the murderous look on his face feels invincible. Like it's his fucking right to take a life just because he wants to.

And I'm about to prove to him exactly how wrong he is.

Starting by shutting the door behind me and flipping the *Open* sign to *Closed*.

"I'll pay you. I'll give you everything I have." The woman's voice is now paired with a face.

She seems to be in her late thirties, standing in front of the counter facing forward. Despite the ancient bell ringing a second ago, she's too terrified to notice anyone else has walked in.

She's lost to the fear that freezes her in place. Poor lady has sweat gluing her auburn hair to her face and causing her to shed tears that ruin her mascara.

"Please, I'm begging you, don't—don't kill me. I have a kid. Please don't do this."

I wish I could say it's her agony that snaps the last of my restraints.

But it's not her.

The disgusting skinny man who wears his tattered, brown baseball cap turned backward behind her that does it to me.

He paints my vision in red so thick it's like blood dripping into my eyes.

He's holding her hands behind her back, shoving her into the dusty counter with his thighs. The fingers of his other hand curl around her neck, slowly sucking the life out of her as the woman fights to breathe.

His violence toward a woman who just stopped by to pump gas brings out the unhinged side of me. Almost as violently as Darlene's friends do.

It's a clear violation of the code I live by. That of being a decent murderer.

I could've turned out like the man in front of me. Ever since the night my parents took their last breaths before my eyes, I've been a monster.

But Eric taught me how to be better.

And what this guy is doing is the worst.

While I thought it bothered me when I simply heard him hurting her, seeing him pisses me off a million times more.

No one lays their stinking hands on the innocent.

As if I'm not raging hard enough, my mind adds fuel to the fire. Instead of the woman's face, I see my little raven's.

A flash of fury bursts through me, picturing my goddaughter here with Lane at her back, hurting her, forcing her.

Though this man right here seems to want to kill the poor passerby, not rape her, it doesn't matter. Hurting people is hurting people.

None of this shit is going to fly with me.

I blink to force Darlene out of my head for now and regroup.

"Let her go." My command rumbles in the small, aging space.

The assailant releases some of the pressure off the woman's throat, averting his attention to where I stand.

His beady, blue eyes narrow at me, trying first to understand who I am.

It's evident that my mask makes an impact on him. Just not how I intended it to be. He's not scared of me. But he will be soon.

Any minute now, my mere breath will have the effect I'm aiming for.

He scowls, thinking that it might somehow scare me when he growls, "We're closed, freak. Get out."

"I don't think so." I inch closer, raising my scissors eye level, snipping them twice. "Release the woman, apologize, and I might give you a peaceful death."

"Please, help me." The woman who tilts her head toward me now cries harder, trying unsuccessfully to shake off her assailant. "Please, I—I ran out of gas. I took a wrong turn and I got lost. I'm not even supposed to be here."

I don't tell her begging isn't needed. Whether she's a passerby or this man's unfortunate wife, I'm still going to save her.

An assault on an innocent is a crime, period.

He's earned the punishment coming to him, and I'm way too eager to be the one to hand it out to him. His spilled blood would, after all, be a wonderful appetizer for my day.

"No one's helping you." The man continues to think he has the upper hand. "You can forget about that."

He resumes applying pressure on her neck, pushing her forward using his other hand until her face mashes into the counter. Until only one of her eyes is visible to me.

Then he yells to me without removing his gaze from her, "Go hunt for an animal or whatever, and take your ridiculous mask, fake accent, and kindergarten scissors with you."

Too bad he can't see my smirk. Maybe he would've considered his words then.

Too late.

"The hard way, I see."

In three calculated steps, I'm at his back. One swift motion brings my scissors to the front of his neck. They press to the spot where I feel his blood thrumming in his veins.

Those that I'm about to cut open.

"What the—?" he grunts when I pull him away from the helpless woman.

I won't grace him with an answer, not yet. I push the open blade until the scent of copper seeps into my nose. Until his squeals filter into my ears like a bloody opera.

"Thank you, thank you so much." The auburn-haired lady rushes to straighten herself, smooths down her dress, and runs to the exit. Her heels clink as she avoids the cracks in the floor.

"Hold up," I call after her.

She hesitates, her hand inches above the door handle.

Eventually, she decides against it, bowing her head to hide her face behind a mass of thick waves. "Please let me go. I won't tell anyone, I swear."

"About that."

I fasten my stare through my masked face to hers. The pull of my gaze causes her to look back at me through squinted, terrified eyes. That's good. That's precisely where I need her to be.

"Anyone gets a word about me, anything at all, believe that I'll have the means to track you down and end you."

To drive my message home, I tear the man's cap off, tugging at his short blond hair to expose more of his neck to my scissors. I press them upward, slicing through the first layer of his skin.

My human onion.

"You psycho! Stop it!"

"I swear." The woman's expression gains an edge of fierceness to it, her voice steady. "No one will even know I stopped here. Wherever here is. Thank you, sir. Thank you for saving my life."

"Good." Hearing her sincerity is all I need. I ignore her gratitude, fixing my attention back on the pig I'm holding. "Now, go."

She does as she's told, disappearing out the door, leaving us alone.

"D-d-do—" the asshole stutters, unable to complete the word with my so-called kindergarten scissors just below his chin.

"Have something to say, little piggy?" I remove my scissors, thrusting his head into the counter and rendering him unconscious.

He falls like a limbless sack of potatoes to the ground, passed out for the time being.

"No?" My boot connects with his back, turning him over to his stomach. "You did say plenty today. Did too much, that's for sure."

He's out, the perfect state for me to tend to my mission. I meander around the shop for anything that might help me kill him without leaving a trace.

Fortunately, the measly rest stop sells more than just sodas and high-carb, processed snacks. I choose one of the ropes hanging around the store, using it to tie his wrists and ankles.

My next mission is spreading a plastic tarp on the floors to cover every drop of blood this fuck spills, and a large piece of cloth for later.

When I'm done, I flip him on the plastic surface. I roll him to his back again, slapping his face a couple of times.

"Wake up, sunshine," I say to his terrified and shocked expression, the bloodied scissors he mocked earlier dangling in his face. "Your executioner is here to give you the retribution you so rightfully earned."

"Fine. Kill me." He understands by now how serious I am. How there's no way out of this. His bleeding throat bobs with his swallow. "Make it fast, please."

"No can do…" The scissors' blades dive into his waist, coaxing a scream from his mouth. "What's your name? So I know whose life I'm about to snuff out."

"Please." Spit dribbles with every word. "I'm Dale, I don't have a family—"

Surprising.

"But I don't want to die. Please."

"You had the chance, remember? Then you threw it away like the idiot that you are."

"You're right! I'm an idiot! Tell me what to do and I'll do it!" He tries to turn on his side.

I spin him right back, pressing my boot to his injured waist. The little piggy returns to squealing and spluttering spit all over the tarp.

Taking a quick glance at my watch, I see time begins to run out on me. Someone might come in, or Darlene's group could send someone up here while I'm deep into the trance of slashing the guy beneath me.

With my gloves on and not a free hand to check the camera on my phone, I have no other option but to hurry the fuck up.

"You may have your wish come true, fucker." My fingers work on yanking his jeans and boxers down to his knees. "Partially, at least."

The man's eyes follow me, his speech slurred. "Why do you have to take it off? You said it's my lucky day."

"It is."

His limp dick is barely peanut-sized, but I'm nothing if not resourceful. I squeeze the soft flesh in my palm, yanking it as high as it'll go.

"You'll be dead a few minutes after I cut off your penis." The scissors glint under the fluorescent lights. I close them in around his dick while my hand moves to stuff the piece of cloth into his mouth. "Not hours like you deserve."

Desperate mumblings rise past his lips.

As if it's going to help him.

Ding-dong, your cock is dead.

CHAPTER TWELVE

Vaughn

"YOU KNOW HOW the saying goes." I throw the last piece of tarp into the burning metal waste bin a few miles away from the rest stop.

My plans, even when being deviated, can't afford to have any glitches in them.

Burning the rest stop creep Dale too close would've alerted the prick they sent here. They would've realized something was seriously wrong, not a mere fluke of slashed tires and no phone reception.

They might've run to the nearby town to save themselves, to call someone.

I couldn't allow that.

"Ashes to ashes, dust to dust, and all that shit. So long, little piggy."

The smell of gasoline permeates through the midday air. Then comes the hint of a human body incinerating.

It doesn't make me gag. In fact, I don't so much as lift my mask to suck in a gulp of fresh air. I relish the cremating of the man I dismembered one limb at a time, reveling at the sight of his blood, guts, and gore.

A ceremony that has to end too quickly for my liking. Because someone might walk up here.

I remove one glove off my hand, finally able to connect to one of the cameras in the cabin's living room. I need to check if anyone's missing, if anyone's on their way here.

I watch them debating between themselves, arguing about whatever it is the bored and wealthy fight about.

Two of them aren't there.

One, whom I'll always look for first, is my raven. The absence of her radiant beauty sticks out like a sore thumb in the bland living room.

The other one is Roy. What a relief not seeing him there or in any of the other rooms or the outside. He's on his way, not trying to hurt Darlene while I'm busy here.

She's safe for now.

Before I turn on the mic to hear what they're saying, I click to go back to Darlene's room. I watch her while I start walking the distance from where I am to the rest stop.

She's there, sleeping on her side like the angel she is. The room is dark, with only a soft glow from the night lamp beside her illuminating her naked body.

I tear my gaze from her for a moment as the rest stop appears close by, as deserted as it'd been when I left it. I round the place, trudging about a mile into the woods.

Nothing, not even a twig breaking beneath someone's shoes. I scan the rest of the cameras on my path back, discovering Roy's nowhere to be found.

Since I'm all by myself, I let my guard down.

My eyes drift to the phone in my hand. My heart sails to Darlene.

Her back is turned to the camera, but it doesn't matter. She lies there naked like she usually naps or sleeps. Without a shirt, a bra, or a blanket to cover her, I get plenty of the view to spark my imagination.

I see each of her soft breaths, each rise and fall of her chest. The mass of dark, entangled hair drapes over her shoulders and back.

A sliver of light filters in underneath the thick curtains. The hint of the sun plays beautifully on Darlene's luscious curves, on the tender flesh I'm craving to sink my teeth into.

My dick jerks in my jeans in response to her. It's the part of me that doesn't give two fucks about my plans, about *our* revenge. It wants one thing and that's to leave its mark all over and inside this woman until I'm emptied. To spread every ounce of seed I have on her again and again and again.

Then there's the brain in my head. The one where all my well-thought-out revenge plans are stored. I'm way too programmed by my history, parents, and DNA to be the killing machine I am today to lose sight of my end game.

Jerking off to Darlene and going over there to tell her who I am then fuck her senseless will have to wait.

I have things to do. Phone lines to cut and CCTV recordings to erase.

After I listen in on these deviants.

When I turn on the audio in the living room feed, I realize how right I'd been to do so.

"You said this shit would be easy," Lincoln hisses at Caroline as he paces on the rug of the living room back and forth. "You said one day, and we're done."

The way he's whispering in anger instead of yelling gives me a good idea of what he's talking about. I reach the wall of broken bricks, leaning against it so my attention is divided between my phone and the road ahead.

"One more day," his girlfriend whispers back in that whiny voice of hers. "She—she talked to me about it. I'm sure a day of persuasion will do it."

"Yeah." Lane stretches on the sectional couch, the smug bastard closing his eyes as if bored. "I'm almost there. She wants it. I can smell it on her."

The hell he can. The vein in my throat pulses like blood is going to spurt out of there any moment now. The only thing he could have possibly smelled on my little raven is me.

Lincoln springs forward and is in Lane's face in a split second. Out of the three men in the group, Lincoln Hopkins is the mastermind as well as the cruelest and most soulless. I can't imagine he'll want anyone fucking with his plan.

I've witnessed it over the months I've followed them. Have seen how he tormented his classmates by insulting them for no reason when no one was listening, punching the others behind the campus.

It'd gotten worse in the days after he talked to his father. And even on other days, Lincoln never showed kindness. He didn't even know the word.

From one heartless sonofabitch to another—this man had been born evil.

"Can you?" He motions with his chin toward her room. "Sleeping in, locked in her bedroom, that's what a girl who wants it looks like to you, you dumb shit?"

None of the girls say anything. They watch the men, fascinated and yet completely and utterly quiet as if they were in a museum.

Can't say I blame them.

If I were in Elle or Caroline's shoes, I wouldn't have breathed a word either.

"Linc, I,"—Lane covers his friend's hand, trying to remove it—"I promise I'll do it. Jesus, chill out."

"I'll say this once, so you better listen carefully," the blond man growls in the other's face. "I refuse to stay here for a second after eight p.m. tomorrow. Refuse to wait for you to fuck her, or deal with her crying about how we tricked her. Eight p.m. I want the papers signed and her..." He makes a *poof* sound while bringing his other fist to Lane's face, then opening it up in one motion. "Gone. Does your tiny, underachiever brain get it?"

"Yes." Lane's brown hair bobs as he nods. "We'll be in the car by eight, tomorrow. Swear."

"Since you're such a fucking loser, I'm speeding up the timeline." Lincoln shoves off Lane, towering over him. "Before Roy returns, I want your dick wet. I want the tape ready. I want to hear her cry in the other room while I fuck Caro's ass tonight."

"Who said—" Caroline starts, but I mute her.

I shut down the phone, having heard everything I need.

And just like that, my plans change again.

Cutting the phone lines dives down to the bottom of my list. The red rage inside me, that shit shoots to the top.

Thanks to his friends, the shadow of the young man I recognize as Roy emerging from the woods will not be the messenger of bad news that'll terrify the group.

He'll be the message itself.

CHAPTER THIRTEEN

Vaughn

WHEN DARLENE CELEBRATED her fifteenth birthday, I discovered a little problem we had on our hands.

A boy at her school was bullying her. Had been bullying her for over a year, as my research revealed to me later on, a chase I started after snooping in her school bag one day.

Her parents had always been trusting. Too trusting. They believed that if anything happened to their only child, she'd come clean about it to them.

One of the family values they were adamant about ingraining in her was honesty. On most days, their daughter didn't fail to tell them everything that'd been happening to her.

Most days.

Obviously, they were both too trusting and had forgotten what teenage girls are like.

They were protective of her as well, but not like me. My possessiveness toward Darlene and my insane care for her wellbeing meant I left nothing to luck and went through her stuff. Regularly.

She must have known it or suspected it at least.

This little clever girl hid the fucker's bullying notes well up to that day. Or she just didn't want her parents to see them.

In either case, she made sure that none of Mister Wyatt's notes—the asshole who went to class with her—were forever hidden. Supposed to be, anyway.

You poor, dumb bitch. No one will ever love you. No one. What are you even doing in school? Get the fuck lost to where you belong —Sincerely, Wyatt Howard, your number one hater.

My first response was rage. Hot and white behind my eyes. One that made me tighten my grip on the note until the paper nearly tore beneath my fingers.

I breathed in and out slowly, forcing myself to settle down so no one in the Pierce family would have realized that I'd been standing where I shouldn't have.

That lowlife wanker, talk about dumb. Had he had the slightest inclination that Eric could buy off him and his whole family and still have enough change to last them ten lifetimes, he wouldn't have breathed a word in her direction.

Then again, Eric had invested his entire life, time, and energy to conceal his true identity.

Which didn't make Wyatt's behavior any more excusable. The stupid piece of shit even dared to sign his name.

Wyatt Howard.

That was how powerful his dad's status led him to believe he was. How goddamn bloody invincible.

Well, that wall curated by wealth and status was very short-lived in his case. Plans began weaving themselves in my head as I returned the offensive note to my goddaughter's backpack.

Plans that included one kid disappearing. *And* that kid's father losing his entire fortune.

"Is everything okay?" Darlene asked, waking me from my sadistic, vengeful plots once I left her room.

She no doubt saw my eyebrows pulled together, my black eyes darker than a starless night. She saw everything, always.

That was her. Had been her since the moment she could put two words together. Caring, compassionate, and in tune with the feelings of those close to her regardless of what she was going through.

My goddaughter didn't have to talk much to express herself. Didn't have to say: *Let's open up and talk about our feelings.*

No, none of that. A trait I thoroughly appreciated.

Her small, affectionate smile and soul-penetrating gaze were warmer than being thrown into a sauna. In her silence, through her attention, I became the king of the world.

The man who'd be her defender at all costs.

I leaned on the doorframe separating the living room and the hall, my head just about touching the low ceiling. My eyes focused on hers as she stood in the living room on their old carpet, scanning for any sign of hurt she might be concealing.

Nothing.

"Yeah, I'm fine," I said, sounding more like the persona I worked so hard on becoming.

By the age of thirty-three, my British accent was barely nonexistent. Unless, obviously, when someone caught me off balance or pissed me off so much that I lost control.

Which didn't happen too often. I'd been smart about it. Truth be told, I'd been smart, period. The genes of my biological parents provided me with a brain and a cunning nature, making me the fatal monster I was.

See, one does not become one of the head families of the gangs of London by sheer force and manpower alone. They needed brains, and Edward and Sophia Graham had plenty of those.

"You seemed…" Darlene wandered off. Pensive, not sad like she should have been after such a derogatory note. "Upset."

Upset doesn't begin to describe it, little raven.

In the unassuming kitchen behind us, her mom arranged the birthday cake on the counter, cutting four slices for each of us.

My best friend, her dad, had been lying on the couch, snoring after a long day and longer nights he worked without his daughter knowing. Poor guy had to be knocked out from dozens of hours of dividing his attention between his real and secret life.

"Don't worry about me."

"But I do."

I forced myself to smooth out my brow, to strain my lips into a semblance of a curve instead of a tight line. It would calm her, help her open up to me.

To be more approachable, I even lowered my voice, telling her it would be our secret.

"How are you? How's school?"

At that question, her brave façade faltered. The corners of her mouth curved down, the color of her eyes somewhat dulling.

"I... I guess I'm fine. Everything's great."

Back then, I didn't love her the way I did later on in life. I didn't want to strip her bare, rob her of her virginity, or claim her as mine.

My impulse to crowd her space and pull her to me was all-encompassing. A superhero in charge of saving one girl and one girl alone.

And I did.

A week hadn't passed after Darlene's fifteenth birthday, and Wyatt had what was coming to him.

Sadly—not—he was told he'd never be able to use his hands again. Meaning, he would never write another repulsive note.

A year after that, his father filed for bankruptcy and sold their luxurious home and everything they owned.

I did it for *her* back then. In those days when I was *just* her godfather.

In the present moment, I'm a far worse threat to anyone who dares hurt Darlene. Because now I'm her protector, avenger, stalker, *and* I am madly, insanely, un-fucking-controllably in love with her.

Those titles have been weaving themselves into my soul for the last two and a half years.

They're a part of who I am. They're also the driving force behind the mission I'm on. I'll annihilate anyone who dares to think he can manipulate her and take her from me.

And being with her yesterday had transformed my feelings for my goddaughter into something psychotic on a whole other level.

Thrusting my fingers inside her ass. Making her come. How she called me Daddy. *Me* instead of some invisible identity when she's alone in her room masturbating.

All of it drives me wild with territorial feelings toward her.

I can't stop visualizing it. The images of my cum smeared on her ass and back, her gaping mouth, how she was so utterly and completely mine.

She is, even if she doesn't know it yet.

I will own her. I will rule her as much as she rules my entire existence.

My dark queen.

Whom this scum below me thought he could hurt.

Thought he could get away with it, too.

He sits in the center of where Dale used to work. I locked up behind us after dragging him in by the back of his neck, punched his kidneys to weaken him, then strangled him long enough to have him faint.

A few minutes later, he wakes up to find himself naked and tied to a chair. Roy's wounded throat doesn't allow him to scream at first, but he does groan. It gives me an excuse—not to mention immense pleasure—to punch his mouth for the obnoxious sounds.

Through his pale lips, he murmurs the word *God* a couple of times until I step on his bare foot, my boot crunching his bones beneath it.

Then he screams.

Much better.

He needs to understand no one's here to help him. The Almighty himself created me, this demon in the shape of a man. I'm His reaper, made to incinerate the evils walking this planet.

I might have been much less murderous had it not been for the trauma I suffered. But I have, I've watched my parents die. And combined with their genes, I've transformed into this monster.

The five people who colluded against Darlene won't be saved. Not in this lifetime.

"Why are you doing this?" Roy squeaks.

Spit and blood coat his chin. His left eye is swollen because he dared to look at me defiantly earlier as though the fucker didn't deserve to be hit.

"Why, indeed?" I huff a humorless laugh.

He hears the malice in it, twitching in his place. He's scared. But not enough.

I have my methods, however, and have never been one to hesitate to use them.

"You tell me, Roy."

The blades of my scissors do a *snip snap* next to his cock. The miserable organ shrivels in horror much like Dale's had.

Chopping off a man's tongue doesn't get them as terrified as this, I've discovered over the years. Nothing beats a good ol' cock threatening.

Roy lets out a cry in fear, then pees himself.

Ah. Now we're getting somewhere.

"Have you been a bad boy?" I drive the edge of the scissors to his abdomen, gliding it lower to his pubic hair.

"No, no," he bellows, shrinking into the chair. "Anything but that, don't cut off my dick, man, it's inhuman."

"I'll tell you what's inhuman."

Lifting the scissors, I chop off one of his brown locks of hair, earning me another terrified groan. Too bad the chair won't move an inch, nor will my knots.

"Trying to fool a young girl is." I tug on his hair, clipping a second lock from the root. "To rob her of her future is. That's fucking inhuman."

His green eyes widen in understanding. "Wait, how do you—"

I'm getting bored with this conversation. The only reason I indulged him in the first place was that talking instills fear into people. The added level of torture just before he's wiped off the face of the planet is what he deserves.

Otherwise, I wouldn't have breathed a word into this exhausting back-and-forth.

Seeing as the hint of color that was on Roy's face slowly drains out, I keep going. He's earned the pounding heartbeats, the uncontrollable tremors breaking on his skin.

Has earned every breath I waste on this motherfucker.

"We're not here to talk about me. We're here to discuss you and your crimes, Roy Lynch." I stab him in the gut in a strategic place that'll draw blood without hurting any vital organs.

Unlike the guy before him, I don't have to rush this one. I locked the door behind me and put *Out of order* signs on all the gas pumps outside. No one's coming here.

"And you've done plenty," I seethe.

"Stop!" His lungs expand as he begins to hyperventilate. "I-I'm sorry. I'm sorry. We'll leave her alone, won't ever look at Darlene again. I swear. Don't hurt me. Don't—don't kill me. Please."

The room reeks of his urine, sweat, and fear. I'm not disgusted by it. I'm content.

"You had plenty of opportunities to pull out of your demonic little plan over the last few months." A second scissor jab parts the meat of his thigh. Blood gushes out, and Roy's agonized scream pierces the otherwise quiet convenience store. "Since you didn't, I'm here to deliver you to hell."

I bend to reach Roy's eye level.

Tears leak down his cheeks. Pathetic coward.

"Every last one of you."

My hand lingers in the air between us for a fleeting second.

Then it lands the scissors into his eyeball, all the way down to his skull.

CHAPTER FOURTEEN
Darlene

"SOMETHING'S NOT ADDING up." Elle shifts on her feet in the living room.

Her hair is a mess; the white nail polish on the finger she's biting into is chipped. "R should've been back already."

She's not wrong. Or at least, not very wrong.

Over ten hours have gone by since Roy left to go call a tow truck from the nearest rest stop.

I wasn't here when he left. I joined them a few hours later, was there by their side when the five-hour mark passed.

We looked over at the spare map—the one Roy didn't take with him. By our calculations, each direction was supposed to be no longer than a four-hour walk.

Knowing he wasn't supposed to walk back here on foot only added to Elle's anxiety. He should've been back here with a tow truck.

Ten hours is way too much time for him to be gone.

Or…given what I witnessed the past day and a half, Roy could be kind of an asshole. It's not impossible that he said the wrong thing, got under a local's skin by just being himself.

Whoever was at the rest stop might've not taken his shit like I had. He could've sent him off to another place or told him to go fuck himself.

Not that it's a theory I care to share with Elle or anyone here.

I don't want to hurt her, even if she does offend me a little. The group has been kind of distant.

Except Lane, who's been trying to get my attention by smiling and asking me to come sit next to him from the second I came out of my room. Uh, no thanks.

Anyway, I still care for Elle. I've never seen her this worried and frazzled, and talking shit about her boyfriend won't help anyone. Her mood least of all.

"I'm sure he's okay, Elle." I place the chamomile tea I made to soothe my friend on the table in front of her and place a comforting hand on her shoulder. "He might've gotten lost, that's all. He'll find his way back."

"No. Roy doesn't get lost." Her gaze snaps to mine, mouth pinched in agitation. "Ever. He's gone on a million hikes, and he always makes it back just fine. He's the best map reader out there. All of his friends say so."

"Yeah," Lane adds. "Roy's good with his maps. Better than good."

At their adamant claim, a scary notion crawls up my spine.

Since it's not a Roy issue…could it be Vaughn? Could the man I love have lied to me and, for whatever reason, have gotten to Roy?

No. No, no, no. Vaughn promised me. He had his fingers in my ass, his cum spread and smeared into my skin. He did what he wanted—what I wanted—in exchange for leaving them alone.

Just like Elle knows what a great map reader Roy is, I know Vaughn. He's a man of his word. He loves me. In a godfatherly way. And he's never lied to me.

Then again, when it comes to protecting me, I might be wrong. I'm not so sure he has it in him to stand aside and do nothing.

While I stay silent beside Elle, the past events in my life suddenly make a lot more sense.

Like Wyatt getting hurt. Like his father filing for bankruptcy.

Or what happened at school last year.

I walked across campus one evening toward the exit that led to my apartment, moving faster than I usually would. It was after an evening class, and while I'd never had a reason to be scared on campus, much less in the darkness that had been a home to me, I did that night.

It was different.

A creeping sensation of being watched hovered in the air around me. The presence suffocated me, heavier than the feeling of simply being watched as I had in my apartment for the past few months.

My home was okay. Cute even, especially when provided to me by my generous secret donor. Yet I couldn't help but feel I hadn't truly been alone there.

I'd checked and double-checked the walls, under the lamps, and behind mirrors. So far, I'd found nothing.

But it didn't take away from that feeling.

Truth be told, I'd been eager to move for several months. I stayed anyway because where would I go? With what money? So, I'd convinced myself the books I was reading were finally affecting my psyche, which I kept reading regardless.

I'd been creeped out, sure, but it hadn't been anything as scary as what loomed in the air that night on campus.

There, outside, on the dirt path leading to one of the college's gates, I couldn't blame my fear fully on my books. Someone could've been following me, waiting for me to be alone when the rest of the students spread out to their dorms or nearby apartments and attacked.

That notion alone lit a fire on my ass. I clung to the strap of my backpack, speeding up my pace as I watched my breaths leave my lips and disappear into the cold air.

The tall gates emerged in front of me, though they offered me no comfort whatsoever. I still had a few streets ahead of me. Some days they were crowded with people; others, not so much. It depended.

Filled with uncertainty and mostly terrified, I started running. Fuck who saw me, fuck if my unpracticed jog made them *laugh. It was one thing reading about violent men and women, being intrigued by the psychology behind what they'd done.*

Being threatened by them wasn't as interesting. It terrified me.

I wanted to live. Being careless with my life would be disrespectful to my parents. Their one singular wish for me had always been to enjoy the days I have on this earth. Live them to the fullest. And with them gone, I had every intention of doing just that.

Boom. Boom. Bang.

A second before I stepped outside into the street, two loud punching sounds echoed. Then something thudded as it hit the ground to my left where one of the campus' stone statues was.

In a weird way, the violent sounds comforted me. As if I could tell the brutality of it signaled safety, not danger.

"Hello?" My voice trembled, but I had to speak.

It might have been my wild imagination fueled by my reading. I might have been making all this up. It didn't matter. There'd been an entity out there protecting me, and it made me grateful. Made me weak with...not desire.

No.

Gratitude.

I had to thank it...or something.

The mysterious man or woman whom I believed saved me stuck to saying nothing. I kept looking around me, straining my head for something, anything, to discover just the statue there.

A long, relieved, and a little disappointed sigh rolled past my lips.

There was no one there. Or there might've been, but they were gone now. I should've been happy.

Yet I wasn't.

I hadn't been loved or cherished since my parents passed, and Vaughn had walked out on me. All I wanted was to have someone to care for. Not like Caroline or Elle. Like a real family.

Reluctant to accept that this was it, I walked forward. Each heavy footstep carried me toward the gate, then beyond it.

I had to sneak one final glance. Whatever happened in the last five minutes had me wound up so tight, it pushed me to sneak another glance.

And there I found what I'd been looking for. A flash of a shadow, a hint of short strands of hair billowing around a man's shoulders before he disappeared into the darkness.

I wasn't making things up. I also didn't want to hang around for them to decide I was worth coming back for. Maybe they didn't want to save me. *Maybe they were just after killing someone.*

Anyone.

Adrenaline surged through my blood, and I ran out of there. I made a beeline to my apartment building, not stopping until I had both the locks of my door sealed shut.

My eyes open wide as I connect the dots. The memory of that night has haunted me for months, who and what really went on that night.

Today, in light of everything going on in the cabin, I know better.

Vaughn had been there. Vaughn came to my rescue.

Could it be that he's had me followed this entire time? Did he know we were coming here, bug the house, and heard how they talked to me?

Was this why he was mad in the woods? Did he perceive that as a threat he had to eliminate?

Is this why he brought up hurting them?

I'm fighting such a violent inner turmoil with all this new information that I can't seem to answer myself.

I do have clarity about a few other things, however.

One is, it shouldn't matter how mad he is. He promised he wouldn't kill them. Roy isn't dead.

Two, despite myself, I'm aroused. A warm tingle spreads down my spine and my heart flutters. Reveling in the fact someone stalked me and had a mission to kill those who offended me isn't rational for shit, but my lonely soul feels it deeply.

Once Roy returns, which I'm sure he will, I'll scour the area for Vaughn. I have my thoughts sorted out. I won't stutter when I tell him there's no need to avenge me for a few misplaced words.

I'm a big girl, and when I'm truly offended, I'll speak for myself.

I'll also tell him that instead of killing people in my honor, he can do other things. Starting with making me feel alive. So, so very alive.

"Then he'll be okay," I say, seeing Caroline nodding at Elle's other side. "Right?"

"He will." Caroline rubs Elle's other shoulder in soothing motions. When she starts trembling and crying,

Eva Marks

Caroline whips her head toward her boyfriend. "Do me a favor and see if he's close, Linc."

"Fine." His blue eyes roll so hard that the pupils nearly disappear behind his head. "Come on, Lane."

"You sure?" He lingers in the living room while Lincoln's already shut off the music coming from the speakers and is standing in the doorway.

It's a strange question, because why would he need to stay here? The last thing either of us is going to do now is party, drink, or trash Lincoln's house.

I won't comment on that, though. This isn't the time or place to worry myself over this.

Lane can be whipped by Lincoln all he wants.

I have Elle to look after, then be brave and find the man I love.

"Yeah, I'm fucking sure," Lincoln growls, his impatience ever evident. "Let's go."

Lane, despite his large physical build that isn't far from Lincoln's, jogs after him almost as if he's scared of his friend's reaction if he doesn't.

I shrug internally, returning my attention to the sobbing Elle.

For less than a minute.

"No!" Lincoln's uncharacteristic shout silences my friend's sobs in a heartbeat. "Fuck! No, no, no!"

My insides just about crash into the ground at the terror in his voice.

For the second time today, I rise to my feet, beating Elle and Caroline to it as I sprint outside.

CHAPTER FIFTEEN
Darlene

AIR WHOOSHES OUT of my lungs and my pulse drops to near zero.

I've seen some pretty horrible crime scenes in my life on TV and in books. Not once have I closed my eyes at these terrible sights or cringed at them.

Then again, I've never had that close of an encounter with one that is *this* mutilated.

I'm not about to throw up or anything, but on a scale of one to what–the–fuck, I'm definitely scratching the top.

And if I'm not okay, I can't even begin to imagine what seeing this would do to Elle.

"Don't come out here." I stumble on the porch, backing up toward the entrance.

In a futile attempt to shut the door, I grasp blindly behind me for the door handle.

One of the girls beats me to it. I'm thrust forward as she pushes, and in a matter of seconds, both of them appear at my side.

Elle's scream pierces my ears, and it's the most heartbreaking *No* I've ever heard.

"Roy! Royyyy!" Elle cries out, leaping forward and down the stairs.

Her long, ash blond locks bounce around her like a halo as she stumbles forward. Her bare feet kick back gravel as she runs toward him.

She continues screaming; the noises leaving her lips are a mixture of gut-wrenching sobs and incoherent murmurs.

They're so fucking loud in the deafening silence. Her wailing blares through the shock that has the four of us incapable of uttering a word.

I mean, it's not every day that you see one of your friends or anyone, in the state that Roy is in right now. And the more I look at him, the more horrified I become as well.

The tall, well-built guy hangs by his neck on a low, sturdy branch. He's completely naked and most definitely lifeless.

His brown curls are a greasy mess like he went out for a ten-mile run.

Puncture wounds mark his taut stomach, his arms, his thighs. Tracks of dried blood run down each sliced piece of flesh, including where his penis used to be.

Yet the terrible view of his abused body isn't the worst of it.

His face had been horribly abused.

There's nothing where his eyes used to be. Just dark, bloodied holes. They're vacant, hollow, giving him the appearance of a horrifying human scarecrow.

It hurts me on a visceral level to think about what torture he was put through before his killer ended his life. How he scared him, tormented him.

No matter what Roy had planned for me, he didn't deserve to end up this way.

To my side, Caroline wakes up from her stupor and runs toward the edge of the porch.

I turn my head to see her gripping the wrought-iron railing as she throws up her lunch onto the ground below. Morsels of food cling to the strands of her hair as she heaves and tries to catch her breath.

I can't focus on her, though. Not when Elle stretches her arms up to reach for Roy's bare feet.

"Stop her," I try to shout to the boys but only manage a whisper.

Lane stands there doing nothing, in no better shape than Caroline and me to help Elle. His arms hang limply at his sides, his jaw slacked, eyes fixed on Roy's mutilated corpse. He doesn't hear me.

Lincoln does.

His detachment and stone-cold heart come to Elle's rescue. He meets her halfway between the house and the tree where her boyfriend dangles for all of us to see, engulfing her in his embrace and dragging her in our direction.

"Let me go!" Her small fists punch his chest, her feet scratching the ground as she fights to stay where she is. "I can fix him! We had CPR classes in school! I can still save him if we just take him down!"

"Shh." A tiny part of Lincoln's humanity rises to the surface to soothe the girl in his arms. "He's okay now. You don't have to worry about anything."

I appreciate what he's doing for her…even the lies.

Because she does have something to worry about. All of them do.

If Vaughn did this—honestly, who else could it be?—then Roy's death won't be the last. I can't deny it anymore.

Vaughn broke his promise to me, and something tells me he's not going to quit until the five of them are gone.

Matter of fact, I'm so sure of it. Every pore in my body gets the clue that this is how this weekend is about to play out. Just like I know that the sun will set sometime soon.

Like I'm aware that the most terrible things come to life in the dark.

And right this minute, in the light, we already have one pretty horrific view staring at us. The notion that more disturbing and cruel deaths will come almost makes me heave alongside Caroline.

The guilt is eating me alive.

Their deaths will be my fault. Mine.

I appreciate Vaughn's territorial behavior, how he takes care of me from afar.

I've missed his presence in my life. Have dreamed about him and came moaning to him, to Daddy, for so many nights.

What I wouldn't have done to feel him beneath my fingertips. To be the one he treated as an adult, as the woman he'd want to cherish and fuck ruthlessly at the same time.

The mysterious and somewhat ominous part of him has never frightened me. It still doesn't. Even now that I've witnessed it for what it truly is—a person capable of a heinous murder.

I'm safe around him. Hell, I love him. Will probably love him until the day I die.

But I can't allow him to slaughter people left and right for saying the wrong thing to me.

I wish there were cracks in my theory. Except there aren't. It's Vaughn, and he's mad.

A vengeful kind of mad.

So am I.

At *him*.

He promised me. Now, not only did he break his promise, but he also hurt someone who was just being rude. At this rate, I'll have dead bodies following me my whole life.

It can't go on like this.

This discussion we need to have has to happen soon—as in, this fucking moment.

"Oh, Lincoln." Elle's sob tears me from my inner debate. She becomes limbless, allowing him to carry her as she clings to his shoulders. "You have to help him. Please, help my Roy."

"I will." Lincoln grips either side of her waist, hoisting her up the stairs while casting his gaze on Caroline and me. "Take her to her room. Look after her. I'll take care of…" His eyes flit to the tree where Roy is hung. "Him."

"I have her." I open my arms to catch Elle.

Caroline doesn't make a move to help us out, standing there dumbfounded. With good reason.

Except her boyfriend seems to hate her for it.

"Caroline." Lincoln glares at her. "It's a dead body. Get over yourself."

His cruelty has my mouth snapping shut.

Surprisingly, it has the opposite effect on Caroline.

She opens her mouth, mumbling to Lincoln, "You said you…"

"I said I'll take care of *Roy*." He takes a step toward her, gripping her chin and forcing her to look at him. "What you need to do is stop acting like an idiot and help your friend."

My eyes dart to Caroline. Other than the traces of puke she has on her top lip, I see a girl gone pale with horror. So much so that she's not even shaken by Lincoln's words.

I realize then it's up to me to take care of them.

Elle just witnessed her boyfriend's mutilated corpse. Caroline is getting scolded by Lincoln for losing it over the murder scene in front of us.

I have to look after them.

Before that though, I have to ask, "What about calling 9-1-1?"

"Have you checked your phone lately?" His lip curves in a derisive smirk. "Right, stupid me, I forgot. You have no one. Who would you even text?"

I don't grace him with an answer.

"Anyway, the Wi-Fi is down for some reason and there's no service. I'll try again later."

"Yes, you're right," Caroline breathes as if she hasn't heard anything of what either of us said.

She's not here with us. Neither is Elle.

I'll delay my search for Vaughn for another hour or so. I have to put my friends in their beds, hum them to sleep, or they'll lose it. The trauma weighs so heavily on them that it seems like it'll happen soon, too.

"I'll take care of them," I say to Lincoln, reaching for Caroline's hand while still supporting Elle.

"Okay." Lincoln glares in disgust at the puddle of vomit Caroline left. "Uh, thanks," he adds, as though it cost him to utter the word.

At least he said it.

"R-R-Roy." Elle trembles in my hold, reminding me of what's important.

"Shh, it's fine." Not without effort, I spin the three of us away from the carnage, taking slow steps into the house. "Everything is fine, you just need some rest, don't you?"

Caroline remains silent at my side, her body a deadweight hanging onto mine. I don't mind it, hardly even feel it. The guilt consuming me gives me the strength to maneuver the two and drag them slowly to the safety of the cabin.

"I guess I do, but…" Elle finally answers when I settle her in her bed upstairs after I tuck Caroline in. "Roy, he's hurt. What about him?"

Air squeezes out of my lungs as the metaphorical rope tightens around them.

"Lincoln's with him." I pull the covers up to her chin, fastening them so she feels warm and protected. "He'll take care of Roy."

Her eyes are wide and incredibly sad, tired, and vacant all at once.

I want to tell her something that'll clear some of it, but I don't want to lie to her, either. "You go to sleep, Elle, that's all you need to do. Lincoln, Lane, and I will take care of the rest."

"S-sounds good." Elle's eyelids grow heavier until they close altogether.

I kiss her forehead, getting up and leaving the room. My sense of mission burns ever strong in my veins, and I don't stop, don't hold back for a minute after that.

I descend the stairs two at a time, lunging outside and into the woods, ignoring Lincoln's, "What the fuck?" at my back.

The blame is mine. So is the responsibility to fix this.

And it has to happen *now*.

CHAPTER SIXTEEN
Darlene

NEVER HAVING BEEN to these woods doesn't mean I can't navigate my way around them. Just like I did on the first night.

My parents, and sometimes Vaughn's, devotion to teaching me everything. That included finding my way in the middle of nowhere.

Their teachings help me guide my path in the darkness.

I remember exactly where I saw my father's best friend.

My heart and senses carry me there as if I'd been walking here for years. I start seeing the signs that tell me I'm on the right track.

Three low shrubs huddled next to each other are the first landmark. Then comes the tree trunk that has a diagonal cut in the center.

I'm close.

Ten-fifteen steps ahead, and I'm there. I march on, hands clenched into fists at my sides. I'm positive I'll reach the location where I met him last night.

Being this near to him makes my stomach turn and I just feel…weird.

Each second that passes by pushes me further toward an emotional edge, both anger and arousal swirling inside.

I push them aside, understanding they won't help the conversation I need to have with Vaughn soon.

Other than convincing him to stop killing my friends, I know I'll have to be honest.

I've hidden so much from Vaughn for so many years. Have played the part of the timid, quiet girl that I used to be. Told myself I was okay with whatever he offered.

Whether it was his curious gazes, his stretched silences, or his disappearance, I acted as though I accepted it.

That stops here.

I can love him and be mad at him at the same time. I need him, yet I have to put it in his head that I'm perfectly capable and have been living life on my own. I'm perfectly capable of standing up for myself.

The thoughts start falling into sentences in my head. One by one, they help me to formulate the speech I'll no doubt give him once we face each other.

I'm lost in thought when three words are uttered my way. "On your knees."

His voice stops me in my tracks. My vision clears in a split second, allowing me to see what's in front of me.

The man I met yesterday is there, arms crossed over his chest, his mask firmly in place.

Since it's far less dark than it was last night, I have a much better view of him. His broad shoulders, the outline of his biceps beneath his black, long-sleeved T-shirt.

The stance I've witnessed Vaughn standing in so many times throughout my life.

Even his voice is clearer without the night creatures chirping and buzzing between us or my earlier panic that messed up my senses.

I don't move. Don't breathe. Still can't believe it's him.

"Get. Down. On. Your. Knees." He tilts his head to the side, black Xs with black eyes behind them assessing me like he's a millisecond from eating me up. "Do it. Now."

As much as I want to, as much the lust in me consumes my bones, my pores, my heart, I hold steady. My fists clench tighter, fingernails digging into my palms.

"No."

"No?" Minus two feet separate us as he steps toward me. There wasn't a lot to begin with. "Is that so?"

I swallow around the lump in my throat. "It is."

He looms above me, so tall that I have to angle my chin higher to look at him when I speak next. "We had an agreement."

"That we did." He curls his fingers around my throat, drawing me toward him. His pupils are visible to me, erasing the zero-point-one percent of doubt I had left.

This is Vaughn. It really is.

"What makes you say I broke it,"—he inches closer—
"little raven?"

I gasp, hearing my nickname coming from him.

"Yes, you're right. It's me."

The confirmation doesn't change anything, though,
doesn't make him remove his mask.

"Why did you kill him?" I ask through my constricted
throat, my voice husky.

"Did he survive the night?" he answers the question
with a question.

"Yes, but—"

"Then I stood by our verbal contract." His fingers
clench a little tighter on my already-choked airways. "The
following day wasn't a part of what we agreed on. I will
entertain your question, though, love. Will tell you why I
killed him. He deserved it."

This is the moment. The time I stand my ground.

I have a feeling what I say now will have an impact on
how our relationship will go forward. Meaning, I have to
stop being a coward and spit it out.

"No, he didn't deserve it."

At that, Vaughn rips off his mask, tossing it to the
ground beside us. His lips are curled in an ominous snarl, his
forehead creased from frowning so hard. He's furious. He's
gorgeous. He's the man I adored then fell for, the one I've
craved every minute of every day of my existence.

"Vaughn," I breathe, my fists loosening, my whole
body becoming limp with the love I have for him.

"We already established you're a clever little one, Darlene."

Full lips covered by short, dark stubble speak against mine as he bends to me. He almost kisses me. His dark, fathomless eyes burn into my soul.

And I'm his.

Always have been, always will be.

"I'm not." I inhale the air his exhale provides me, my eyes tearing up at the onslaught of emotions from his proximity. "I don't know anything. I don't know why you're doing this."

"Bend your knees and to the ground you go." He pushes me downward by pressing his gloved hand to my shoulder.

I let him force me to do as he says until my knees hit the sand and patches of grass.

"You do know," he adds. "You've sensed it, felt something's off with these...people."

I'm wet. Despite the humiliation of being positioned to bend before him, of having his hard erection staring at me through his black jeans, I need him.

Arousal soaks through my panties, my clit sensitive against the cotton.

The slightest move would thrust me to the edge of an orgasm. Another few would definitely deliver me to an explosive climax.

I'm high on him, and it fucks with my resolve.

He sees it. His hungry yet satisfied gaze tells me he sees all of me. Even the parts I'm trying my best to hide.

"My friends, not *people*," I whisper as I fight through the cloud of desire.

"My darling."

With one hand and a very smooth move, he unbuckles his belt. Next, he unbuttons and undoes his fly without breaking eye contact for a second.

His erection is now very evident through his boxer briefs. My gaze dances between his crotch and his dark, devouring glare.

Swallowing is hard when he grasps my throat again the way he does, but I do it anyway.

Watching him this mad, this violent, with his hard-on in my face, it's everything I could've wanted and more.

"They aren't your friends." A hint of care slips into his voice, though his anger is still very much present. "Nor are they to be called *people*."

"They..." I cover his hand in mine, tugging it back to get some air. He relents, letting me have my tiny inch of space. "They said some mean things. That doesn't turn them into my enemies."

"But they are." Vaughn's nostrils flare. "Like I said, you noticed. Are you going to sit here and lie to your Daddy by telling me I'm wrong?"

The title Daddy registers harder than anything else he said. It sends goose bumps across my skin, hardening my nipples. The heat of awareness flares lower down my belly.

A moan escapes me when Vaughn bends toward me. His shoulder-length hair drapes on each side of his face when his teeth lock onto my bottom lip, sucking it into his mouth.

"Well, then?" He smirks, letting my lip go but not my throat as he straightens to his full height again.

Through my haze of arousal and desire for him, I think about what he's trying to tell me. I return to Caroline and Elle's changed behavior, to Lincoln's creepy stares, to Lane's sudden attraction.

None of it makes sense.

None of it is criminal, either.

They're not being themselves. They're tired, drunk, and bored. That's what I get from them, not anything of what Vaughn's implicating.

Since I don't have the answer he's seeking, I go for a question of my own. "Where have you been?"

The answer to it will do one of two things. It could confirm my suspicions and tell me I'm not crazy. Or, it could break my heart into a million pieces knowing he just didn't want to be around me anymore.

"Watching after you," he admits bluntly, his free hand whipping out his cock.

My eyes are drawn to the movement, widening at the girth of him. At the glistening drop of precum on the blunt crown.

"Taking care of you." Vaughn slides a hand up and down his length, over the veins as he points the tip at me. "Loving you when I fucking shouldn't be from a safe distance."

He *loves* me. Like *that*.

I'm on the ground and yet my soul levitates at hearing his confession. He wouldn't have looked so fierce had he meant an innocent kind of love. No.

This is the real thing. Knowing it makes me even more delirious and high on him than before.

Roy's dead body is forgotten; my anger is set aside. There's no explaining the way I feel. I don't want to analyze it, either.

I just want him.

My mouth opens for Vaughn as I sway closer to his dick, my tongue slipping out to lick my lips while wishing I could taste him instead.

"Please," I whisper.

"That's a good enough response for now, my beautiful little whore." His growl is my undoing, and I sigh with blissful contentment at the blend of praise and degradation.

"Please," I repeat, painfully desperate to have any part of him touching me in any capacity, anyway he'd allow me.

"I'm gonna enjoy shoving my cock down that throat of yours." He drops to his knees, his fingers threading through my hair in a punishing grip. "But only after I've had my taste of you."

He doesn't give me a second to marvel at how our needs align so fucking perfectly. He doesn't, because he clashes his mouth to mine, giving me my first-ever kiss.

I want to scream. I want to stop time. I want anything and everything. Most of all, I want this to be good for him.

It's that desire to be a woman instead of an inexperienced girl that freezes me in my place. Sucking him off is way less intimidating than this. Opening up and hollowing my cheeks isn't as complicated as kissing seems to be.

I stay there and do nothing. It beats trying and failing.

"Open up for me, little raven." Vaughn pulls back an inch, speaking against my lips. "Open the fuck up and give me what I need. What we both need."

My lips start to part. It isn't fast enough for him.

"Come here." He presses his thumb to my chin and forces me to move like he ordered me to. "That's it," is the last thing he says, then his mouth is back on mine.

Truthfully, I don't know what I'm doing. I don't know if I'm getting it right when I try to follow his lead by letting my tongue seek his. When I open wider for him or the way I move my wet lips against Vaughn's.

I don't even know my name anymore, let alone remember the gruesome sight I witnessed back at the house.

Blood, guts, and mutilated body parts cease to be a part of my existence.

There's only Vaughn. There's only his touch, his hand slithering to the back of my neck to pull me closer to him, his body heat radiating into mine.

He engulfs me in his hold, making me his, ripping away my fear of being inadequate.

Vaughn gives me more than just love in these moments. He grants me the freedom to act on my own impulses without fearing judgment or belittling.

To be myself and to be loved for the person I am.

Having my dreams turn into reality turns me on even more. I stop thinking of what I should do and just fucking do it.

Empowered by his touch, I arch my back, angling my head to allow him better access. Our tongues chase one another's, teeth seeking lips to cling onto, to mark.

He grunts into me like it hurts him to want me this much, to admit to it. The moan I give back is equally desperate and emotional.

We're drowning in each other, hypnotized by the moment as we devour one another.

That is, until I lift my hands to grip his neck. He tears himself from me, stands up, and pulls my hair. His dick is erect and proud and the sexiest thing I've ever seen.

Other than Vaughn's eyes, where I'm looking as he commands, "Hands behind your back."

I comply in a heartbeat, still high on our kiss and everything it means to me. To him.

"Good girl." Vaughn's other long, lean fingers wrap around his shaft, slapping it on my swollen lips once I've done what he asked. "Now, this cock won't suck itself, little raven."

He's not exactly asking. I don't need him to. I want it.

I let Vaughn shove his length all the way down my throat while he holds me steady by the back of my head. For him, I fight the gag reflex just so I can have every inch of him inside me.

He's thick and pulsing in my mouth, tasting even better than I imagined. So virile and incredibly him. His silky, hard dick slides across my tongue as he draws out of me, only to push back inside forcefully.

This time, I don't choke or gag. I accept it, feeling for the first time in a while that I'm finally whole.

"Fuck, darling." Vaughn's fingers tighten around my strands of hair, tugging at the roots. "You take me so well."

He pumps himself in and out of me, owning his pleasure with rough, elegant thrusts.

"For three years I've fantasized about what it'd be like, fucking those pretty little lips." Dark eyes glare down at me. Vaughn continues to talk as he pounds at me without mercy or tenderness. Taking me by force like he *knows* I want it that way. "Been jerking off to you, imagining all the violence I'd unleash on you. On what a filthy, compliant fuck doll you'd be to take everything I give you. But nothing compares to what a good fucking sex puppet you turned out to be."

My thighs clench at his words. A moan emanates from somewhere deep within me reverberating on his cock.

"Yes," he groans in appreciation, grinding harder into me until my lips graze his groin, until his balls slap on my chin. "Just like that. Exactly like-fucking-that."

Minutes go by of him fucking my mouth, of my arousal soaking my panties. He doesn't stop or let me breathe, his cock stealing my ability to suck in air.

I blink away the tears that form in the corners of my eyes. Vaughn's smirk cuts through his predatory expression.

"Gorgeous." He tightens his grasp on my hair. "You look bloody stunning when you cry, raven."

Regardless of his admiration, he pulls out. He leaves the head of his cock on the tip of my tongue, his salty precum leaking on me.

He places his hand on my jaw, keeping my mouth open. Instead of breathing, I press them together to have another taste of him, of his arousal.

Saliva trickles down my chin, my head spinning. But when Vaughn's eyes pierce mine, allowing me a moment of clarity.

"Wait," I whisper when he presses my head forward to suck him again.

He doesn't wait at all, rocking his hips, his length dragging in and out of me.

For a minute.

"Pretty little puppet."

The sliver of tenderness in his voice compels me to call him, "Daddy."

"Fuck." He tugs on my hair harder, his other hand releasing my chin to jerk himself off. "You were telling me to wait because?"

My previous lucidity disappears in an instant.

I'm lost in the need to have more of him, to listen to his depraved praise, to enjoy this ride he's taking me on. To come undone for him and only him.

"Answer." He drops back to his knees next to me. My arms rise on their own while Vaughn whips my shirt over my head. "If you want Daddy sucking on your clit and making you come, you better start talking, darling."

His strong hands yank the cups of my bra down, exposing me to him. That's it, though. I'm aware he won't give me anything unless I do as he says.

"Answer or I'll get real fucking mad, real fucking soon." He tweaks one nipple between his talented fingers, slapping the other. "I need to know everything there is to know about you, and you'll tell me."

All I do is moan.

"Not good enough." Vaughn's voice darkens like his eyes. "Talk."

For him as well as for myself, I open my mouth again, and I talk.

CHAPTER SEVENTEEN

Vaughn

"THEY DIDN'T DO anything wrong."

My jaw tics as I keep my mouth shut.

"They were rude, that's it," Darlene repeats, rushing to get the words out. "It wasn't their fault, they were just a little out of it."

She's quiet again, breathless from fearing me. From the pending orgasm that has her throat constricting. From her admirable bravery.

Tears run down her cheeks, her body kneeling and submissive to me and only me.

She's utterly beautiful.

She also enrages me in ways no one else has.

She still doesn't suspect them. Her need to protect them makes it that much more obvious. And while I want to scream the truth in her face, I don't.

As the only adult and educating figure remaining to look out for her, I'm responsible for her life lessons. And I take my job very seriously.

Understanding people's ulterior motives on her own is high on that list. The first thing she needs to understand by herself. I can't lay out the truth to her just yet.

A horrible truth that has me fuming all over again. They would've tortured and killed her had I not been stalking her.

I'm infuriated all over again. For how innocent and trusting she is.

Especially because of that.

Her blindness to her friends' underlying cruelty makes me want to punish her. To spank her while I fuck her relentlessly, to feel that tight little pussy clenching when she screams for her Daddy.

I'm blinded by the desire she stirs in me.

And I take her.

"On your back." I place a hand on her bare sternum, folding her and guiding her to the ground.

My all-consuming lust transforms into a wild, loose beast when I feel her pulse quicken beneath my fingertips. She's trying to fight back and it's hot as hell.

"I'm not done." Darlene's wide eyes bore into mine.

She should be scared. Should be confused at the very least.

She's none of those things as she finally gives in and reclines back. Not fearful in the slightest. Her tears dry up, and she glares at me defiantly as I loom on top of her.

Fierce and majestic, that's what this woman is. More so than I could've expected, neither from the girl I used to know nor the adult I've been stalking.

In two words, absolutely perfect.

But for now, she should remain well aware that I'm her owner. I grip Darlene from under her right knee, then the left to maneuver her legs so they're splayed straight on the dirty ground.

"Tell me, then." I shove her knees apart, lowering my mouth to the wet, sopping space where her thighs meet. "Tell me what makes you think they're so innocent."

I'm going to claim her, make her entirely mine as my wife someday soon. I decided it yesterday, but if I'm being honest with myself, I've wanted it for years now.

She's always belonged to me.

And as such, she should be aware of who I really am. How being gentle won't ever be in the cards for us.

Not that she wants it like that.

And not that it matters.

I strip her off her boots, socks, leggings, then panties.

My breath lands on her sensitive skin and she whimpers, thrashing her head back. I dig my fingers deeper into her supple flesh, introducing pain to the pleasure she's experiencing.

"You know the rules by now, little raven." I sink my teeth into the line where her thigh and cunt meet, sucking on it to the sounds of her strangled cries. "You'll speak. Either that or you'll be on the verge of an orgasm for so long, you'll weep in pain."

"You weren't honest about not killing them before."
Her palm bangs against the ground, grasping onto the grass
and fallen leaves. My good girl understands she can't touch
me unless I allow her to. "I get you're being protective, but I
need you to stop it. Please, don't do this anymore. I have
this, I can handle them."

She says she gets it. She probably thinks it, too. Problem
is, she has no idea what exactly it is she's facing.

I'm still mad about it. And I still fucking love her like a
man obsessed regardless.

I close my lips around her pink, taut clit. I suck her off
as a reward for being honest, then use my teeth to punish
her naiveté.

She pulls her lips in, her chest rising and falling
violently. And all the while, she's quiet so she doesn't alert
the other monsters that we're here.

"No, *I* have this." I place my hands beneath her ass,
pushing it up.

My tongue finds her sweet asshole. I lick around the
rim, up to her slit, her pussy lips, and clit where I circle her
until she's swollen with need.

My little goddaughter struggles to get away, just
enough to prove to herself she's trying. "Then I won't, it's
not okay…"

She gives it her best, and I admire her for it like I adore
everything about her. But her submission, her visible desire,
they're stronger than her reluctance. Her sigh when I suck
her clit hard and how she falls to the ground confirm that.

"I didn't mean"—I play with my spit in my mouth, spitting on her tight pucker and spreading it inside using my index finger—"that I don't agree with your terms. As infuriating as they are."

"Then?" A feral groan rises from her when I nudge my tongue into her pussy while I keep pleasuring her other hole. "Oh God, please, please."

"Tonight, no one else will die."

"Okay." Darlene is too far gone. Once more, her turned-on state makes her ignore the fine print.

I haven't and won't apologize for my so-called dishonesty. Because I didn't lie.

Then again, I haven't exactly agreed to anything she asked of me.

I know for a fact she wouldn't have asked for it, knowing what I know.

All in due time.

Until then, there's one promise I can give her. Making her come. Again, and again, and again.

"See, you can talk to me about anything." I scrape my teeth along her folds, grazing her clit as I go higher. Fastening my stare to hers, I say, "You're Daddy's good girl. And good girls get their reward."

"Please." She writhes, pressing her heels to the ground to ride my face.

"You'll come for me, then?" I draw back, spit on her pussy, and look at it as it drips down to where my fingers slip in and out of her ass. "Come for Daddy when I suck you so hard it hurts?"

181

"Anything." Darlene's black, ravenous eyes don't leave mine for a second. "I'm yours."

"Mine to play with?" I watch my saliva coating the finger that moves in and out of her, then add a second one to stretch her wider.

"Yes." One of her hands reaches for her hair, tugging on it as the pleasure consumes her.

"Mine to torment?" I let her down to the ground, tapping my thumb on her glistening clit while I speak.

"Please. I'm begging."

"Mine to make you both my whore and queen?"

She slaps a hand to her mouth, drowning out a moan when I pinch and twist her mound like the cruel sadist I am. But she nods. Fuck yeah, she does.

"Then come, darling." This time when I close my lips on her clit, I suck her harder than before.

For a brief moment, her body clamps all around me. Then she shakes and quivers, her clit pulsing in my mouth, her ass clenching and unclenching on my fingers.

"Vaughn," she groans into the evening air.

My name is being repeated by her, chanted, a desperate prayer rather than a word. It's not what I'm looking for, and she should be aware of it by now.

"Daddy," I grunt out, looming over her.

My hard-as-fuck cock parts the swollen lips of her pussy. I push two clean fingers down her throat. She gags on them, making me impossibly harder.

"It's Daddy, Darlene." I drag my fingers out slowly, feeling the texture of her soft tongue on my way out. "When you come, you come for Daddy."

She's choking, blinking away more tears that run the lengths of her sexy, plump pink cheeks. She's overwhelmed, beautiful in her struggle, and exactly where I aimed to have her.

My degraded, majestic queen.

"Say it." I remove my fingers. My breaths tangle with hers while I rock myself over her dripping cunt. "Call me by my fucking name and you'll get more of what you want."

Her throat works to gulp spit, to help her speak despite the damage I inflicted on it. I curl my fingers around her neck, sensing she's about to say it and needing to feel the word under my palm.

"Daddy," she rasps out. "I...I love you."

Then another tear comes, trickling slowly down her cheek. This one's not a result of physical pain, it's solely emotional. Her heartache mirrors the one my cold soul has been battling for years.

Unlike Darlene, though, I'm not that open about it.

I don't do crying. I fight. And she'll learn to be a warrior too.

For tonight, I'm touching her, taking her, claiming her. She can be emotional once the danger is behind her.

"That's right." I angle my cock to her entrance, to that tight little hole I'll own when I claim her virginity. "I'm here for you, but I can't allow any more self-pity. Not tonight."

183

She nods once, wiping the tear. Her jaw is set firm with resolve, her black eyes darkening. "Yes, Daddy."

"Good girl." I sink one inch of my length inside her. Deep enough to have her folds close around me, not too deep to rupture her delicate hymen. "You make me so proud, little raven."

"Are you going to…?" She barely utters the words as the wide head spreads her pussy further, her thick thighs pressing firmly around me despite the trembling in her hoarse voice. "Oh, oh…"

"Not tonight, little minx." My teeth scrape the crook of her neck, nibbling on her flesh until I reach one perky nipple. "Daddy's gonna sink just the tip in, take just a little. You're not ready for me yet."

"I am." Her needy whine is so fucking hot. "I've wanted you to do it for years. Daddy, please."

"Everything will reveal itself eventually."

I fight the insane urge to thrust into her. To sink into her, tear her apart, pleasure her through agony. Instead, curbing my desire, I suck on her other nipple, bite, and tug on, tasting her blood on my tongue.

"But I will finish inside you." Her wanton, inexperienced, and goddamn-perfect tongue meets mine when I kiss her, giving her a taste of herself. "And you will take my cum."

"Anything." She writhes beneath me, reacting to the circular motions my thumb makes on her clit. "Yes, yes, Vau-Daddy. Whatever you say. I'm yours."

"Yeah, you are." Strands of my hair drape around us, closing us off from the world for a few more seconds. "Daddy's whore. Daddy's lady. Daddy's everything. *Mine*."

"I am," is the last thing she says.

Darlene comes again with my cock buried an inch inside her. One of my hands restricts her wrists over her head, the other massaging her taut mound furiously.

"So tight and wet for me," I sneer between clenched teeth. "I'm gonna enjoy pushing my cock up to your womb, shoving it to the hilt, filling you up with my babies."

She doesn't say anything coherent in response. She's groaning, mumbling, and cursing as wave after wave of her orgasm rattles her.

I keep going, moving in and out and rubbing her clit. Her body strains for the third time against another rising climax, her eyes rolling upward, her lashes fluttering when her eyelids close.

I'm not having any of that. "Look at me. Look into my eyes when I take you."

The harshness of my command snaps her attention right back to me.

"Ready to come, aren't you?" My cock swells, almost bringing me there too.

"Yes." Her tits sway beneath me, large and soft and red from my torment.

"Ready to come when I do?" I bend my head, my forehead resting against hers. "To be my cum slut and take my semen wherever I put it?"

"Please."

I swallow her moan with a kiss, sucking hard on her tongue. "Then do it," I grunt. "Come all over me."

The moment her body starts rippling, the second waves claim her body, and that's when I lose control and release inside her. It's the most powerful climax I've ever had, hitting me straight in the gut. For a short while, I forget how to breathe.

A few minutes pass, and I return to myself.

To the icy, detached killer I am.

Almost.

A small part of me rebels, demanding I give her *something*.

"You are loved. Always have been." Using two fingers, I push the seed that seeped out inside her, mingling our fluids, and sucking on them. On her.

Darlene's gaze dances between my fingers and my eyes. She's still lost to her orgasm.

"Even if it's a tough kind of love,"—I repeat the motion, letting her taste us on her tongue while I get hard all over again as she sucks eagerly—"know that you are loved."

With these final words and my fingers clean, I help Darlene get dressed. I kiss her forehead, and clear the dried leaves and dirt from her hair.

"I am?" Big, round, vulnerable eyes follow me.

I told her I loved her before I even touched her. Yet, after so many years that I've gone AWOL, I understand why she feels the need to ask again.

I get dressed, grab my mask, and squat before her.

"Yes." I tug on her hair until she's looking up into my adamant expression. "You are. Loved. And you are mine."

My lips mold into hers one last time. My teeth mark the plump bottom one. My fingers sink into her skull.

That's all she'll have for today.

I get up to leave.

"Wait!"

I should leave. I really should.

But when she calls me, my twisted, blackened heart can't say no.

CHAPTER EIGHTEEN

Vaughn

DARLENE MIGHT BE sitting. She might be physically beneath me. Definitely not in a position of power.

Except she is.

Leaning on her hands, arms straight, shoulders pulled back, and chin raised high, she looks like a queen.

She owns me.

I admire it. I'm fucking hard from it, and my dick's still wet with her juices.

I won't let it go to her head, though. She has much more to learn this weekend until I allow her to rule me just as much as I rule her.

"What is it?" The speed with which I crouch down in front of her.

Grabbing her chin finally puts a dent in her strong façade.

She bites her plump bottom lip as if she's unsure of herself. Her gaze, however, tells me something else. She keeps it fastened to mine, willful and fierce.

I'm drawn to her like a hypnotized man. I shouldn't. I have things to take care of. She has to let tonight sink in, to connect the dots and start seeing her reality for what it is.

By herself.

Still, I can't leave her. I walked away from her once. My obsession with her won't allow me to repeat this mistake.

I lower to my knees, bracing myself for whatever she has to say.

"Who are you?" She speaks every word carefully, her tone unwavering and commanding me to answer her.

It hasn't dawned on me until this moment how much she reminds me of her father. The dark eyes and hair, the identical shape of her nose—they're all her mother's. Her demanding approach, that part she certainly inherited from her dad.

See, Eric was a kind man, a friendly man. Unless he faced serious matters—like when we'd argue about where Darlene should go to college. Then he became this almost unrecognizable serious figure. This persona he worked so hard on hiding as the elitist ruler of a law firm.

And though Darlene rarely saw that side of him, I'm ecstatic that he somehow passed it on to her. It means she's not as sheltered as I believed. It'll make my task that much easier.

My eyebrows knit together, my head tilting at her when I think about her question.

She knows who I am.

She *loves* me.

"Elaborate."

The leaves on the trees bristle in the light wind of the evening. From the corner of my eye, I spy a small animal I'm unable to recognize crawling quickly up the bark. There's a lingering scent of sex and bleach on me, and now on Darlene as well.

An abundance of stimulation overloads my senses. As the predator I am, I'm acutely aware of it. However, none of it demands my attention like Darlene's furrowed brow, like her clever eyes as she contemplates what she's about to say.

Once more, I realize how she owns every bit of me.

"Your accent," she starts after a couple of minutes of contemplation. Our faces are close, barely inches apart. Most people tremble in my presence. Not her. "This isn't something you picked up because you're fascinated with the UK, is it?"

Despite my best efforts to school my expression, my lips hike to the side.

Years ago, her parents and I decided this was the best explanation to give her if and when she brought it up. Telling her the truth would've meant another set of questions, ones we weren't ready to answer. And we hated lying to her.

The truth would've been just as bad. A sweet girl, the girl we both swore to protect, didn't need her mind muddled by the ugliness of my past.

Neither her parents nor I wanted that for her. Hence why I pretended to be an Anglophile.

She believed it, too. Why wouldn't she? She trusted all of us, her parents and me, and we've never given her a reason not to.

Then this weekend happened.

I revealed aspects of my personality she's never been exposed to before. Sides of me that made her question everything.

There's no use in lying to her anymore, nor do I want to.

There should be no secrets between me and my future wife.

"Clever little one." My tongue runs along the top set of my teeth.

What a pretty thing with wide doe eyes she is, glaring at me for answers. No one but her could derail my plans or cause me to put them on a temporary hold. Not like I have any for the next few hours. I did promise her I'd lay off the murders.

For *tonight*.

"I'm right." She nods to herself. "You weren't born here."

"That's true." While I will tell her everything eventually, I keep my answers short. Letting my guard down in one blow is dangerous, might even scare her more than I intend. "Born and raised in London until I turned nine."

The creases on her smooth forehead deepen.

"By Otto and Julie?" She refers to my adoptive parents, the ones she met.

Judging by the question in her voice, she already realizes the answer by herself.

"Tell me, love, what do you think?"

Darlene shakes her head. After that, she keeps silent as she tries to draw another truth out of me. She's tricking me into elaborating on my own.

Can't say I'm not tempted to fuck the intelligence out of her.

Then again, if provoked enough by her, I just might.

"You want me to tell you who my real parents were?"

Her infuriating nod is Darlene's second attempt to draw more explanations out of me. It sends me right over the edge I've been careful skirting around.

"You'll have to work for it." I rise to stand, walking backward to a tree about ten feet from where she gapes at me. "For every one of your questions, you'll have to do something for me in return."

"Okay," she purrs, her teeth sinking into her bottom lip again.

This isn't an innocent gesture, I see it now. My goddaughter has a few skeletons in her closet, sexual ones. She might be a virgin, but she's a seductress nonetheless.

My seductress.

"Crawl to me." With my index finger, I beckon her to where I am. "Be a good girl, come to me on your hands and knees, and I'll tell you who they were."

There's not an ounce of fear or humiliation on her features when she shifts to all fours.

She thrives on the depravity of my order, swaying her hips as she crawls to my feet.

And it's not just my dominance that turns her on.

My goddaughter witnessed a mutilated corpse up close and personal not an hour ago. My doing. On top of that, she found out about my mask, that I like rough sex.

She also, without a doubt, is aware that I've been stalking her.

And still, she's intrigued by me. She wants me, wet and dripping for me and me alone. Darlene is willing to act like an animal to unveil my history. She cares.

"There's so much to you that you hide, little devil," I drawl. I watch her knees drag on the ground, marveling at her dark hair gleaming beneath the scarce moonlight beams that filter through the trees. "Twisted and depraved as well."

"Maybe." By the hint of amusement painting her tone, it seems she doesn't remember Roy's corpse anymore. Or perhaps it didn't much bother her in the first place.

Another step closer, and her fingernails graze the front of my boots.

"Who were they?" There's no smile in her voice anymore, no remnant of it in her face, either. There's curiosity there and a hint of...love? "I want to know. I *need* to know."

As I stare down at her, at Darlene's defiance and eagerness, I wonder if my desire to be inside her will ever be toned down.

Fuck no.

It'll be a cold day in hell before I stop wanting her. Before I stop *loving* her.

"They were Edward and Sophia Graham." Since I'm even aware of how lackluster this answer is and how unfair I'm being, I add, "They were the head of a crime family in London years ago. Today they're buried on the outskirts of Boston where they died."

"Boston?" she whispers from what must be a shock. "How did you get to Chicago, then?"

"That's a second question, darling." I pop my pocketknife out of my jeans. It, too, smells of bleach, even though days have passed since the last time I cleaned it.

My desire for destruction rages inside me. It's ever strong now that I hold the small weapon. "Sit high on your knees."

Darlene does as she's told. I bend the slightest bit, starting to tear her T-shirt from top to bottom.

"They'll notice, Vaughn," she murmurs but doesn't resist me.

"I don't care." My cheek rests next to hers. I feel each of her hot, shaky breaths on my neck, her pulse against my temple. "None of this is for them."

The old shirt rips without a shred of resistance.

I promise myself that once this is over, I'll give her nothing but the best. The best house, the finest clothes, take her to the fanciest restaurants.

When this weekend's behind us, I'll spoil her rotten.

"It's for me."

194

She groans when I bite her earlobe and grab her waist, when my fingers bite into her feminine curves.

She's mine to cherish. Mine to torture. Mine to fuck. All mine.

"But—"

"You'll manage." My dick jerks from her heaved breaths in my ear. "Make an excuse. I'm confident you can do it."

"O—" she moans. "Okay."

"To your question, the Fletcher family gained power. They had enough of it to make my untouchable parents run scared." I pull away from her, straightening myself again.

She'll undoubtedly have more follow-up questions, and I will give her more in return. "For over a year, they took over the drug supply in the city. By the time Mum and Dad became aware of it, it was too late. Everyone had turned on us. That was why we moved to Boston."

"What happened to them?"

"Pants and underwear off, then back on your hands and knees again." My finger twirls in a spin-around motion. "Then let me see that gorgeous ass of yours."

Darlene's whimper is as involuntary as her, "Yes, Daddy."

And fuck, do I thrive on both.

She sits down, removing her clothes and spins to me on her hands and knees. Even in the darkness, the redness on her bottom from being *almost* fucked on the grass is visible.

"That's my girl." I swipe my thumb along the cum dripping from her slit.

"Oh." Darlene presses into me.

The fire in her doesn't allow her to beg for more or complain when I remove it.

We're going to have so much fun, the two of us.

"The oldest of the Fletcher boys, a real sadist motherfucker,"—I don't miss the irony of pressing my blade to her wounded flesh—"Harvey. He hunted them down. Hunted *us*."

Darlene sucks in a breath. It could be a reaction to my story. Could be the steel pressing against her left butt cheek. I don't care which of the two it is.

Just that she gasps.

"And?"

"Your cheek on the ground, your fingers rubbing your clit." Through clenched tight teeth, a groan escapes me after I free my cock out of its confines.

It's throbbing, begging for her, a bead of precum glistening at the tip. "While I nick your lovely behind."

"Are you sure?" She hesitates, touching herself nonetheless.

Half of her face mashed to the dirty ground, making her the most sensual vision I've ever come across.

"Never been surer in my life, my sex puppet. Now hold still until I'm done using my knife." I position my cock between her legs, looking her dead in the eye the moment I make that first cut.

A streak of red blood trickles from the straight line I slice into her. We groan in unison. Her fingers rub her clit faster, her head grinding slowly against the sand.

Pure, fathomless lust simmers through me, seeing how much closer to another orgasm that pain gets her.

"He killed them." I sum up the night my parents died, sparing Darlene the rest of the details.

She's had enough for one night. The rest of the story and how I finished him off can wait for the future.

"My parents heard him coming, knew they didn't stand a chance. They hid me in the space they had ready behind one of our bookshelves."

"Then your…" A moan slices through her question when I drag my knife along her precious butt again.

Her thighs clench, and I lick my lips as her thighs squeeze my dick harder. As more juices seep down her thighs. Then I make a third cut on her other cheek.

"Finish your question."

That fourth bloody cut on her skin and her labored, pained breaths nearly send me over the edge.

"You were adopted by the Grimms in Chicago?" Each word she lets out is strained and spoken between moans. "That was how you… How you and my dad met?"

"Indeed." I throw the knife to the side, leaning forward. I swat her hand from her clit, replacing it with mine. "But that's a story for another day."

She cries and clenches her thighs around my cock as I thrust it back and forth on her pussy.

"Be my good little raven," I groan in her ear. "Don't move and only come when I tell you to."

"Yes, Daddy."

The way she clenches around me is borderline criminal. The wetness that's soaking my dick makes my balls tight and ready to burst.

I pinch her clit, slap it. I don't stop touching her the way that makes her bite her lip and flex her fingers on the ground.

She chokes back the screams I know she's dying to let out. Other than clothes and luxury, I'll build this woman a soundproof home. She won't ever have to hide her true self again.

"You ready, love?" I go faster, rubbing her harder.

Darlene's blood smears on my pubic bone. The hot, sticky liquid brings me closer than ever to coming on her.

"Daddy," she whispers into the night air. "Yes."

It's all the approval I need.

"Come on my hand. Let me feel those sexy round thighs squeezing my cock harder when you do." My command is quiet and leaves no room for debate.

And my little puppet responds like the good girl she is. She opens her mouth in a silent scream. Her desire drips on my cock, her clit flutters beneath my thumb.

I finish a few seconds later, grabbing my cock so my cum sprays on her back. Marking her again as mine.

"Stay," she begs when I lift from her, her eyes meeting mine in the darkness. "Please. Let's get out of here. Just you and me."

"No can do." I pull on her hair, tilting her head higher and claiming her mouth.

Her lips taste of earth, blood, and her. I want to drown in them for eternity. Soon enough, I will.

"I'll be around, though."

"Can I come with you?" Her plea is more of a demand.

Once more, she proves to me she's evolving, growing into a powerful woman when she's not submitting to me.

"Not yet." I swipe my thumb across my stomach, licking her blood off it. "If you follow me, if you find me, our deal regarding the others is off. I will not hesitate to have all their heads on a platter by the end of the night."

"Why?" Quickly, she sits straight, reaching her hand out to grasp my leg, to stop me. "Please, let's leave here. I don't need any of this vengeance. I only need you."

"You do need it. And not. Yet," are my final words.

When the statement leaves my mouth, I collect my knife and my mask, and into the night I disappear.

She'll need the night to digest the information on her own. It hurts to leave her, and yet when I remind myself it's for Darlene's own good, the ache in my chest becomes duller.

Besides, it's only temporary.

Soon enough, I'll have her all to myself.

The threat will be gone. She'll know better, at last.

Darlene will finally be what she was meant for from the moment she took her first breath.

She'll be *mine*.

CHAPTER NINETEEN

Darlene

THE REST OF the world's definition of *confusion* goes along the lines of bewilderment, of being uncertain about something.

Then there's what I'm feeling right now.

As I walk back to the cabin, what I'm experiencing can only be described as confusion on steroids.

I'm so lost inside my head that I can't connect the words floating up. My emotions spiral out of control, faster and more violent than they had last night.

Yesterday, a bulldozer named Vaughn pummeled its way through my heart. The weight of him was heavy and scary and exhilarating which shocked me to my core.

That was nothing compared to the overwhelming pressure that crushes me beneath its weight this evening.

It's as if I can't breathe from the metaphorical weight on my soul. But weirdly, I've also never felt this light, this happy. My hormones are scattered everywhere, have not rested since Vaughn treated my body as if it belonged to him.

Still, nothing could've prepared me for this out-of-body experience from having multiple orgasms. From having Vaughn's face so close to mine. From his cock entering me just barely...

Shivers rake my body. I grasp tighter onto the two torn ends of my T-shirt, pulling them together to cover myself against tremors coming from inside of me.

Being with him, held and ravaged, it's what I've dreamt of forever. I shouldn't be surprised at what it's doing to me. And yet it's a lot to process.

Because even though I momentarily forgot about Roy, what happened to him, what Vaughn did to him, it all starts to resurface. I'm fully aware and can put a name to what Vaughn did to him—he *murdered* him.

He wasn't quick about it, either. He tortured him before he robbed him of his last breath, and it's all my fault. I could've saved him by telling the boys to shut up the second they made their crude suggestions. Roy might've been alive now if I'd done that.

Vaughn would've heard these conversations and would've seen how they'd apologized to me.

Yes, I couldn't foresee that the man who abandoned me was full-blown stalking me.

Yes, number two, I could've said something to Vaughn after what he did to the car. Except I didn't for the life of me believe he'd do anything worse than slashing their tires. I would've never in a million years guessed that my late dad's best friend had a taste for blood—literally, too—and revenge. Ever.

Logically, I know I'm not supposed to carry the blame for Roy's death.

My conscience, however, begs to differ. It dismisses my brain's attempts to rid me of the guilt.

I should've believed Vaughn the first time. Should've realized this isn't a game to him.

I should've warned the others of a threat without telling them who the threat was. I could've done that.

Should've pushed them, somehow, to go to the rest stop as a group. To persuade them to check into a motel or something and return with a tow truck in the morning and get the hell out of here.

Amidst the jumbled thoughts, the cabin appears behind the mass of trees. I slow my pace, fastening my torn shirt tighter around me.

I squint to check who's out there.

No one. The lights are off in the rooms, the porch, and behind the cabin.

I stop in front of it, shifting on my feet.

What will I tell them when I walk in? How will I explain why I ran off or why my shirt is tattered, my hair is disheveled, and my lips are swollen?

How can I warn them? Vaughn's threat isn't an empty one anymore. I need to tell them to leave, except I have to find a way to say it without telling them I'm in love with Roy's killer.

Well, not all of them. Caroline and Elle, I could tell them. They might yell, scream, and force me to go turn myself in at the nearest police station. I might deserve it, too. I could handle it.

Lane isn't an issue for me, either. I'm not sure what his reaction might be like, but how he acted around Lincoln showed me I have nothing to fear regarding him.

Which brings me to Lincoln. Even though I have Vaughn close and monitoring me, Caroline's boyfriend terrifies me. After seeing his glacial stare, I don't need to be told twice that he's dangerous.

Vaughn's eyes and intensity, as cruel as they might seem, have his love for me permeating through them. Lincoln's are empty, void of any emotion whatsoever.

Roy's death didn't impact him other than making him angry for a brief moment. Elle's sobs were something to take care of, his soothing of her a job to be done. And worse still was that Caroline's shock didn't register for him in the slightest. Or it did. It disgusted him.

And those are people he's supposed to care about.

What would he do to me if he found out I've known about a murderer planning to kill them? Me, a person he doesn't mind mocking, doesn't care to throw on his friend to fuck simply because he can?

He'd ruin me, that's what he'd do.

Less than six feet separate me and the house.

The voice in my head finally starts making sense, talking louder now.

Yes, he will kill you, Darlene. He'd do it so fast that even Vaughn with his bugging equipment and animal instincts wouldn't get here fast enough to save you. Lincoln Hopkins would slaughter you without batting an eye, and the result would be the same—Vaughn would still kill them, except you wouldn't be alive anymore.

No. I can't tell them. I have to trust the only man I've ever loved will stay true to his promise for tonight. Tomorrow, I'll wake up at the crack of dawn and tell them I'm sick or something so we can get out of here.

My resolve soothes the panic bubbling inside me. I head toward the house, to get in through my room's unlocked window. It slides open easily, and I climb inside. I'm grateful it seems everyone's asleep. I'm also grateful for the bathroom next door.

I tiptoe my way in there with a change of clothes. My heart breaks a tiny bit to wash Vaughn's smell and fluids off me, but I convince myself this won't be the last time as I step into the shower.

Under the hot water's stream, I caress each and every cut he engraved into my ass, then apply antiseptic cream on it before putting on my underwear and an oversized T-shirt.

Back in my room, I look at the time on my phone. I gasp when I realize it's nearing one in the morning. Evidently, hours ran away from me while Vaughn and I were together.

I have to catch some sleep before I put on the show tomorrow.

In the pitch-dark room, I lie on my back, staring up at the ceiling, wondering whether Vaughn will stay true to his promise now.

To be honest, I'll be really fucking pissed if he doesn't. I want a future with him, a future I can't have if there's no trust, if I need to fear innocent people will die because of me.

I want to trust him. I want it so fucking bad.

My conscience can't take on the guilt of another death. I twist to the nightstand and set an alarm for seven a.m. I'll wake up the girls, tell them I caught something, and beg to go home.

We'll be out of here by the afternoon. They'll be safe.

I'll make sure of that.

CHAPTER TWENTY

Vaughn

HALF-CLOSED BLUE eyes stare at me, pleading.

"Please."

Why must they always turn to manners in their final moments? What is it about saying *please* to a man wielding a knife or another weapon in your face? They believe I'll simply say, *Oh, now that you asked so nicely, you can leave?*

One day I'll have to write an article about it. Some sort of a public service announcement.

It'll be titled: *Being polite hasn't and never will save anyone.*

The text itself will go something along the lines of:

Dear soon-to-be sacks of flesh and bones,

The best way to depart from this world when facing a cold-blooded killer is to tell them to fuck themselves. Or whatever it is you'd like. Because asking for another breath sure as shit won't work.

Yours truly,

V. Grimm, representative of the Hitmen and Serial Killers Association.

Straight and to the point.

Until I do that, I've got Miss Head Traitor to deal with.

"No," I seethe, keeping quiet to avoid waking anyone up.

Especially *her*.

While I want Darlene to be aware of every aspect of my character, I don't want to do it all at once. Witnessing me murder these people won't get my message across.

It's how the others will react to it. How their lips will loosen from the fear that'll make Darlene see them for what they are.

It has already started happening. Like how Darlene's brow furrowed in the living room when Lane questioned Lincoln about joining him to search for Roy. Or how her lips twisted on the porch after they discovered Roy.

My little clever raven can't ignore these signs. The meaning behind their weird behavior starts to sink in for her, just how I envisioned it would.

And the results of Caroline's death will be no different.

My left hand wraps around the blond's fragile throat. The right one uses the knife to carve a message into her torso.

Her body remains stock-still after the shock it went into seconds ago. Her catatonic state helps, but I would've killed her either way.

After all, I have the upper hand on her. I have a hundred pounds on this petite girl, the element of surprise, and the fury pulsing through me.

Nothing will stop me from carving my message into her body.

That's the easy part. A child's play, really. Snatching Caroline from the bed at dawn where she slept next to her painfully uncaring boyfriend, that was the challenging part.

I know men like Lincoln. He would've killed her eventually. Him, and no one else.

But I managed.

I worked fast; every step was calculated and precise. From treading into their room undetected to shutting Caroline's mouth with my gloved hand.

The evil cunt stayed quiet after that. I guessed my threatening knife shoved to her neck did the trick.

Now though, she's loud again. Miss Let's-Kill-Our-Trusting-Friend can't stop pleading for her life.

It's really fucking annoying when I'm concentrating on carving the final letter *r* into her taut, bleeding belly.

"Please," she murmurs again.

"You will die, Caroline. Let me comfort you, it'll be a merciful bloody death for the crime you planned to commit." I move back to my heels, scratching the mask and hiding my chin as I admire my handiwork. "Compared to the punishments we had back in the homeland, you know—disembowelment and whatnot—I'd say you got off easy. You should thank me."

Her silent gasp does nothing to me. No pity or urge to have some sort of mercy on her rises in me. I didn't lie. The stuck-up cunt has much worse coming her way.

But then, where would I write my message? What good would her death be to me?

Yeah, I'd find endless satisfaction in torturing her, or any other spoiled brat like her. I met dozens of those. That's how Darlene's dad and I became friends. I can never forget that or them.

Eric was the only one who loved me for me. The unpolished kid who didn't fit into the preppy school his foster parents sent him to.

The rest of them mocked me for cursing, for not mincing my words.

They beat me up in the locker rooms. Stuck gum to the seat of my chair. Pointed, laughed, and tripped me in the hallways.

They'd done it until Eric, the most popular boy in school and one of the richest, put an end to it.

We both despised the others for being jerks. For thinking they were so much better than everyone else. Eric's loathing had always topped mine, even though none of them dared to hurt him. They disgusted him to his core, and he was tired of them.

That's why...

I shake my head at the memories. I have to focus on the task at hand.

At getting back at the worst bully I've ever known.

My lips curl in a snarl, my hatred bubbling inside me until it's all I know.

Fuck them for considering it. Fuck them for planning it. Fuck them up their fucking asses for putting their murderous scheme into motion.

They and I will burn in hell when our lives reach their end. Only difference is I'll enter Satan's halls wearing the biggest, nastiest bloody grin across my face, knowing I did right by the universe, and more importantly, by my Darlene.

What will they have to be proud of?

Nothing. Less than that, come to think of it.

"I don't understand," Caroline breathes out, still dangling between consciousness and the eternal blackness she'll stride into soon. "Why?"

"Maybe this will clear things up for you." I pluck the phone out of the back pocket of my jeans, snapping a picture of her stomach.

Caroline's vision must be blurry by now. I do her this one last favor and bring the photo I took close to her hazy eyes.

"Do you see, Miss Caroline Anne Phillips?"

She cringes. I let out a derisive laugh.

Both of our reactions are driven by the same reason. Calling her by her full name means I've done my research. That I know who she is. That this isn't some mistake she can weasel her way out of.

That I'm here because of her, to end her here and now.

"Y-yes." A tear rolls down her left temple.

Again, it does nothing to my dark soul.

All that matters is that she understands, and she most certainly does, given her following question. "Why do you care?"

"You little nitwit." My voice doesn't rise above a growl.

Don't need it to go any higher when the rest of my actions are a sufficient threat on their own.

I climb on top of Caroline, leaning on my hands as I'm too disgusted to touch her further. I need to be the last thing she sees on this earth.

Not the sun above. Not the maintained green grass around the cabin. Not the chance to catch a butterfly flapping its wings.

Me.

She'll die a miserable death soon, but I'd still like to torture her some more.

"You and your pathetic group didn't bother with research, did you?" Since the answer to my question is obvious, I don't bother waiting for her reply. "You missed the fact that Darlene *does* have a family. Though we're not blood. We're much thicker than that."

"W-what?" Her pathetic whimper ends the back-and-forth game for me.

I don't owe Caroline explanations.

The only thing she'll get from me is her death sentence.

"Time to depart from this world." I carry my knife to her throat while clamping a hand to her mouth to shove down her screams. "I would've let you say your final goodbyes, except I need you to be quiet."

Spit and Caroline's desperate cries sputter against my glove. They dribble down both her cheeks.

Let her fight. Let her whine. I'll be waiting here to personally give her a ticket to hell.

I start slicing along the length of her throat. Caroline's eyes grow wild and frantic with adrenaline. It hurts her, and it's also the end. It seems to terrify her.

Oh, well. She should've thought about it sooner.

"Enjoy burning in hell, Caroline." As much as I'd like to prolong it, it's time to finish her.

I wink at her behind my mask, then slice her open as deep as I can.

Blood gushes on my hands, around Caroline's head and shoulders.

It pours all the way down to the ground, turning everything red.

The fluttering body of Caroline stills slowly until her soul leaves this earth, and she lies there lifeless.

"Good riddance."

I unfold myself from the ground, standing up to my feet with my hands on my hips.

Caroline's corpse is my work of art. Her hands are tied behind her back, her ankles strapped together. Crimson blood taints her outer pristine façade, showing the world what she really is.

Beneath the manners, the designer clothes, the hundred-dollar haircuts. There she is, a heartless, cruel bitch who wouldn't hesitate to sell out another person's life for money.

My raven's life.

And just like that, I'm hard. Obviously, Caroline isn't what's causing my dick to strain in my jeans. She's definitely not the reason all my blood is pumping to my cock.

It's Darlene.

Protecting her turns me on. I'm fucking throbbing for her, raging to be inside her. To ravage every inch of her sweet, delicious body.

Once this is over, once they're gone and she knows the truth, I'm shoving myself deep inside her mouth, her ass, her tight, virgin cunt every single day for the rest of our lives.

Every breath she takes will be mine.

My palm runs over my length, squeezing the tip.

Soon. Very, very, soon.

"Vaughn?"

I'm not startled when she calls my name. Darlene's voice reaches from behind me. Her scent wafts to my nostrils until she's next to me, mixing with the copper ones swirling in the air.

There's a sense of serenity surrounding me. My little raven is clever. She'll see my message, and get an insight into a large chunk of the truth.

"Yes, love?"

"You promised," she mumbles.

Her shock doesn't last long as she stalks forward, her voice raising an octave, anger fusing into her whisper when she turns to look at me.

"You promised you'd stop with Roy. Caroline is"—her fist hits me square in the chest, her sob tearing what's left of my soul—"*was* my friend."

"I didn't break my promise." I swallow her rage, wanting to comfort her while being furious about how she defends them. "I told you I wouldn't hurt them *tonight*." Briefly, I tilt my head up toward the sky. "It's already morning."

"Why?" Another punch, her other fist slamming into me as hard as she can. "Why did you do it?"

"Look. At. Her." I grab this fierce girl by her shoulders, maneuvering her to face the message I wrote on Caroline.

"No." She twists her head, pinching her eyes shut while wriggling in my hold. "No. I won't! *You* tell me what this is!"

Any other obstinate person would've probably frustrated me. They might've found themselves equally dead as Caroline. But my patience for Darlene is endless. I won't ever give up on her.

I wrap an arm around her waist, pinning her back to my chest. Once she's partly subdued, I curl the fingers of my other hand around her throat, controlling her breaths rather than choking her.

"Look. At. Caroline."

Darlene's red face has me ready to fuck her here and now. I don't. She has her lesson to learn.

My good little girl opens her eyes to truly look at it.

"It doesn't mean anything." She shakes her head now that I released the grasp on her throat. "Doesn't mean anything at all. You wrote it, so what?"

I walk us to the cabin, where I spin her and throw her flush against the wood wall. I cage Darlene by placing my hands on either side of her face.

She stares back at me, her gaze searing into me.

She knows. She bloody knows I didn't just mutilate her friend for the heck of it. She can tell I'm right. That's why she's not yelling anymore.

The puzzle starts piecing together for her. It's still difficult for her to see the bigger picture, but she's trying.

Christ, I love her.

She still has a lot to learn, and it can't happen now.

One lesson at a time.

"What does it say?" I grunt, breathing heavily with my forehead to hers.

"No." Darlene's teeth sink into her bottom lip. "No."

"Say. It. You need to say it."

"I can't!" she whisper-shouts.

In a swift movement, I have one hand under her T-shirt, reaching for her breast and tugging on her nipple punishingly. While I do that, I control her movement by cupping her jaw, angling her face up so that she looks up to meet my eyes.

"What's the word on Caroline's stomach, little raven?"

Her dark eyelashes flutter on her cheeks when she blinks. She's deeply perverse yet incredibly angelic all wrapped up into one fire of a package for me.

215

I'll have her to myself soon, but not a moment before she *sees*.

"Traitor," she finally answers. "It says *traitor*."

CHAPTER TWENTY-ONE

Darlene

SOMETHING INSIDE ME screams, yells, shouts until my ears ring.

It's a mess. It's a fucking shit show.

But it starts making sense.

Just barely.

I have to think.

To try, at the very least.

Because nothing is harder than focusing on Vaughn robbing my air and space by looming over me the way he does.

For the millionth time on this trip, his presence turns me on rather than scares me. Being around him fires up my core and weakens my knees, making them feel like Jell-O.

He glares daggers at me behind his mask and tortures my nipple to the point I'm blinded by the pleasure and love I have for him.

His voice tells me he wants me to understand. The rest of his body demands that I submit and lose myself in him.

Another moan escapes past my lips. I can barely concentrate anymore. I have to think, and I have to do it fast.

So there are the facts that first, he's a lawyer. A criminal lawyer. He inspired me to be one as well.

I worshiped the ground my father walked on, and yet I chose to be a lawyer because of his best friend.

It wasn't that my dad wasn't good at his job. He gave his clients everything as far as I knew, staying late nights and sometimes even weekends.

He just wasn't Vaughn. I wanted Vaughn to be proud of me, to consider me as his equal.

But I digress. I don't have much time to let my mind wander. By the way Vaughn's eyes turn darker than black, I'd say I have to come back to the present moment right now.

Or else.

So, yeah, what matters is that Vaughn is a good lawyer, a great one at that. He knows where murderers get sent. What the inside of a maximum-security prison looks like.

No way would he have risked his freedom for me. He wouldn't have made such a blunt statement as carving into Caroline's body just because she mocked me.

It doesn't make sense. There's got to be more to it.

"That's right, little raven." The material of his mask grazes my cheek as he rests the side of his face against mine. He thrusts his erection into my belly repeatedly.

Methodically. "She's a traitor. The five of them are. Well, Roy was, but I took care of him."

Vaughn raises his head, pulling his hips back just to pummel them into me once more. My back hits the siding of the cabin, trapping me between it and Vaughn's thick cock.

"Do you see it now?" He moves his hand down my belly. His fingers coast along the waistband of the leggings I slept in. And then shoves it inside to cup my pussy. "Or do you need further explanation?"

Hot and cold waves flutter across my skin. Goose bumps come to life over my legs, arms, my neck, everywhere. He looks terrifying and hot wearing his mask.

It doesn't take anything away from how terrifying he is. Of how adamant he is to prove whatever it is he insists on to me.

That, or fuck me.

Or both.

Shit, I have to think.

"I don't get why them pushing me into Lane's arms, mildly so, would make you want to…to kill them."

That's the one explanation I can come up with. It's the best I've got, when I'm nearly blinded by Vaughn's thumb circling my clit.

I let out a heavy breath, trying so fucking hard to stay straight and not collapse down to the floor.

By myself. Through the sliver of sanity I have left, I remember he didn't like me holding onto him.

Instead, I spread my palms flat out on the wall behind me to hold on to it. I pray like hell that it and my very angry godfather will keep me in place.

"*Mildly?*" he whispers behind the mask. The angrier he gets, the more the Brit in him slips out. "They *forced* you, Darlene. You noticed it, don't say you didn't. Don't lie to me."

"Isn't it…" A moan escapes me as my body responds to Vaughn's fingers gathering more arousal from my slit and sliding along my crack. "Isn't it what you're doing to me? Forcing yourself?"

He's not. I'm aware of how much he's not. Of how I want it, maybe even more than he does. The need I've had for him has blossomed inside me for so goddamn long. Every bit of me aches to have him. Every part of me wants him.

And Vaughn knows he's not forcing himself just as well.

"I am not, nor will I ever, force myself on you." The fingers he has wrapped around my neck clutch harder, demanding me to fix my entire attention on him. "You *belong* to me, little one, because we were meant to be. I'm only taking what's rightfully mine. Don't pretend otherwise."

"I'm not." Frustration rises through my lungs, up my throat, and into my eyes. Two tears leak out without my consent. "But you have to tell me what's going on. Why did you kill her? She didn't do anything to deserve this."

Vaughn nods his head once. The pitch-black eyes that pin me into place roam over my face.

I'm drawn into it, intoxicated by his scent, and at the same time mad at myself for craving his touch and attention despite the scent of blood surrounding us. Caroline's blood.

"Answer me," I breathe. "Please."

"You're my clever puppet. You don't need me to spell it out for you. I can see in your eyes that you understand that I'm not coming at them for no reason." His gloved fingers trace the lines of my tears, though his voice isn't any less gentle. "The rest, I'll show you soon enough. The most valuable lessons are those you learn the hard way."

"What…" My breath catches in my throat when Vaughn discards his glove and bends toward me.

He yanks down my leggings, leaving me exposed to the fresh morning air.

"Lessons?"

I'm answered with a low, feral growl, then with my leggings shoved lower. He lifts my bare feet one at a time, forcing me to slip my pants off. To expose my legs to him, and to whoever might come here.

To flash my friend's dead body.

Which doesn't bother me. I'm feral for Vaughn, dead body or not.

In the back of my mind, I know I should be bothered by it.

But I'm not.

It is what it is.

A noise cuts into the air just then.

Of a zipper being pulled down.

My toes curl and an uncontrolled moan builds in my lungs. I need him.

"Lessons in unraveling people's hidden motives. Lessons in seeing the insides of their rotten minds. Lessons in finding out who *you* truly are, raven."

Vaughn grabs one of my hands, tugs on it, then shoves it into his boxer briefs. His cock throbs in my palm, the veins smooth as I stroke the length of him.

I shouldn't be doing this.

Not next to Caroline's body.

Not before I have a decent answer to what's really going on.

It doesn't get any more wrong than this.

With any other man, I would've stopped this. My common sense would kick in then and there. I would open my mouth wide and scream for help.

Except Vaughn isn't any other man.

He's more than my dad's best friend, my guardian, and the love of my life. He holds the key to the truth that everyone seems to have been hiding from me.

Suddenly, I get why I want him in this painfully inappropriate moment. Why I feel the ache of love I have for Vaughn. Why desire bursts inside me to get him off, to wet my thumb with his precum and rub it along the silky crown of his cock.

I moan in return to his satisfied groan. And all the while, Caroline's blood dries on either side of her neck.

He's the one singular comfort I have in my life right now. He's the only one I'll be able to lean on once the tidal wave of hurt hits me when I unravel what the other five people in our group planned to do to me.

Just the idea of being fooled and manipulated makes me want to cry, let alone the thought of them wanting to hurt me. I can only guess it has something to do with me losing my virginity. Yet I can't even fathom why they'd do it.

Actually, I don't know what good it would do to *anyone* to coerce me into doing it. Into taking the last thing I own after I've lost *everything*.

I have nothing left, other than Vaughn. I haven't had him either until now. For the longest time, I've been sure he too left for good. I'd had nothing and no one.

The tears I held back unleash themselves. They rush down my cheeks as I blink my eyes hard. There's nothing I can do to stop them.

"No," Vaughn grunts, gripping the crotch of my panties and tearing them right off. His hand then supports me underneath my thigh, picking my leg up to drape around his waist. "Don't you dare cry over them. Over this human pile of garbage that'll be gone soon."

"Wh-what?" I frown, my eyebrows drawing close together.

I'm not crying over them. I also don't want them dead.

There has to be another way to resolve this…situation. Vaughn still hasn't given me answers to whatever *this* is, and I think it only serves to annoy me further.

"We can go to the police." Despite my confusion and anger, I try to sort through my thoughts. To think of a possible, peaceful solution. "You're a lawyer. Help me build a case and arrest them for whatever it is they have planned for me."

"Fuck the law." Vaughn's hand works me harder, his gaze boring holes into me. I swear I feel his fury permeating through the mask he's wearing. "The remaining three are breathing. For the time being. You might as well consider them dead."

"No! Why would you do that? You want me? You have me!" My frustration leaks from me as I whisper-shout into his masked face. Not like it makes me move my hand from his cock. "We don't need to kill anyone else."

"Be angry all you want. Hate me even, see if I care. Whatever you're feeling, it's temporary." Vaughn covers my palm with his, positioning the thick head at my entrance. "This—what I'm doing here? This is permanent. The lessons, their deaths, they'll be over soon. You *will* go along with my plan. You *will* join me in the end."

I'm panting—short, clipped breaths that are a product of need and indignation. I want him. I want to fix this. I want to be a fucking part of the decisions that are being made for me.

"Tell me."

I leverage the pause Vaughn's given me in his silence, cupping the cheek of his mask. I lift it to reveal his sculpted lips and his strong nose.

Blood splatters appear on the bottom of his chin, red mixing with the black scruff adorning his jawline.

Then I raise it higher, exposing the dark hollows of his eyes.

"Please." I trace his face with my fingers. "Please, Daddy."

"Shut up, little raven." His eyes brand me, possessing me to do what he says without a second's hesitation. "You've said enough. Until I tell you otherwise, you're gonna shut up and take it like the good girl I know you are."

Time slows almost to a full halt. The world, my life, my very thoughts quiet, making the blood rushing behind my ears roar. It sounds like a waterfall that gushes fervently into the river, of water breaking on the rocks over and over again.

Nothing else exists in my universe besides Vaughn and me. I'm dripping on the tip of his cock while he consumes me with his glare, followed by his lips when he kisses me hard.

"Tell me you love me." He grinds out the words, fighting to say them.

Easiest thing I ever had to say. "I love you."

"Tell me you trust me." His hold fastens on me, his request spoken between harsh, demanding kisses.

"I trust you." My hips move the slightest bit forward, eager for him to take me. "Daddy."

"Fuck, how I love you."

As I'm moaning into his mouth, he bites my bottom lip harder. Vaughn tugs on it until I can taste blood on my tongue.

He shoves his entire length all the way inside me.

And just like that, I'm no longer a virgin.

CHAPTER TWENTY-TWO

Vaughn

MY LIPS DEVOUR Darlene's mouth to swallow her agonized cry.

Her no-longer-virgin cunt was wet and ready for me. She tore for me. Bled for me.

I broke through her hymen without the courtesy of making her come first. Took what belongs to me without a single apology on my tongue or in my eyes.

She's officially mine now. All of her.

I'm balls deep inside my goddaughter. One hand is beneath her thigh, the other clutching the side of her neck. Every part of me owns her. With my teeth still fastened to her lip and my dick still buried in her, I open my eyes.

And I see she understands that too.

It's the look of shock mingling with complete submission. How she melts into my hold despite the horrors

I've done. Regardless of the evidence of what I'm capable of lying just behind me in the form of Caroline's lifeless body.

This pretty little raven understands exactly what this means for her.

Things have changed permanently between us.

She's bound to me for good. The knowledge pulls out the monster inside of me in full force.

"You like this murderer's cock fucking you?" I start moving, pulling out an inch just to push myself in with more tenacity when I come for her again. The shred of mercy, of tenderness that I had, had been ripped apart the second my dick broke through her hymen. "Like it when I hurt you, when I treat you as my possession?"

"Vaughn." Her breath fans on my wet lips and I kiss her again, molding my mouth to hers.

My tongue rubs hers, and my fingers dig deeper into her flesh. I'm claiming Darlene's heart, body, and soul, finally going after what I've wanted for so long.

She answers my silent demands with another of her cries of pleasure. With her thighs clenching to suck my cock deeper into her.

It should be enough. Except it isn't.

"It's Daddy." My glare and my body work in tandem to pin her further into the wall. "Don't you ever forget that."

"Yes," Darlene complies, the eagerness in her voice making me pound into her harder. "I like it. I love it. Thank you, Daddy."

When I draw back, her folds wrap around the crown of my dick. My highly trained senses pick up on a scent other than her musky arousal and Caroline's corpse.

My goddaughter's blood.

I hold myself exactly where I am. My gaze races down Darlene's reddened cheeks, her soft neck, the delicious curves of her body.

I end my trail by landing where our bodies meet.

Crimson red paints my cock.

"I'm sorry," she rushes to explain. "I–I'm a virgin."

The hold I have on her intensifies, hurting her more than before. It's the only way I know how to get my point across to her. That I care. That I'm here for her.

Her mother would've probably hugged her tight.

Unfortunately, I'm not as gracious as Helena. And I'm all Darlene's got.

"Don't be sorry. I know." I drive myself back into her repeatedly, showing her nothing about her blood bothers me. "Being marked by you just as you're marked by me seals our bond tighter. I would've owned you either way, virgin or not, but I'm fucking honored to be the first. The only one."

I talk between each stroke; each time her walls squeeze me in.

Her tits bounce against my chest in the thin T–shirt she slept in. I lean deeper into her, feeling her shuddered breaths flick across my skin. Her thighs clench harder when I run my tongue along her jaw.

She's perfect. Truly, truly perfect. I want to eat her alive, to cut my name into her skin. For now, I settle into fucking her brains out.

Each time I draw out of her, I slam back harder. I need my cock in her womb. Need my seed inside her.

"You feel that?" We let out a heavy breath in unison when I drive myself all the way in. "That's where I'm going to put babies, little puppet. Our babies."

The entirety of her quivers, her eyes widening in shock.

"I lo—" she starts.

She never gets to finish.

"Enough of that for now." With my hands holding her firmly to me, we move together as I haul her off the cabin wall.

I lower her to the ground, careful to keep her face away from Caroline's corpse.

In the very near future, when Darlene realizes what her *friend* and the rest of them had planned, she'll accept Caroline's death. At the moment, I need her to focus on me, on us. I don't want to upset her.

I'm making her mine for the first time, and that should be her main and only focus.

My cock throbs inside of her, cementing our connection and pushing her deeper into the grass and ground.

Darlene's swollen lips part, air bursting out of her lungs. A soundless moan, a heave of desire.

"Life isn't just sunshine and rainbows and fluffy love declarations." I release her neck to remove my second glove, then grab my knife to slice Darlene's shirt down the middle. "Especially not when I fuck you. You'll moan and cry. You'll call for your Daddy. You'll be my fierce dark queen who loves being degraded. Are we clear?"

"Yes," she rasps.

She's consumed by lust but is so close to coming. It's visible by the way her eyelids droop in stark contrast to how alive the rest of her body is.

Her pink nipples are taut and straining, goose bumps prickling her delectable skin. I drift my eyes lower to her clit. To her clenched thighs that take every torture I lay on them.

"Yes, what?" I fling her ankle over my shoulder, not sparing her an ounce of mercy.

Even in the new angle, I'm able to bend her to my will. I stretch her leg, lowering my mouth to her delicate shoulder and bite while fucking her harder.

"Yes, Daddy." She thrashes her head back, arching up for me to give her more. "Please."

There's so much beauty to the pleasure she derives from the pain. She's been right to wait for me. She couldn't have guessed whether I would return to her life or not, yet she waited.

No one in this world could deliver her the erotic torture I do. No one will make her scream until she's blinded by her orgasms every. Single. Time.

"Fuck, you're tight." My tongue swirls along her shoulder, then my lips close in on it and suck. "Your little pussy knew to wait for your Daddy, didn't it?"

Sweat, dirt, and the pure taste of my Darlene rise as I keep biting her shoulder. I get harder, thrusting deeper to scratch the itch after years of dreaming of this day.

"I did," she says. "It did."

"Because you're mine. All of you. Now, your spit." I return to her mouth, hovering an inch above her. "Give it to me."

Through her darkened gaze, I see the pools of her desire and trepidation. She's not sure, though, of how filthy she can be around me. It's time she realized how disturbingly dirty I can be, and not just by ramming into her next to a dead body.

"You won't like the consequences if you make me ask twice, little raven." I draw myself out of her, resting the crown of my pulsing dick on her pucker.

My cock is coated by her blood and arousal. Hardly any lube.

As much as she gets off the pain, going in almost dry is on a whole other level of evil.

I don't need to tell her that.

My silent warning works as it should, and she's quick to fill her mouth with saliva.

"Good girl." Praise and my cock slamming back inside her are her rewards.

Though I'm not nearly done with being rough with her.

"Open your mouth." I grab her chin, tugging on it until she relents to me. I press my forehead to hers, whispering while I keep stretching her pretty cunt wide, "Good fucking puppet."

Her thighs clench around me the instant the words are breathed into the air between us. Then her tongue peeks to give me what demanded of her.

I slant my lips on hers, sucking off her spit. A groan of pleasure rises in my throat as I roll her saliva on my tongue. I revel in this sick kick I get out of having another part of her to myself.

I'll swallow it another time. Today, it's for her pleasure.

I sit up on my knees, my head bent low right above the pussy that I'm still fucking, still claiming.

My hair clings to my damp nape. My lips pinch together while I aim at her tight, wet hole.

With my thumb and forefinger, I spread her swollen lips to have a full view of her clit. The pretty little thing flutters for my cock.

"My beautiful, compliant sex puppet." My gaze rakes up her delicious body once more, feeling my balls tighten as I look at Darlene's face.

Her black hair is splayed around her like a halo. She's sucking in her bottom lip, looking at me with the desire for what's next.

I won't waste another second, focusing back on her cunt and spit.

A strangled cry escapes her, one she tries to mute knowing we can't be overheard.

"Fuck, yes." Her hands clutch onto the patches of grass below where she lies.

"So fucking filthy." I pinch her clit, then rub it in circular motions in intervals, being her torturer and source of comfort. "*My* filthy girl."

"Yes, Daddy," she whispers. "I am."

"That's it, you're getting it now." I smirk, pounding into her hard. "You're Daddy's dirty whore. Mine and only mine."

The full light of the morning swallows down what remained of the night. Everyone will be up any moment now.

I should pull out and put Darlene in her room, make sure she's safe. Hide the evidence so no one has any idea we had sex here, a mere few feet away from Caroline's corpse.

Doing it would keep her safe until my plan is executed. Except it's impossible to break free from her.

I'm not pulling out a second before she comes. Her first time should be special.

Looking at her, I'm mesmerized by how stunning she is. Sunlight glimmers on her skin, her perspiration glistening on her heavy breasts. I want to suck, slap, and devour them.

Which I will. We have an entire future for me to demolish and devour her body. Piece by piece, one breath after the other.

"I am."

The friction with the gravel, grass, and sand beneath her must hurt. Not to mention the abrasions I left on her yesterday. She doesn't seem to notice though, with the ball of her foot sinking into my shoulder, egging me to fuck her harder.

"I'm yours."

"You want to be my good little puppet and come for me?" Raising my thumb, I tease the little bundle of nerves while pounding into her. "To spasm all over my cock to milk my cum out of me?"

"Please, Daddy," she cries, her needy voice accompanied by a tear running down her cheeks. "It hurts to hold back. Please."

Watching her beg and weep does a lot for a depraved man like me. Another reason to reward her.

"Twist your nipples, both of them." My lips curl in a sneer. "Make it painful. When I see the suffering on your face, that's when I'll let you have what you want."

I don't have to finish the sentence for her to comply. Her fingers reach up, closing around the swollen mounds. Darlene pinches, torments, and pulls at her nipples which are now red from the torture.

Her smooth brow wrinkles with pain, but her gasps are those of intense pleasure.

"I knew you were made for me." I press my thumb to her clit, rubbing in quick and deliberate circles that will take her over the edge. "Daddy's perfect little whore. Come for me, let me feel that pussy clench around me until I fill you up with our babies."

Her eyelashes flutter, the word *yes* being whispered like a prayer. Darlene's whole body stills while her dark eyes pierce me with their shock and devotion for a second that lasts an eternity before she lets go and her orgasm rakes through her in a succession of silent moans and labored breaths.

"Such a good girl." Lengthening her climax, I continue massaging her, readying myself for my own ending. "Gonna come inside you now, put babies in that beautiful belly of yours."

With wide eyes, she says, "Yes," and, "Please," repeatedly.

It's then, as I tether on the precipice of an orgasm, that I see the world more clearly than ever before. And in my current reality, I see her and our future. I have her trust, I have her love, and once this weekend is over, I'll have all of her, including her forgiveness.

"Fuck, I love you." Though I forbade her from saying it when I took her, the confession is being ripped from me as I release my seed inside her.

I'm so fucking high it's like I'm being injected with some sort of drug, and its name is Darlene.

Worn out and sated, I lower to my forearms. I'm spent and the most vulnerable I've ever been. But I don't hate it.

I'm here, thoroughly satisfied, kissing Darlene's lips. I pull my hand back, running my fingers up her thighs, to her waist, ending with cupping her cheek.

And I find myself amazed yet again by how badly I need to tell her how I feel.

"I fucking love you, little raven. Always have, always will."

She blinks, another set of tears springing out of the corners of her eyes. It's heartbreakingly beautiful. *She* is heartbreakingly beautiful.

I would've stayed here on top of her for an eternity.

If not for him.

"Caroline?" Lincoln calls from somewhere within the house.

My thoughts of spoiling her rotten on the ground are cut short. My brain reverts to where it needs to be, to my eternal need to protect Darlene.

"Time to go." I lift myself and her up off the ground and tuck myself in.

I bend to collect our things, helping Darlene into her clothes then pull on my mask and gloves.

On our walk to her bedroom window, I hold her hand, gripping it hard to make sure she listens. "You'll put on a new set of clothes and hide inside there. Pretend you fell asleep."

"What about you?" she whispers, her pace matching mine.

"I have everything in order." We reach her window and I slide it to the side, then help her climb in, watching her walk in safely. "Keep to yourself. The less you say, the less likely they'll be onto you, and you'll be safe while I'm gone. Be Daddy's good little girl, and I promise it'll all make sense in the end. I'll be back for you."

Darlene pulls her lips in. I wish I could use the seconds she thinks this through to admire her body, to get hard again and fill her sore pussy with me.

There's no time for a second round.

We've run out of time.

"Don't disappoint me." My voice leaves no room for argument, as does my tough-love glare.

"I won't." She rests her hand on the window, obeying me by sliding it shut. "I won't."

CHAPTER TWENTY-THREE
Darlene

I'M NO LONGER a virgin.

I repeat, I am no longer a virgin.

Vaughn took this gift I apparently kept for him. He tore from me what I was so willing to give to no one but him, and left me complete.

I'm finally whole, yet it's the most lonely I've ever felt.

I miss Vaughn already, hating that I'm not with him. I hate that he's gone, and I hate getting dressed with the first T-shirt and sweats I could find instead of cuddling into him.

I don't just miss him. I *love* him. Owned and possessed by him.

Having him near me gives my life some sort of a purpose—my soulmate has found me, and I'm his.

I'm not even upset by the stalking and cameras he installed to track me. To be honest—and fuck, why does my neck burn with arousal thinking about this?—I like it.

I've longed for his attention since I can remember. And he's really been there. Following me, watching me, spying on me at home. It's beyond thrilling—it's every dream I have come alive.

For years he'd been a completely different man. So much so, that I began to think it would never happen for us.

He'd always been the one my family and I could count on to be there. He'd fix things around the house, sit with Dad after a long, exhausting week at work, listen to Mom rehash their school days.

It had been nice to have his constant presence there.

He'd talk to me too, just not that much. He'd always been reserved.

I wanted more. Prayed it for it every single day.

In my fantasies, he'd come and take me, claim me. He'd tell me the nastiest things like he had this weekend.

And now he's exactly that.

My lover. My protector. My everything.

Mine.

I should remember that. Should latch on to it while he's away and use it as a constant reminder that he's not going to run off and leave me.

Okay, so maybe I'm not so lonely, I tell myself.

I don't have to be this clingy when he tells me he'll be back.

I have this. I'll see him soon.

The question is, what am I supposed to do until then?

An hour has passed since Vaughn left. I haven't heard from him or anyone else in the cabin. I'm pacing around the bedroom, my steps silent on the wooden floorboards covered with carpet. I'm being quiet like he asked me to. Staying safe.

But the mess in my head doesn't want to quiet down. I can't stop thinking about losing one of my best friends and the fact that she somehow planned to hurt me.

Vaughn has to have a reason.

Going back to my past, I think about who Vaughn is. About his presence in my life before the disturbing conversation he and Dad had at the campfire.

Way before I discovered to what lengths he'd go for me. Before I found out he'd kill for me and not bat an eye about it, as if it's just another side of his personality.

I remember this one time I returned from school. This particular instance should've alerted me that Vaughn wasn't just broody.

That he'd been my shield against the world all along.

It happened one day during my sophomore year. I walked through the front door of our home, holding onto another geometry exam I aced.

My straight As were no surprise to anyone in my close-knit family, and yet whenever I told them about it they were over-the-roof excited for me. I needed them to experience it, the pride and joy they had when it came to me and my grades on that afternoon in particular.

I needed it desperately because otherwise, they would've seen right through me. They'd figure out what I'd been through that day. It would ruin their mood in a second.

Obsession

They were such good, amazing parents, always. They paid attention to everything I'd done, to my changing moods. We spent hours together playing board games and sharing dinners.

Generally speaking, they were the most loving people the universe had ever created.

That was why I hid the bullying I'd experienced in the school cafeteria. Most days, I didn't let it get to me. Some days, though, were downright awful.

Like that day. Someone from behind me had tugged on my old, tattered school blazer.

Another girl a few feet away yelled out, "How's Daddy handling the overdraft, poor girl?"

Almost everyone laughed.

I understood why my parents had me enrolled in a private school with a scholarship. For my future. Similarly to everything they did, they wanted the best for me.

But it was those incidents that sometimes had me praying I could've gone somewhere I belonged.

Bringing it up to Mom and Dad would've meant telling them about the bullying. My pain would become their pain.

A hard pass from me.

"Mom, Da—" My greeting died on my lips.

They weren't there.

Vaughn was.

He stood in our kitchen in one of his sharp, navy suits, scrolling through what probably must be work emails.

He'd received so many of those, all of them important according to him. So important that every couple of weeks he had to cancel dinner plans with us. I hadn't understood why a lawyer would have to fly across the country, but it was none of my business.

That afternoon, though, the emails weren't as important.

Vaughn put his phone down on our counter as soon as he heard my greeting.

"Little raven." He turned his eyes to me, his lips curling only slightly to one side.

I stood there, crushing hard on him as he snapped the paper in my hand.

"Another A, I assume?" He examined it.

The cinch around my heart tightened some more. I faked a smile, hiding what had happened that day from him.

Telling him rich kids laughed at me felt like I'd be accusing him too. It wasn't his fault. Vaughn came from a rich family, true. However, not once was he condescending.

I didn't want him to pity me, either. More so because I looked up to him. His opinion mattered to me.

"Yeah." I dumped my bag on the floor next to me, my shoulders sagging.

My smile lingered while my attitude showed what I really felt about life.

"What's that about?" His lips tilted an inch higher. "Were you aiming for a D?"

Humor wasn't a Vaughn thing. He didn't crack jokes, like ever.

He was trying to cheer me up.

Next came pity. I could feel it.

"Sort of." I cast my eyes downward and to the side.

Away from him. I didn't want to be consoled. Didn't want to break down and tell him what happened.

"Umm, where are Mom and Dad? They didn't text me about not being here."

His dark eyes stared so intently at me that I felt it despite having my eyes glued to the floor. I tilted my head up. I was right.

Vaughn stood there, leaning his forearms on the counter. He assessed me like he was seeing right through me.

My skin prickled under his scrutiny. An unfamiliar heat bloomed in my heart. It spread downward until I had to clench my thighs together to ease the pressure there.

"To your question, your dad got held back for a last-minute meeting with a client. He'll come home late," Vaughn offered blandly, as if this part held zero interest to him. Because it wasn't me. "Your mom stayed to say hi before she drove off with dinner to take to him."

Tap, tap, tap, Vaughn's fingers went on the kitchen counter. What was he trying to tell me?

"I think I'll go up to my room." I swallowed around the lump in my throat, starting to walk past the human X-ray machine.

I didn't care that my lips were parched from thirst, or my stomach started rumbling with hunger. I hadn't eaten anything since breakfast.

But I wasn't about to hang around so he'd peel off my layers and have a real reason to go boo-hoo on my behalf.

"Wait." Strong, long fingers grasped my bicep on my way to my room.

"Yes?" No part of my body twitched, moved, or flinched; my gaze included.

I remained still, needing him to let me go, to process this day on my own. And also...I needed him to hold on.

"If you ever need to talk about anything..." The tone of his voice morphed into one I hadn't recognized. A hundred times more serious than usual, laced with a cold, scary edge. "If anyone in that school of pricks did anything to harm you, you can tell me. I'll take care of it. Your parents would want that, too."

"Thanks, I'm good," I murmured, shaking him off and racing to my room.

He hadn't followed me there. And yet I felt so much better.

I release a sigh, falling on the bed. My face winces at both my stupidity and the sting on my ass as it lands on the mattress. I push away the pain, drop my head in my hands, and analyze the situation.

How could I have missed the signs?

Vaughn has been the same man all along. The violent edge in him has never been aimed at us. Nevertheless, it's been there. A rage that intensified anytime he thought someone was hurting me.

I trust him, I believe him.

Still, I'm curious whether he's overreacting. I have to find out what I'm being shielded from. I have to be in charge of at least a part of my future.

It's obviously not the boys' teasing.

Maybe, though, it's something close? An offense that is just as mild and wouldn't warrant these horrible murders?

What could it be?

I need to know. He can't keep hiding it from me. He has to tell me, and he has to do it right now.

Or whenever he comes back. Definitely before someone else dies.

"Caroline! Darlene!" Elle, Lincoln, and Lane call in the distance.

They won't hurt me. Nothing and no one will when I have Vaughn looming around.

I ignore them, doing what he instructed me to by staying quiet.

That is, until a devastated scream reaches my ears.

Elle.

Instead of staying here, I rush to put my socks and boots on. I slide the window to the side and am about to jump out when I hear the door to my room being pushed open.

Angry footsteps are headed toward me.

They're here.

"You," Lincoln growls, his cold tone never reaching a higher octave than necessary which is all the more scary.

Then he says something that really has me freezing with terror, "Do not take another fucking step, murderer."

CHAPTER TWENTY-FOUR
Darlene

"CLOSE THE GODDAMN window and get back inside here."

Though I only hear Lincoln's voice behind my back, there's another set of footsteps accompanying him. Strong ones, heavier than Elle's.

They're Lane's.

It makes me wonder, where is Elle? Did they just leave her there to deal with what's left of her best friend by herself?

Despite knowing the five of them colluded to do something that would hurt me, I don't resent the girls. I don't wish anything bad on either one of them. I can't, not when less than a day ago I considered them my second family.

Everything's happened too fast for my heart to switch from the love I had for them to the hurt I'm experiencing now. Hating them without knowing what exactly it is that they had planned for me is virtually impossible.

On instinct, I open my mouth to ask them where she is.

"Back. Inside," Lincoln repeats himself; his sharp tone is a whip that has me snapping my mouth shut. "If you force me to do it, trust me that you won't like the outcome."

I have no choice but to do as he says. When I turn around, I find one pale-faced Lane and another cross-armed, emotionless Lincoln glaring down at me.

Lane remains in place while Lincoln takes two ominous steps in my direction.

He could've scared me, this man-boy with the glacial stare.

Could being the operative word, since I've just been subjected to a man equally ruthless and cold.

The other side of Vaughn is the stuff horror movies are made from. I faced it and came out alive, feeling a million times stronger and more capable of dealing with Lincoln.

Although, they're not really the same. At all. I have to remind myself that as I stare at Lincoln's icy blue eyes, I can't compare him to Vaughn.

Vaughn would never touch a hair on my head. I'm sure of it. He's never treated me the way Lincoln has Caroline.

Even when he degraded me, ordered me to kneel, touched me, and penetrated me, he did it for me. And I *wanted* it.

Looking back now, I'm positive Vaughn knew. He must've learned that about me from watching me over the years. My calls for *Daddy* when I came were always for him.

248

A lot of my tears too. I consented to him long before he asked.

And it's not just me he wouldn't harm. It's the other innocent people of the world.

I have no proof to back it up, but I do have a hunch.

Because of my parents. My dad mostly.

They were so close to him that they were practically blood related. Mom and Dad had to have known Vaughn's true character. And they wouldn't have allowed a man who could flip like a switch and hurt just anyone for no reason to be around their only child.

Vaughn wouldn't have killed Caroline and Roy and hated everyone here for no good reason.

As far as I'm concerned, they've done something. They're trying to trick me into giving away my virginity.

Personally, I don't think he should kill them for it.

But I've seen how protective Vaughn is being. I get where he's coming from.

Sort of.

He's not an inherently bad person. His past might've shaped him into the man he is today, but he's not bad. He just isn't.

He cares. He does it from the goodness of his heart.

Lincoln, on the other hand, is all wrong up there. His dead girlfriend lies outside the cabin, her body mutilated, and he acts as if she's a part of the scenery. A bloodied wicker chair or whatever.

He's hardly mad, either. He seems as detached as he'd been yesterday as he towers over me without a speck of emotion in his eyes.

He's messed up. I'm just shocked I'm only realizing it now.

"I'm not a murderer." I lift my hands on reflex, showing him there's not a drop of blood on them.

"A murderer *and* a liar." Lincoln inches closer, his lips tilting into a sneer. He cocks his head to the side like he's examining an animal he'll devour soon. "I didn't think this little nothing of a human could have it in her."

Vaughn's warnings come back to haunt me, to warn me about Lincoln and this group. How I should be careful of them, to pretend I did nothing.

"I'm not a liar, either, Lincoln." My voice quivers.

It's not an attempt to act innocent like Vaughn instructed. This is one hundred percent me being scared of what Lincoln would do to me.

Then I remember Vaughn's fierceness and how I faced him head on.

I power through my fear and try to throw Lincoln off. "I didn't kill Roy."

Saying I know Caroline is dead would frame me. They would realize I saw her and said nothing. They'll call me an accomplice.

There's a twinkle in Lincoln's blue gaze. He's entertained, a predator readying himself to pounce.

His threatening presence slowly erases the security Vaughn provided me with earlier. There are cameras in my room, sure, ones Vaughn uses to stalk me. Yet the man who should be watching me could be busy doing…I don't know what.

All I know is that if he was watching, he would be here by now.

And he's not.

Lane's no help, nor will he ever be. He stands there idly, probably paralyzed by the shock of what he had to face outside. By the way he's been behaving this weekend— wanting nothing but to touch me—I see him for the weak boy he is.

He's there to do Lincoln's bidding. Just like the rest of them.

But he could've said no. Could've defended me earlier. Yet he hasn't.

Asshole.

"You hear that?" Lincoln doesn't twist his head to talk to Lane, his shadow pinning my back to the window. "You hear her lies?"

"Y-yes," his friend stammers from his place, sounding miles away.

"She's. A. Liar," he seethes.

"I am not!" The best defense is a good offense, they say, so I have a go at that with as much confidence as I can muster. "It was probably one of you guys. Roy was much stronger than I'll ever be. There's no way I could've overpowered him."

"See, now that's what a liar would do, isn't it?" Lincoln's mocking laugh mixed with his evil glare tell me exactly what he thinks of my meek attempt at denial.

And how much he still doesn't give a damn that his girlfriend was murdered.

He eliminates the rest of the distance between us, pressing me to the windows. The front of his sneaker touches the tip of my boot, his hands bracketing either side of my head.

The glaciers surrounding him envelop me too, and I'm shivering at the sudden coldness.

"Do what?" I whisper.

"Lie." His fingers curl around my throat, barely touching but the warning of violence is there.

Lincoln's cruelty is all-encompassing, drowning me in its endless depths that he's kept hidden up until now.

"I'm not lying." My teeth grit as I spit out the lie. "It makes no sense to blame me for Roy. I was sleeping when Roy was...was..."

"That's exactly what you'd expect a liar to do, wouldn't you? She'd pretend she never left the room," Lincoln growls. "She'd lie she didn't intend to sneak out, even though we just caught her in the act. You heard us down the hall, didn't you? We were coming to get you for Roy *and* Caroline's murders and you *knew* it."

I gasp, clutching on to the front of my shirt.

I'm the first person who saw Caroline drowning in her own blood. For fuck's sake, I lost my virginity next to her corpse. I did it happily, too. Because I believed Vaughn when he called her a traitor, even though he hadn't shown me a single proof to back it up.

Still, hearing that she's dead and being blamed for it—which I kind of deserve—hurts like a motherfucker. I never wanted anyone to die because of me. In fact, that's the main reason why I was heading out of the room to talk to Vaughn; to help me understand, to temper down the insane shock to my system.

To help me put an end to it.

None of which I can say to Lincoln.

"Oh, she's a good actress, our Darlene." Chills run down my spine from the way he says my name, from the venom dripping into his voice. "Pretending again. Acting as if you're shocked to hear Caroline's gone and lying about being asleep. Who can corroborate that, huh? Who do you have to vouch that you were here sleeping when either of the two were murdered, or when my tires were slashed?"

"I-I-I…" No excuses, no line of defense. I'm stuck on one word that only serves to have Lincoln's hand close in on me. "I had no idea Caroline died."

"Murdered. Not died, fucking murdered. Which you know as well, loser," Lincoln growls, his sudden rage focused solely on me as he slams both hands against the window. "You heard Elle scream, then you tried to escape. Stop lying."

Her scream probably reached the people who live in the nearby town, it was so loud. Denying it is futile at this point.

I think hard about how to get away from him, but I have nothing. "I—"

"Lincoln, maybe we shouldn't—" Lane mumbles.

"Shut up, Lane." The blond, raging man in front of me raises a finger to silence his friend.

His lips tighten into a fine line, and he sucks in a deep inhale through his nose. The enraged emotional storm in him disappears as quickly as it appeared, his features morphing into the picture of terrifying calm again.

"You didn't do it by yourself, though, right?" He lowers his head until our gazes are at eye level. "You were onto us, and you brought someone here to help you. An angrier someone. Tell us who it was and where to find him. Now."

Horror and fear for Vaughn's life race through me like black ink. It spills out of its cartridge into my lungs and guts, reaching every part of my body right down to my fingertips and toes.

Vaughn might be built for destruction. He sure as fuck has the strength to overcome a huge guy like Roy. But can he subdue two guys his size? When they're prepared to take him on? Lincoln won't be anywhere near as surprised or docile as Roy must've been.

But he'll be outnumbered. They might actually hurt him.

They'll take him from me.

"No," I deny his accusation with everything in me. "No. I don't know anything. I haven't told anyone to follow us. I was about to step out because I needed some fresh air by myself. That's it."

"Right, like I'll believe anything that your lying mouth says. Way I see it, *murderer*,"—he spits out—"you have two options. One, we tie you up and keep you locked up here until we get new tires and drag your ass back home to deal with you there. Two, you submit to us and we start what we came here for. You'll lie on the bed and keep your mouth shut while I record Lane fucking you, and then maybe, *maybe*, you'll be forgiven."

It's become paralyzingly obvious that this isn't about Caroline or Roy dying anymore. Not entirely.

It's about ruining *me*.

I just have to choose which option would destroy me less.

I wouldn't hesitate to tell him to tie me up if I believed it would end there. Vaughn would come for me, or the cops would clear my name. There's no evidence I ever touched either of the bodies. I'd be free.

Except Lincoln didn't say he'd hand me over to the police. He said *they* would "deal with me" back home.

He'll take me there, inflict cruelty, and punish me any way he deems fit. He could kidnap me to a place where Vaughn wouldn't be able to find me.

Not a single part of me trusts Lincoln to not cause me permanent damage.

As if that's not disturbing enough, he presented me with a second, possibly worse choice. This obsession they have to force Lane on me suddenly sounds dangerous.

You'll lie on the bed and keep your mouth shut while I record Lane fucking you.

The fear in me sends shivers coursing through me. But I'm subdued by it.

I become more alive thanks to it. It delivers me the clarity I need.

Lincoln confessed, give or take. He confirmed what Vaughn had warned me about.

It becomes so clear that Vaughn wasn't lying or exaggerating. They have a secret agenda that they'll execute after filming me having *consensual* sex with Lane.

They mean to hurt me, and Lincoln isn't sorry about it. He revels in it.

By taking this road—having sex with Lane and have Lincoln forgive me—I just might survive this.

Lincoln dealing with me at home sounds horrifying. I'm sure he won't be quick about it, either.

But fuck, there'll be a tape. A tape Lincoln will spread.

I don't have much left other than my dignity, good grades, and now Vaughn. Having a sex tape released would destroy my reputation. I might still stay in law school, but no law firm on this planet will hire me.

Hell, I wouldn't be able to leave the house.

Or maybe…maybe there's a third option out there for me.

Maybe I can appeal to whatever humanity still dwells within Lincoln's heartless soul.

"Please, Lincoln," I turn to begging, to the one ammunition I have until Vaughn catches up to what's going on here. "You don't have to do this. You *know* I couldn't have killed them and that I have no one in this world. Let me go. Please."

"Lane it is." Lincoln twists to the side, giving me his profile and a view of Lane as he addresses him, "She's yours. Have at it."

"Please don't," I repeat, then turn to the option that would be less destructive for me. "Tie me up. I choose option one."

"Too late." Lincoln doesn't spare a glance my way. "Lane here will fuck you, won't you?"

"Lincoln." The white shade on Lane's face changes into a sick kind of green hue. "After Caroline... Outside... I don't... I can't."

"I said do it." Lincoln stalks toward him, lifting him from the collar of his gray T-shirt.

Lane raises his hands in surrender. "I can't, Linc."

"What's the matter?" The sight of Lane's wide eyes doesn't bother Lincoln one bit. In fact, I think I hear a smile lacing his tone. "A little blood and you're having trouble getting it up? You need me to put on porn in the background to help you forget about my dead girlfriend?"

"N-no, no." Seeming like he's fighting a surge to heave, Lane gulps audibly. "I can't. I won't be able to do it."

Their arguing distracts them, and I take it as my cue to get out of there. I sneak my hand under the curtain, flattening my palm on the window's handle.

"Don't you dare, Darlene." Lincoln's hiss reaches my ears before I step outside. He drags Lane back to where I stand trembling, manhandling him until Lane's being thrust in my face. "Now, put your hands on her, lose our dearest virgin's clothes, and fuck her already."

Lane's clear blue eyes look down at me. He's horrified, disgusted.

This guy isn't going to rape me. Not today, anyway.

"No," he breathes out.

Relief flushes through me when he confirms it. I might still be saved by Vaughn, depending on how long they keep me here. Depending on how long it takes him to open the camera app again.

He'll have a chance to find me.

To save me.

To avenge me.

"I'm surrounded by useless idiots who can't seem to survive on their own. One's screaming like a fucking chicken with her head cut off. The other can't perform because of one miserable dead body."

Lane stumbles backward when Lincoln releases him with a disgusted grunt.

"Be useful, Lane, and go get me the rope from my room. Think you can handle that?"

"Yes. Will do, Linc." He sprints out the door as if chased, leaving me with the impassive blue-eyed monster.

"After that, you're going to the rest stop to get some fucking help, you hear?" Lincoln yells behind him.

"Yes." Lane's voice echoes in the distance.

My survival instinct drives me to start bargaining again before Lane returns. "Lincoln, listen, we can work it out. I promise you can let me go."

Lincoln grabs my shoulders in a punishing hold, swerving me around so my back is flush against his muscled, unrelenting chest. He has me by a stranglehold, cutting my air supply almost completely.

"Nice try, loser. You're not free," he whispers in my ear. "You might be off the hook as far as fucking Lane goes, but I promise you on my life that this isn't the end. I *will* have what I came here for. I *will* have my money and cut loose from my dad. Nothing will stop me, especially not an emo freak like you."

My eyes pop open, my mouth following suit. I want to ask him *What money?* so I can explain to him that I have none.

I would've, too.

But then his hold around my neck tightens.

The light in the room darkens.

Everything becomes dark.

And I black out.

CHAPTER TWENTY-FIVE

Vaughn

AS I SIT here in the woods after hours of making myself scarce, I think about my goddaughter. How is it possible that I haven't seen Darlene for what she truly is?

I'm not a man easily caught off guard.

I plan meticulously, ready for every twist and turn along the way.

Whether it's when I prepare for a case at the law firm, or to hunt down a mark, I know my shit. I know it fucking well.

What I didn't anticipate is Darlene and the profound effect she'd have on me.

The darkness I've seen by stalking her for years had me suspecting her and I were soul mates. I knew we were when her parents were alive, but I didn't *know*.

In the years I'd gone through her bags and private belongings, I hadn't come across anything like the books she reads these days. I hadn't heard from her room the music she has on her phone, too.

I wouldn't have left her had I known my darkness complemented hers.

She would've loved it, like she does now.

The few moments we shared on this trip opened my eyes to what lies beneath the layers of my goddaughter. What she doesn't bare to the rest of the world.

My Darlene is more than clever, beautiful, and kind. Fire blares from that girl. She's courageous and fierce. Her resilience to my temper turns me on, enchanting me.

And to my complete surprise and utter delight, it doesn't end there. Her sexual depravity matches mine in ways neither of us suspected it would.

That's a whole other level of perfection, giving away her virginity several feet from the bleeding, mutilated corpse of someone she used to call her friend.

For me.

Only for me.

She lives for me, breathes for me, opens her legs, and takes it like a good girl for me.

We're so bloody right together. The very soul of her was created specifically to fit into mine. Her flesh was sculpted by God—better yet, Satan—with the intention to mold into my embrace, her hair growing thick and black to be wound around my fingers.

I love her.

I want to fuck her. To possess her.

The obsession for her damn near blinded me to my world.

Thoughts of her consume me over the hours I spend lurking behind the trees as I stalk Lane. The asshole walked to the rest stop, and now I wait for him to return.

I stare blankly ahead instead of watching the group in the cabin, daydreaming about all the shit I'll do to Darlene.

Which is very unlike me.

Usually, when choosing a threatening tactic on my targets, I enjoy watching my results.

People's fear and misery top my list of favorite pastimes, and I try not to miss out on them.

Unless the sight distracts me. Watching Darlene for hours would cause me to miss Lane on his way back.

I can't afford the distraction.

My eyes follow Lane as he walks past me, trudging through the woods. He's finally back.

The cunt. Fuck him. He won't have her.

She's mine. Tucked safe in her room. They must think she's napping again, while I'm out here knowing they suffer.

In no time at all, though, the waiting will be over.

Darlene will be in my arms. Our souls will be as entwined as our bodies, and the wait will be over.

We'll have an explosive reunion after the years it took for us to reach this point.

I would've never believed I'd end up like this when I cradled her as a baby in my arms. When I watched her play with toys in her family's living room.

We shouldn't have happened. The lust, mature kind of love I have for her. Society would condemn it, would point fingers. Blame me for dating a child.

Like I care. Fuck everyone else.

There's no one else out there for her like me. No one in this universe will ever be this perfect for me either.

The two people whose opinions I would've cared about were Eric's and Helena's. They would've approved, surely.

They would've seen my endless devotion, how no one would love her more.

They would've been content knowing Darlene would forever be protected by me.

My craving for murder and my proficiency in violence will shield Darlene for as long as I'm alive. I will slay anyone who dared look at her the wrong way.

Like Lane, who disappears from my view.

My little one understands it. I'm glad she does. Though she remains mildly confused and in the dark about certain aspects of *why* this is happening and what they had planned for her, she knows they're wrong.

She'll see it too in no time.

Until then, I've got a job to do.

I keep watching the lowlife who was supposed to bring Darlene to her knees and rob her of her virginity. Of course, his shoulders are slumped on his way back, much like his now-dead friend Roy's had been. The convenience store is empty, phone lines are dead.

Lincoln will tear him a new asshole.

Not unless I do it first.

The tormentor in me is eager to smell the fear on his skin.

He doesn't notice I've gotten close to him. He holds something.

Oh, I see it. The glint of a blade. I have to stifle a laugh.

His knife could barely slice a tomato, and that's his version of being armed.

Pathetic.

And comforting. It tells without a shadow of a doubt that I've been right all along, that Darlene is safe. They must've come to a conclusion the real killer is out there, since she hasn't left the cabin. She would've come for me if she had.

I continue watching Lane the coward. His measly, almost kids' knife won't save him. Nor will his muscle power.

Nothing will, once I set my mind to do it. And I have, the second he became a part of the group who plotted to destroy my Darlene.

My little raven.

The mere thought of her name chokes me in a pleasant way.

Maybe I can have a look at her. I've earned it after ten hours of holding back.

And Lane is on his way to the cabin. It'll take him some time to reach it, to tell them the bad news. I have a few minutes until his entertaining act comes on.

While he continues on his march forward, I swipe the phone out of the back pocket of my jeans. I unlock it, quickly navigating to the camera app.

It takes less than a second for my nerves to explode.

Fury doesn't begin to describe the emotion that rakes through me. I'm being devoured by rage as the stream of Darlene's bedroom lights up on my screen. I'm consumed by anger so visceral, I could bite someone's ear off like it was nothing.

These bastards have her wrists tied above her head. My Darlene, *mine*, is pinned to the wrought-iron headboard and consequently the bed. Her ankles are bound together in front of her.

Tape is clamping her mouth shut, a fabric covering her eyes.

I'm looking at this queen as she's being held down, as she's fighting the restrictions. Her mouth moves slightly against the tape as she no doubt does her best to scream.

Who knows how many hours she's been bound like this. How many excruciating minutes she had to suffer through.

By herself.

Fuck. Fuck, fuck, fuck.

The confidence I've had until recently dissolves to nothing. For the first time in my entire life, I despise myself.

My focus on my plan has blinded me to this third option.

Sure, Lane may be dumb as bricks, but Lincoln isn't. He knows this isn't some low-budget horror flick. He knows I'm not killing them randomly.

He's fully aware that someone has it out for them. That the *Traitor* engraved on Caroline's body was a message that I'm not done with my revenge.

Since Elle would never hurt Roy or her best friend, and Lane is nothing but a lackey, only one suspect remains. One girl who they wronged. Darlene.

What a bloody, disastrous oversight on my part.

I'm still immobile as I'm devoured by my agony and self-loathing. I scold myself over and over again.

Killing them isn't the goal here, as entertaining as it may be.

She is the final goal. Her safety, her life. And I've neglected it.

Suddenly, I don't see her on the screen, hurt and silently begging for her savior.

Her image transforms into being that of my biological parents. They're sprawled on the bed in a pool of blood. Their mouths are open, eyes gaping and devoid of life.

Their bodies are scattered around the room like Harvey Fletcher left them so many years ago. The bastard wasn't satisfied with simply murdering them, no.

From my hiding place, I had to watch him take his precious time carving out their guts, cutting out the tops of their scalps. I forced down my vomit while he emptied the contents of their brains on the old tan carpet, then snapped photos as a trophy or to show off back home.

The vivid image of their corpses as if I'm really looking at them now doesn't surprise me. I don't need to see a therapist to connect the dots.

The impact my history has on me is clear to me. I'll never forget what happened that day and its role in shaping me into the man I am today.

I'm a product of my trauma. The hollow faces of my dead parents and how they were brutalized and torn into pieces will haunt me for life.

No kid should be exposed to the sights I've seen. No adult, either.

But I have. And now the rest of the world will just have to deal with the fallout.

I shake my head, forcing myself to return to the present. To the here and now where I fucked up royally.

This—Darlene becoming their victim, again—wasn't how the events of this weekend were supposed to turn out.

She's *mine*. Mine and only mine in every aspect of the word.

Blood surges to my cock in my feral need to defend and claim her. To take back what belongs to me.

I'll strike them after I ensure my cum is deep inside her. When she's safe and sheltered while I slaughter them one by one then come for her.

My muscles function again, stronger and more pumped with blood and adrenaline than ever before. They propel me to run, carrying me as I sprint past high roots and low shrubs, over potholes in the ground, past random animals.

To her.

They captured her like a prisoner, my mind keeps reminding me, fueling my rage. *Hurt them. Torture them. Kill them.*

How dare they tie her up?

As if the monstrosity of what they have in store for her isn't enough. As if they just had to find another way to humiliate and hurt her on top of everything.

They think they can fuck with my woman?

In their motherfucking dreams.

I run where Lane can't see me, leaving him behind.

Dry leaves crunch beneath my boots as I head forward in the early evening. My sharp set of eyes is able to detect where I'm going despite the darkness beginning to set around me.

One thing and one thing alone comforts me throughout these torturous minutes—they won't lay a finger on her before Lane gets there. By then, I'll get there to serve as Lane's welcome committee.

Because Lincoln wouldn't go after Darlene by himself. This tidbit of knowledge was brought to me thanks to the time I spent listening in on them. He would've fucked her himself if it weren't for his fear of being recognized in the recording or having his DNA on her.

Self-preservation meets Daddy issues.

He thought everything through, including the shell company the money of Darlene's inheritance would go to, that coward.

I'm thankful for that. He won't go into Darlene's room. Won't step inside when I ravage her body right before I destroy theirs.

He won't have any idea I'm coming for him. For all of them.

No more fucking around.

It's showtime.

CHAPTER TWENTY-SIX

Darlene

THREE SECONDS TICKED by since Lincoln left me tied up in my bedroom.

Or five minutes.

Maybe an hour.

That or four hundred days.

Fuck if I know.

Being bound and blinded robbed me of any sense of time. It also made me seriously pissed off.

I hate lying helpless on this bed, tied up and left alone like a prisoner waiting for her sentence. I hate that Vaughn abandoned me again, that I'm about to be tortured and probably killed.

For what? I'm still in the dark about that one. Because Vaughn didn't tell me, and now he's gone.

God-fucking-dammit, I will not cry for him or myself.

I will not.

The window slides open, the whooshing noise drawing my attention and saving me from self-pity.

Someone whistles.

The cool air of the afternoon's breeze spills into the room, caressing my ears and cheek.

A footstep of a heavy boot followed by another causes the floorboards to creak as he climbs inside my bedroom.

Lastly, his virile scent tinged with that of copper swirls and swivels in the air, landing in my nostrils.

"Little raven."

Vaughn.

Warmth barrels into me like the first sunny day after a long, windy Chicago winter.

But it doesn't last.

Fury, heat, and compassion rise to play tug-of-war on my heart.

Vaughn does so many things to me at once, confusing me to the point that my emotions almost tear me apart.

"My lovely little raven," he repeats. At the sound of his hoarse voice, I surrender to him.

I have to believe that he had some sort of plan. That this is why he let me rot for hours.

Vaughn is both my owner and he's mine. And in the end, he came for me.

I can't stay mad at him. I love him.

I whimper his name, fighting the tape constricting my speech and let out the most pathetic, "Hmph."

"Did they touch you?" he asks, his voice restrained and far away from me.

Too far.

I'm still not mad. He'll touch me when the timing is right.

I shake my head.

"I would've killed myself if they had. Them, then myself." He exhales, the honesty in his words brutal and blatant.

Then, just as fast, he's back to being my impassioned Vaughn. "I'm sorry, raven."

Another set of hmphs comes out of me. He doesn't hear what I mean to say, can't possibly understand what I'm trying to tell him.

Yet somehow, he does. "I'll earn your forgiveness later. For now, I want something else."

Thank fuck I didn't eat or drink before Lincoln tied me up. Otherwise, I would've had to ask him to take me to the bathroom after hours of sitting here by myself.

It would've meant peeing instead of hugging him.

I don't have this kind of patience anymore.

He doesn't seem to either, adding after only a second's pause, "I want to play a game."

I want it too. I ache for it, actually. To be able to talk to him and say what's on my heart. Once he releases me, I'll be free to say the words I intended to tell him before Lincoln trapped me here.

First, I should tell him that regardless of Lincoln's cruelty, I still prefer to take the lawful alternative.

We shouldn't risk our souls and freedom when we can get the fuck out of here. We can go to the police and hand

272

over the evidence Vaughn holds, then leave them to deal with these people.

I should tell him that. When my mind isn't high on lust and my pussy is sated.

Over the past weekend, I stopped being the girl I used to be. Or better yet, I'm the improved version of her. Vaughn's special kind love has permitted—no, demanded—that I put myself, my needs, and my well-being first.

And as I started prioritizing myself, it became really easy to articulate what it is I crave. I've always enjoyed pain when I chased my orgasms. I just couldn't bring myself to talk about it. I've been too scared to be shamed for my kinks.

Now, I embrace my dark necessities.

I'm not ashamed when he says, "You little minx, have waited for me. You lie here totally compliant, just waiting for me to abuse your body until you black out when you come, don't you?"

The answer to what he asks is a definite yes.

I want him to maul me just the way I am now—restricted and helpless and under his command. I desire nothing more than to have Vaughn on top of me, touching me, hurting me, possessing me. Doing anything and everything with my body.

"No one can hurt you now." He keeps talking in the distance. "This, the way they left you, isn't the worst they had in mind. I hope you see that, little one. There will be no more bargaining between you and me for their lives, no more stalling. They'll all die for even thinking about hurting you."

Something snaps in me when I hear him. Maybe they do deserve to be punished. After the horrors they intended to unleash on me, I'm not so quick to run to their defense. And I'm okay with it.

Matter of fact, I'm not just okay. I'm angry.

Though I don't know what it is yet that they planned, they've had something in the works that would've ended up hurting me.

The boys are in on it. My so-called friends too.

I feel it.

I know it.

The roaring in my blood calls for me to believe Vaughn, to do whatever he tells me to.

To follow him blindly. Only ever him.

Rage fuels me, desire floods my soul. The sense of being *home* finally lands on me with the promise to keep safe and defiled simultaneously.

I nod to answer his question.

My ears prick up as I listen to the four extra steps trudging on old wood.

Right, left. Right, left.

"You have any idea how beautiful you are?" The air of his all-consuming presence tells me how close he is before he touches me.

I shake my head. This is the first time anyone's ever talked to me like this other than my parents. I know feeling beautiful should come from within, and it does. I know I am.

Then Vaughn—whom I worshiped and adored—took off. I couldn't help but think there was something wrong with me.

And while I would've loved for him to fix my self-esteem like he made me accept my sexual needs, I'm aware this isn't something that'll happen overnight.

His coarse knuckles graze the side of my face, running down my temple, caressing my jaw.

The skin on his hand feels rugged, coated by something that had dried out. Maybe it's dirt, maybe blood. Each option or a combination of both turns me on just the same.

"You don't?" Vaughn's voice is louder when he speaks next, his hot breath fanning my cheek.

I smell him when he's this near. The scent of the woods, the copper, and his hunger for me. Feeling beautiful doesn't matter to me at this point.

All I can think of is the incessant craving to be his. To launch at him, scream and shout how much I'm desperate for his affection.

But I don't.

Not because I physically can't.

I'd much rather have him *take it.*

"I do," he whispers, though there's nothing gentle about it. My godfather sounds absolutely bestial.

As if being in this position enrages and arouses him as much as it does me.

"You're fucking gorgeous, that's what you are. They might have tied you up thinking it'd be a punishment, when in reality, they set you up to be my present."

Another strangled whimper rushes to the space where my lips meet the tape.

"My little sex puppet…" Despite my bound ankles gluing my thighs together, Vaughn manages to sneak a hand below my leggings. "Fuck. Me. You still have my cum and your blood on you, soaking through your panties. That's the hottest fucking thing I've ever felt. Almost enough to have me consider passing on our game."

My teeth clamp on the inside of my cheek. I tasted Vaughn. I witnessed what he could do to me. I'm not scared of Lincoln anymore. I'm empowered.

A motherfucking queen.

"My precious little soaking prize. Mine and all mine, for as long as I shall live. No one else will have you," he speaks again, his lips at my ear as he rubs my sensitive clit. "No one else will even dare look at you without suffering the consequences."

I quiver, breathing hard through my nose as shivers rake my skin. The longer he massages me, the harder his thumb presses to my swollen nub, the more deliriously needy I become.

"These people have no idea what's coming to them for wanting to ruin you." His tongue swipes across the length of my neck. I nearly come undone from the ferocity of his teeth as they bite my wet skin. "I own you. I protect you. And they haven't seen nothing yet."

Breathing is a hardship by now. I'm panting, my nose gasping for air. My breasts rise and fall with every labored inhale and exhale.

Vaughn presses his nose to mine, his lips moving on the tape separating us. "I'll burn the world for you."

Though I'm bound to the bed, I'm floating. I don't doubt him, not for a minute, and my God, what a heady feeling this is.

I'm not being sheltered by Vaughn. I'm being elevated on a throne.

His property and his queen, freed and owned. After years of believing I had no one, of being neglected and unwanted, at last, I'm in the arms of the one person I ached for the most.

I would've survived without him. But I wouldn't have lived.

I'm complete, I'm loved. I'm finally whole.

In a swift movement, he shoves my shirt over my breasts. Vaughn's mouth latches on my nipple while his deft fingers pull on my shoelaces and throws my boots on the carpet below us.

I barely register the low thud as they hit the plush material. I don't hear much of anything when my blood whooshes between my ears and Vaughn's wet, suckling noises are feral and loud. He drives me that much closer to the edge.

"Are we clear, little raven?" I feel him turning his head up to me, the scruff on his chin chafing my abused flesh.

My nod serves as a yes.

"That's my good girl," he groans.

Vaughn lifts himself from my chest. I whimper angrily at the loss of his warmth. He tsks and just like that, I'm docile again.

My desperation to please him makes me summon my last bit of willpower to stay absolutely still.

"I'm going to release your ankles, and you're gonna keep being my submissive little puppet. You will not move unless I order you to."

A knife—maybe the one he used on Caroline—brushes along my exposed ankle. Less of a dangerous threat for me, more like a skin-prickling, exciting promise.

I bob my head up and down before he asks whether I agree or not.

"Your compliance makes me so fucking hard, love." Vaughn snaps the rope using his knife.

It happens fast, less than a millisecond, really. I'm suddenly driven to imagine how easily he sliced through Caroline's flesh, and Roy's. It sends warmth through me.

I'm sickened by how my lover's revenge sends warmth throughout me.

I should be.

The girl I was before would've been ashamed of it.

Me? Who's been mocked by everyone here, played by my friends, and has been locked in a room after being threatened?

I don't give a flying fuck. I own my lust and my depraved thoughts.

Thanks to him.

"Your responsiveness, too." Vaughn kisses my exposed ankles, rising higher along my body.

My leggings and panties are being yanked off me along with my socks.

"So appetizing." The sound of Vaughn sucking in a breath is as sensual as his following crude words. "Jesus, I could sniff and taste these bloodied panties for an eternity."

The bed dips to one side, a belt buckle opens. A zipper slides down. After that, to my absolute delight, Vaughn's thick, heavy cock glides up and down on my slick clit.

"Which I probably would," he growls at my cheek, his fingers peeling the tape gagging me. "I'd inhale your panties day and fucking night, but first I'm taking advantage of the predicament you're in."

"Vaughn," I sigh his name, my mouth captured in a rough, demanding kiss for a few moments before he breaks it.

"Raven." He leans forward, cutting the rope and tying me to the headboard. "For years I've touched no one else. I've fantasized about you every waking and sleeping moment. I'll never be a gentle lover. I'll never give you a sweet, tender love. I will, however, be yours, be the man you need, the depravity you crave."

It's my turn to inhale deeply through my bruised lips. The knowledge that he stayed celibate for me soothes the jealousy I didn't realize I had within me.

I couldn't have asked him to put his life on hold and wait for me.

And yet he has.

For me. For us.

"I love you," I say, my eyes closed. "I love you so fucking much, Vaughn."

"I love you too, little one." He nips, tugs, and kisses my lips, his tongue running along the seam as he says, "And you'll do well to remember it when I violate your body when nothing but the word 'enough' will stop me from hurting you in the best sort of way."

CHAPTER TWENTY-SEVEN
Darlene

"NEVER," I SEETHE into the face of my savior. "I'll never say it."

My thighs clench with need, and desire pools in my core. Even blindfolded and subdued beneath Vaughn's weight, I'm not afraid. I'm running headfirst and agreeing to be a puppet he can use however he desires.

Consequences be damned. Conscience be damned.

The living, the dead, my history, and my future. None of those I care about.

So why am I crying?

"What are those for?" Vaughn's tongue laps at my cheek, tucking away a wayward tear, then the other. "I won't count it as 'enough'"—he growls while dragging his cock along my bloodied slit, pushing the throbbing head to arouse the bundle of nerves at the top—"but I want to know why."

Seeing what I've been through, I should be stronger than this. I shouldn't just give him what he wants. I should demand answers too.

Which I can't.

The question that's been on my mind weighs heavier on me than the insult stemming from my friends' betrayal. It consumes me more than finding out about my godfather being a ruthless killer.

There's no quieting the sudden pain that surges when I remember the night of my eighteenth birthday.

The emotional whirlwind must've triggered it inside me. All the confidence and anger I had a minute ago withers to almost nothing.

I'm rattled, offended all over again. Most of all, I need answers.

If I don't have it sorted out, if I don't understand why Vaughn said what he did, then he and I can never be together.

We need to trust each other.

And for the sake of our future, I start.

"Why—" My treacherous voice cracks at the end of the word.

"Go on." Vaughn's teeth nibble at my cheek where my tear mingles with his spit. His deft fingers twist me to undo the knot around my wrists. "Why what?"

His presence commands each and every one of my senses. Through his control over me, I know I'm loved. He lends his strength to me while holding me down.

Above all, it gives me that extra push to talk past the tears. "That day at the campfire, on my eighteenth birthday…" I take a deep breath.

"Yes?" He edges me on using his fingers, digging them into my jaw and holding it firmly.

"You…" I go at it again, remembering his words of love from a moment ago.

We have to stay together. And without honesty, without transparency, there'll be no us. I have to finish this.

"You wanted me gone. You told Dad he should encourage me to attend a college in another state, not around here."

"I did." That's the only explanation he gives me.

Vaughn's weight on me shifts until he's not lying anymore. He sits between my spread-out thighs.

The next sound I hear is of him gathering saliva in his mouth, then spitting it on himself, because I don't feel it.

"Go on." The hand he had on my jaw trails lower to clasp on my thigh, sending a delicious kind of pain through me. "Tell me what you want to know."

I swallow around the lump in my throat, begging my heart to slow and my mind to focus. It's my dire attempt to not let my insecurities show, to maintain my confident and unwavering tone.

"Was it…" I start asking, "Was it me?" and then think better of it.

He'll never allow me to second-guess myself around him. To sound like I'm blaming myself.

In fact, given how his fingers burrow deeper into my flesh, he probably hates it.

I rephrase my question. "Why send me off?"

"Remember our deal?" The tip of his now spit-slick dick nudges at my tight pucker briefly before Vaughn pulls away. "You'll have to pay to hear the truth."

This feels better already.

Our conversation has brought tears to my eyes.

Our twisted games, on the other hand, spark my arousal anew. I like this discussion better already.

My whole body arches up to meet him in response to his words.

I'm begging Vaughn to penetrate me again. His impressive size breaking through my hymen hurt like hell this morning. I can't imagine what it'd feel like, even lubed, in my ass.

I can't, and yet I ache for it. I'm desperate for Vaughn to fuck and claim this hole like he has the other ones.

Anything he has to offer is something I want. I'll do anything to have all of him.

"No, no, no, little raven." With a strong hand, he lifts my thigh so my ass is in the air. With the other he slaps one of my cheeks so hard I'm sure the skin reddens. "We play by my rules or there'll be consequences."

A moment of lucidity strikes me. I wonder why Vaughn doesn't hurry, why he doesn't seem to care someone might barge into the room.

"Do. You. Understand?" Each word is emphasized by another strike. Each one of those is more painful than the last.

This must be his method to coax me back to reality, to answer my unasked question—Vaughn fears *no one*. By spanking me and taking his time, he tells me he doesn't care who walks in on us.

Whether it's one man or twenty, he'll find a way to kill them.

"Yes," I gasp.

"'Yes,' what?" He dips one finger into my pussy, curling it inside me and stroking my walls.

I writhe, the pleasure consuming me. "Yes, Daddy."

"Good girl." A second finger is being jammed inside me without warning, pressing and rubbing me in the spot that has my toes curling.

"Now that I have your pussy,"—his intense and honest voice sends ice down my spine—"I'll answer you about the night you eavesdropped on me and your father around the campfire."

CHAPTER TWENTY-EIGHT
Darlene

MY QUICK INTAKE of air exposes me. He knows I listened in on them, that it wasn't Mom or Dad who told me about their conversation later.

Somehow, he saw through my closed eyelids that night. And he *still* said the things he said. The newfound knowledge piques my curiosity tenfold, pushing through the dense haze of arousal and embarrassment surrounding me.

"Don't act so surprised, little raven." He bends down to lick my shoulder and up to my earlobe, sucking on my tender flesh when he reaches the end. "Whatever you do, wherever you may be, I'll feel you."

Vaughn pushes his fingers deeper inside me, then stretches me wider by introducing a third finger. Each is thick and meticulous in its quest to pummel through me. The fact that I'm sore makes it all the sweeter, and I'm salivating for more pain.

He keeps moving when he murmurs, "I see you. Always."

My nipples harden into tiny diamonds, grazing Vaughn's soft T-shirt. I want to tell him how good it feels, to beg him to never stop.

Instead, I ask, "You do?"

"Yes. Every damn day since the moment you took your first gulp of air." His smooth, seductive voice contradicts his sharp movements as he lifts himself from me.

"But that isn't your question, isn't it? You asked why I wanted you gone."

Vaughn stretches me in a different way by pinning one of my ankles to his shoulder and shutting my mouth with his palm. "I wanted you out of the cocoon your parents weaved around you. Wanted you out of your comfort zone and where it's safe to evolve into the strong and fierce woman you've always been beneath your quiet mask. And I wanted you to learn it by yourself. Just like I want you to learn why I'm killing these privileged fucks now."

His answer barely sinks in when he stretches my wet, aching pussy with a fourth finger.

I scream into his palm.

"My little sex puppet, you take it so well." His hot breath teases the wet skin of my breast until his teeth clamp on my nipple. "Before I allow you your next question"—Vaughn speaks, his lips moving on my bruised flesh—"you're gonna come for me. I need that hole drenched and ready for my fist to fuck it. To have it wide and gaping for my cock to rut hard and fast into you."

Behind the fabric Lincoln used to blindfold me, my eyes widen in horror. I can't—I won't be able to fit anything else in my pussy, let alone another one of Vaughn's large fingers.

I shake my head as much as the pressure he's applying on my face lets me, murmuring, "No" into his palm.

"Yes." There's an air of triumph in Vaughn's voice. A sense of his ownership of me as he lashes his tongue and teeth on my other nipple.

My lips begin to form the word "no" again. My throat demands me to insist that no amount of pleasuring will ever make me ready for his fist, regardless of how much I want it.

"Yes, you will take it," he insists faster than I can deny him. "You will spasm, suck in, and tremble all over your Daddy's fist like the filthy good girl you are."

His thumb starts flicking my clit at a relentless pace. It sends sparks of burning desire through me as he continues to bury his fingers deeper into me with every shove.

I'm incapable of resisting Vaughn's commands. My thighs quiver, my insides coiling as my impending orgasm builds at a frightening speed.

The pain Vaughn unleashes is a mind-boggling pleasure. He sucks on the sensitive area beneath my nipples, switching from one breast to the other. He punishes and lavishes me in tandem with an insatiable need he himself can hardly contain.

I can't. I'm about to explode any second now. My breath hitches the closer I get to the finish line.

"Gorgeous little whore, you're there, aren't you?"

He comes back up to my lips, his mouth taking the place of his palm. He kisses me hard and passionately. Vaughn's tongue invades my mouth and consumes me like his fingers do, massaging my tongue with his furiously like his thumb works my clit.

"Yes," I breathe between his assaulting kisses. "Make me come, Daddy. I need to come. I need your fist, your cock, all of you."

"You do." I feel his body heat leaving mine, then his fingers being removed from my pussy.

I remain still and quiet despite my impulse to search for him, remembering how he wants me. My owner.

My throbbing desire will be satisfied. Despite how badly it hurts to wait, I do it.

He releases my butt back down on the bed. A spitting noise follows. My inability to see cranks up my hearing, and I pick up on another sound of Vaughn stroking his length quick and hard.

Except, I remember he said he'll fist me before he fucks me. I'm not sure if I'm relieved or disappointed.

A question I don't get to marinate on.

Vaughn presses the slick crown of his dick to my crack. His approving groan follows the moan I let out into the air.

"What a horny little puppet you are." With my ankle resting on his shoulder, he continues to press his cock to my ass while slamming four fingers into my pussy.

My neck arches; my swollen lips part in a silent scream.

"That's right." He's merciless and demanding, so powerful that I'm not scared of being fisted anymore. "I know all the ways to make you open up to me. Gonna tease that tiny hole the way you like it. Make you spill juices down my hand, have you ready for me to defile you."

Sweet and dirty sensations claim me as I'm being driven higher and higher toward the peak Vaughn is vehement about taking me to. I'm almost there, almost reaching the crest of the metaphorical mountain. I just need the tiniest push.

Vaughn hears this unvoiced need, thundering, "Come. Now."

It's all I ever needed. I'm writhing and clenching and gasping, burning up from the inside out as I spasm around Vaughn's fingers with his dick pressed to my asshole.

"That's it." Vaughn backs away, his weight shifting differently on the mattress. "So fucking hot. I'd lick your juices dry, but it defeats the purpose, doesn't it? We need you wet."

Blank. My lust-filled mind goes absolutely blank in search of an answer to his question.

"My fist, little raven." He reads my confused silence easily. "Gonna use every drop of your orgasm to push me deep into that sweet cunt. To mark that beautiful pussy that belongs to me. Open your legs wider, spread them for Daddy."

The moment Vaughn stops talking is the moment another mouthful of saliva lands on my clit. He pinches it between his slick fingers, rubbing and twisting it to the sound of my cries of agony and joy. He probably watches every inch of me unraveling for him.

"Be careful with those moans, little raven." The ministrations on my clit continue as he swirls two fingers back into my pussy. "Unless you want me to hold off your second orgasm so I can slash someone's throat when they walk in."

Vaughn's third and fourth fingers rip into me in one quick move. My juices and Vaughn's spit make the invasion easier than before, although I feel the stretching.

It hurts and I'm struggling.

For him and my own pleasure.

As another orgasm builds inside me, I find that I care even less now than I did before if another member of the group I came here with dies.

Even the thought of gore and blood doesn't bother me at this point. The only things I have in mind are the man I love, the violent connection we share, and how I'll never trade being his for anything in the world.

I only want Vaughn. And maybe…maybe I'm also turned on by imagining him destroying someone who tries to come between us.

As soon as the thought rises to the surface, I bite my bottom lip hard to subdue my moan.

Then again, I don't want him to pull out when I'm this high on him. Never.

"I'll be a good girl, I'll be quiet," I whisper breathlessly.

"You turned on by the idea of me killing someone for you, my twisted puppet?" He pinches my clit harder, spinning and turning his four broad fingers inside me. What was left of the pain is gone, giving way to immense pleasure.

"You do. I see the look in your eyes and I can tell that you do."

Thinking about it and saying it are two different things. Uttering the words will make my depravity real, and that I can't do.

"Deviant little thing." Vaughn's name for me is being spoken right above my knee where he bites and sucks on my flesh. "Tell me. Admit how much you'd like it."

I don't want to admit it. I can't admit it. I *won't* admit it.

"Say it." The last of Vaughn's knuckles hit my slit as he pushes his fingers deeper. "Say it, or I won't be so considerate when I fist you."

"I am," I groan, the truth leaving my mouth and it's so incredibly freeing. "I am, Daddy. I love you. Everything about you turns me on. Every single thing."

"Especially when I annihilate the people who are after destroying you." His thumb plays with my slit, nudging at my entrance to join the other four fingers. "I'll do it again and again, and you'll be wet watching their blood soak my clothes as I do."

My pussy is being torn from the way Vaughn twists his wrist left and right. It's a stinging kind of pleasure, one that's heightened by Vaughn's murderous promises.

I can't talk. I'm just…happy.

"That's my girl." I'm not surprised anymore that he can read my mind. Instead, I thrive on it. "Now that you're quiet, we don't have to worry about being caught."

Vaughn's thumb slips into me, his insistent maneuvering finally adding the fifth finger inside me. Still not fisting me, but damn, that's a lot.

It's a kind of madness I thought I wouldn't be able to take.

The torture is delicious, an agonizing delight. I have no other choice except to listen to my body and lift my butt up off the mattress. A silent plea for more.

He doesn't scold me verbally for disobeying him this time. Vaughn just slithers the hand that's on my clit higher up. His touch is his command as he flattens it on my belly, forcing me back down to the bed.

"Right now, let's get you properly fisted."

In another swivel of his hand, a suction, sloppy and wet noise echoes in the room. And then, he's inside me. All the way to his wrist.

A guttural, almost inhuman groan barrels its way out of my throat. "Daddy, it hurts."

"Let me in." He spits on where his hand connects to my pussy again, never stopping the circular motions of his fist. "You love the pain. You love your Daddy. Do not resist me."

I take a deep breath, releasing my clenched muscles. A switch flips on in my head and the pinching, tearing, and searing I'm experiencing transforms into a pure form of pleasure.

I enjoyed pinching and hurting myself while I pleasured myself, but it'd never been like this. This fullness—

this insane sense of being complete—is something I haven't experienced in my entire life.

Every time I think Vaughn can't make me more whole than I already am, he pushes my limits to engrain himself deeper into my soul. I'm consumed, elevated, flown right out into space with him by my side.

"Yes, like that, fill me, Daddy." My gasps are shallow when my need overpowers the pain. "Fuck, I do love it. I'm coming, Vaughn, I'm so close."

"Good girl." He draws back by some to shove his fist in me again, spinning his wrist to have his knuckles graze every inch of my walls. "Do it, soak me, little raven."

My fingernails sink into the sheets, clutching and damn near tearing them as my orgasm pummels through my body. I'm shaking harder than before, drawing air in rapid, desperate inhales that burn my lungs in the best possible way.

His satisfied hum is everything. "What an obedient puppet you are."

Vaughn pulls his hand out of me, kisses my clit, sucking on it to prolong my orgasm. When the waves settle and my breath calms a bit, he moves again. I feel his knees on either side of my stomach before he places his thick shaft on my chest between my breasts.

"You make me so proud." His wet fingers clutch around my blindfold, ripping it off my eyes. "Taking my fist like that.

I blink a couple of times to adjust to the light.

There he is.

My body reacts to the sight of Vaughn immediately, goose bumps raking across my skin.

This dark king who's all mine kneels on top of me in all his glory.

His looming, enchanting figure casts a shadow on my chest and face. His eyes are pitch-black, and his straight hair drapes on either side of his face.

My gaze darts lower across his black T-shirt, down to his massive erection directed at my face. Vaughn's cock throbs, a menacing weapon against my soft flesh.

It's perfect. It's mouthwateringly sexy.

It was made to lie between my breasts and fuck me there too.

Anyone else would—and should—be terrified at how ominous he looks. I'm not. I admire him, worship and adore him.

He looks fierce as fuck, majestic and all-powerful.

This man is my everything. And I love him.

He smears the dried blood of my hymen and arousal across my temple, my cheekbone, my jaw, until he reaches my lips. Vaughn prods them open and I open up for him, accepting the pads of his fingers as he presses them to my tongue.

"Now, you're gonna make *me* come." He furrows his brow, slithering his hand down to my throat, curling his fingers around it. "Hold on to your tits, squeeze them hard while I fuck them, little raven."

"Yes, Daddy." I rush to do as he says.

I feel his girth on my large breasts, the veins of his dick before he starts thrusting.

"My love." Vaughn tightens his grasp on my throat, his balls slapping on my stomach with each movement. The pressure he has on me cuts some of my air supply, which only serves to turn me on more. "You're a dirty little thing. We'll get so bloody filthy together."

I swallow, barely, keeping my eyes open and staring up at him. I don't want to miss a second of this. His mouth curves into a sneer of pleasure, his breath more labored the closer he gets to his orgasm

His undoing is my doing. His grunts of desire tap into mine because he's using *me*. There's no denying our love, how we were meant to be for eternity.

"I'm going to come, darling." The previously elegant, derisive thrusts become errant and messy with his need.

I press my breasts together, reveling in each of his strokes, in the feeling of his cock swelling on me.

"Yes, Daddy." I lower my chin as much as I can with his hand clutched around my throat, offering myself to him by parting my lips and batting my eyelashes. "Please, Daddy, do it, mark my face. Let me taste you."

"Bloody hell." Vaughn's grunt is no less animalistic than my moans of insatiable desire.

He releases my throat to grip my hair from behind. Then he tightens his hold on my roots, pressing my head so that my chin touches my chest.

"Close your eyes," he says, just barely.

The moment I do, he finishes all over my face. Hot spurts of cum splash on my chin, my cheeks, my eyelashes, in my mouth.

I slip my tongue out to swipe across my lips, moaning with how much I love the taste of him. Vaughn groans, releasing another torrent of his sticky semen on my jaw.

"What a hot little fiend you are," he whispers as he slides down my body.

I'm waiting for him to clean me up, to wipe the sweet memory of him off me. He doesn't. He doesn't do anything for what seems like forever.

"Vaug—" I start to ask what's happening, what's wrong.

I never get to finish. His mouth crushes into mine, his tongue invading me as he kisses me, licking his own cum off me.

The whole thing is incredibly visceral and raw, and I don't want it to end.

I want us to lie here and exchange fluids forever. Truthfully, I could've let him take me over and over again, to pass a full year and then some in his bed like this.

I would've said it to him, too.

If it weren't for Elle, who makes herself known out of nowhere.

She's screaming from somewhere outside the bedroom, her feet thumping on the wooden floor as she storms toward the room.

"I'm going to kill that bitch, and don't you dare fucking stop me, Lane!"

CHAPTER TWENTY-NINE

Vaughn

ALMOST TWENTY-ONE years ago, the day
Darlene was born, I made a vow to my best friend, her
father. I told him I'd spend the rest of my existence
protecting her. Until I leave this earth, I swore to him his
daughter would be safe no matter what.

I was deadly serious when I made the oath. Given the
familiarity I had with the monsters lurking around in the
shadows, I readied myself for every possible threat.

Eric, the lawyer who was best friends with a serial killer,
AKA me, also knew life could get dangerous for his only
child. But he was a good man. A shielded one.

He'd never imagined anything as dramatic as this
happening.

He would've never dreamed of someone wanting to kill
Darlene.

It made no sense. Her parents didn't have any enemies. She was brought up in what most people would deem a "normal" environment.

Eric and Helena made sure she got the best education too. They lied by telling her they petitioned for the scholarship that landed her in the best private school in Chicago. In truth, they only did it because they cared. Because they were worried.

They loved her like the doting parents they were.

Aside from the boy who was dumb enough to try to rape her in college, their wishes had been fulfilled. No one had posed a threat to her.

Then *they* entered the picture.

And then I did.

I'm the only one who's ever been prepared at a second's notice to leap to her defense. To do whatever it takes, including to kill for her.

Like I do now.

From lying naked on top of Darlene, the sound of Elle's roar pushes me straight off the bed. I jump to the floor like a predator shielding his mate, reaching for my discarded clothes before Elle manages to finish her war cry.

I neglected Darlene once. There won't be a second time.

Over my dead body.

"She thinks I did it?" Darlene covers herself quickly under the blankets; her tone is a mixture of horror and shock as she discovers the true character of her friends. "That I killed Caroline? Her too?"

"You have no idea who you're dealing with,"—I tuck myself in, tug my T-shirt down, and reach for the mask and knife I placed on one of the wood floating tables—"do you, darling?"

"Don't patronize me," she hisses, leaning forward. "We've been through too much for you to throw me back to square one and treat me like an innocent, stupid girl. I was never her, even if I might've looked like that to you."

"I'm not patronizing you." I stalk toward the bed, stroking Darlene's jawline.

Using the sheets she's grasping, I clean her eyes of my cum.

Only when she's clean and opens her eyes do I say, "I never thought you were anything other than perfect. What you saw was me sheltering the young girl whom I vowed to protect. You were, are, and forever will be my treasure. But now you're older, and what I'm saying is for your benefit, not to condescend you. You have to connect the dots and you have to do it now."

Her cheeks are ruddy and still a little damp with my cum. Her thick, black hair is wild and tangled.

The questions, accusations, and wrath in her eyes are endless. I'm sure she aims some of it at me as well as the people outside this room.

She's entitled to her rage. I prefer it that way. I need her riled up and vigilant. It doesn't hurt that she's insanely gorgeous with the fire blazing in her eyes.

"You're almost there, too."

The scratching on the floor outside tells me that Lane—who got here faster than I gave him credit for—is trying to keep Elle in place. I have another minute or two to talk to Darlene.

"Do it for me. Think."

"Why me?" Realization clears the doubts in her gaze, making space for the question I've been waiting for her to ask. "They want to kill me, don't they? Wanted it all along? Why?"

I kiss her forehead in an unusually warm gesture, murmuring, "Clever girl," and pushing off from her.

My mask slips on my face in preparation for what's to come. I don't need it to hide from them—I need it to sow terror into their final moments on this earth.

"You'll find out soon enough." The steps in the hall grow louder, more adamant. This Elle cunt sure knows how to stomp. "I just have this small matter of annihilating the imbeciles outside the door and we'll continue this."

Slow and deliberate, I spin on my heel, clutching harder to the knife's handle. I'm rife to attack, my senses working overtime to listen, see, and hear.

To prepare me for the unexpected assault.

Shame I have to change my plans. I had other lovely, exquisite ideas on how to end these three. Beheading, removing their bowels, skinning them, and dragging them by the hair while they're naked around the cabin while their insides slip out. Twice.

They've earned it. These conniving, entitled, wannabe murderers.

301

Alas, fate decided to put us all on a different route. For once, I'm not disappointed. I can't regret any second I passed with Darlene that I wasn't torturing them. Can't wish to undo the moments of degradation, love, and sex we shared.

Other lowlifes will get to be the target of said plans in the future. Problem solved.

Until then, I have my beautiful goddaughter to protect.

"Wait." Darlene's call halts me in place. "Maybe there's some other way to solve this."

A low growl rises up my throat as I turn to see her straightening on the bed and throwing her feet to the floor, still covered by the sheets.

"Darlene, we've been through this," I threaten her with her real name, not any other term of endearment. "Don't test me. This is the end of the road for them. It won't be long until I tell you everything. You figured it out on your own, most of it, with the information you had. You deserve this revenge. Once you know why, you'll agree with me."

Thump, thump, thump.

The wooden door nearly breaks at the violent knocks. "Open the fuck up, Darlene! I'm going to kill you eventually, so just let me in."

Elle might seem skinny and fragile, but I guess I underestimated her love for her degrading boyfriend and her bond with that scum, Caroline.

May her soul *not* rest in peace.

"You'll thank me for the painful, horrible deaths I'm unleashing on them." My tone speaks louder than my words, harsh and demanding her to listen. "Now, my love, if you don't mind…"

"I do mind."

"Who are you talking to in there?" More bashing on the wooden door, followed by a violent shake of the door handle. "You bitch! Lincoln's right, you have an accomplice! You brought all of us here to die!"

This lock won't hold for much longer. We don't have time.

Not even to tell the cunt on the other side that *they* were the ones who dragged *Darlene* here.

My fierce little raven doesn't care about us running out of time, though.

She and I are at a standoff.

Her gaze demands I stop attacking them.

Mine tells her, "When hell freezes over."

She won't approve of what I'm about to do to them without a thorough explanation. Me, I'll die a thousand deaths before I show any of them a shred of mercy.

It seems like we're stuck.

"We'll tie them up." Darlene stands up, reaching her hand up to stroke my masked cheek. "Hand them over to the police. You have the evidence to bring them down. I see it in your eyes. I do trust you. I do believe you. We can do it, it's better this way. For your sake."

The foreign warmth after years of solitude prickles the hairs at the back of my neck. I shake my head, ignoring it.

If I don't, I'll throw away my plans, hoist my queen over my shoulder and get the fuck out of here.

We'll disappear to another country, another life.

God knows we both have the means to do it.

We'll have a beautiful future, but I'll never be able to forgive myself for letting the others here live.

No one, and I mean no one, in this house will go on as if nothing happened. As if they haven't planned to annihilate Darlene.

"No." My fingers wrap around her wrist. I drag her to me, pinning her chest to mine. "Retribution is coming to them, little raven. Retribution and hell."

"Dad wouldn't have wanted it," she whispers when more of Elle's loud banging and indecipherable screaming comes through the door.

"Your dad would want me to do whatever it takes to protect you."

Despite, or maybe because of the havoc and danger to Darlene, I'm hard as steel. The animal in me gets off on the blood in the air, on the imminent attack.

Once the threat is dismantled, I'm fucking Darlene again.

"Not for them. Fuck them. He wouldn't have wanted it for *you*." Darlene's finger stabs at my chest, trying to dig into the soul that only she can reach. "You don't have to scar yourself for my benefit. The cops will handle them. They'll be in jail for a long time for attempted murder."

"That's where you're wrong." The knife in my hand stops me from gripping the finger she's pointing at me. "Eric recognized who I was the moment he laid eyes on me at school. You think this is the first time I'm doing this?"

"I know it's not. Wait…" Her mouth gapes open. "Dad? He knew?"

It's a struggle to decide whether I'm eager to shove my cock or my tongue between those parted lips. No, I can't do it. I have shit to do. People to ruin.

"Elle, please. There's no one there with her. I would've seen it," Lane murmurs, a pathetic sound to add to his attempts to soothe that raging bitch. "Lincoln is out there. He's looking for this guy's campsite. Whatever he's hiding there, weapons or I don't know what else. Linc will have it here soon."

Once again, I'm proven what a clever snake Lincoln is and of Lane's unperceptiveness. I'm not surprised by what I heard, yet I do grow more nervous.

He'll be here to kill her. He might even hurt her.

"Your dad knew, yes." I walk Darlene backward toward the bed where she'll be safe. Thank fuck her shock is too great that she doesn't fight me on it. "I trusted him. Told him that was what happened when one lies in their parents' blood and guts for hours."

"Vaughn." She loses her fight, her voice gentle. Too gentle.

I can't stand her look of pity, the furrowed brow, or the *poor Vaughn* expression on her face.

Unfortunately, it's also a look of *I'm not backing down*. I don't waste time, launching into the short version of her family's and my story. Hopefully, it will quiet her until after I put down the evil bastards out there.

"We fled to the US before I turned nine."

305

Darlene's brow smooths, and her lips relax so they're not pinched into a tight line anymore. She finally relents, sitting her round, sexy ass on the bed.

"By that age, my parents had already taught me everything there is to know about cruelty, murder, stealing, smuggling."

When she opens her mouth to say something, I sink two fingers in it, dragging them in and out across her tongue to keep her quiet and go as fast as I can.

"As if that wasn't enough to destroy my young, impressionable mind. They were murdered right in front of my fucking face a few months later. I stayed in the hiding place by myself, soaking in what remained of them for two long nights until one of the neighbors reported the stench seeping from our apartment."

A fist slams over the wooden door. The incoherent mumbling of Elle and Lane filters into the room.

One tear runs across the dirty cheek of the woman I intend to love forever.

"Don't you fucking pity me." I sink my fingers deeper, hitting the back of her throat, and groan in satisfaction. "No one has. My adoptive parents haven't. Your father sure as shit hadn't. Matter of fact, Eric with his wealth and resources helped me find Fletcher, the man who slaughtered my parents, since I didn't want my adoptive parents involved."

Her eyes widen. Mine must gleam remembering how satisfying it'd been to get back at him for everything he did.

"*I* was the one who dealt the final blow, as I mentioned. Who avenged my parents."

"Dad...Dad helped you kill him?" she repeats.

"Yes, your father." With her chin in my grip, I force her to look at me. "He never judged, or more like— appreciated the murderous side of me. So long as I didn't spill innocents' blood, he wanted to help me punish the criminal and morally corrupt. Your father was honorable. He was *justice*. He was and forever will be my best friend for it. And by God, little raven, you will love me for it too."

Eric's memory reminds me of the day we met. How he took one look at the skinny, full-of-fight boy I used to be.

How he helped me up and said, *"You're unlike anyone else they have here. I fucking love it."*

My rich-beyond-means friend never intended to fit in with the crowd he was born into. He hated how stuck-up they were, the underlying cruelty of their nature. He loathed how they couldn't stop talking about their big house, their cars, their clothes.

Despised it, really.

Later in life, he refused to manage his business in the public's eye. He continued to put in work into his family's business, but he'd never shown his face to his clients.

The man craved a humble life. That was that.

All he ever cared about was to be there for his loving family and his honest, homicidal best friend.

I blink twice when Darlene waves her hand in my face, her dark eyes telling me I've been silent for too long.

Thank fuck she woke me from my daydreams or I would've missed the footsteps and angry murmurs nearing us from outside the window.

"Hang on, love." I press her into the mattress. My fingers trail the length of her body in a soothing gesture, from her collarbone down to her cunt. "Get dressed and stay here for me."

She nods, though I feel the resilience rolling off her in waves.

"Nothing is going to happen to me." My tone is harsh, much unlike the compassionate words I've never spoken to anyone except her. "But you need to be safe, right here where they can't reach you. So, *please*, listen to me and hang. Fucking. Tight. Daddy's here, and he's gonna fix everything for you."

CHAPTER THIRTY
Darlene

WHAT DO I want?

If I look deep inside myself, to the very core of my being, right here, right now, what. Do. I. Want?

Ever since the moment I took my first breath, I'd trusted my father. I'd believe he'd sort life out for me, and therefore hadn't doubted him or my mother.

For years I'd believed he and my mother were paving the best path for me. From how they raised me to the stories they told me about who we were.

With good reason. My dad drove to work every day and came back for most of our dinners. My mom stayed home to help with my homework, talk to me, or just be there, her smiles ever so soothing.

To the best of my knowledge, they had no siblings and their parents died years ago. Then again...I never did visit their graves because they said they laid in California, and we didn't have the budget to travel all the way over there.

Crap.

I'm starting to doubt my entire life. Everything they'd told me might have been a lie.

I inhale long and deep, clearing my head.

It doesn't matter. I don't care if my last name is made up.

My parents loved me. That's the truth, the only important thing I'll carry with me forever. I never missed having grandparents or uncles or even money. I never wanted for anything; the love they gave me had been more than I could've ever asked for.

I still trust that they'd done it for my own good, for the benefit of our family.

The only thing that saddens me, that I wish I knew before so I could've been there for him, is Vaughn's past and present.

This poor, poor man. My Vaughn.

He had to constantly wander this world wearing his mask, a metaphorical one. It might explain the physical one he has on.

The man who'd guarded me in every way that matters had no one to protect him. To love him like I do.

Sure, he'd been loved by Mom, Dad, and his adoptive parents. I can tell, however, that he never let anyone see the layers beneath the obvious rage. When he told me about how he sat in what remained of his biological parents, it was like a knife sliced into his ruthless façade.

The brutal murder of his parents and the memories of it have been festering in him for years—that much is clear. His eyes reflected his hurt for a millisecond when he told me about it, something I feel like he only ever showed me.

Truth be told, I bet no one's ever looked hard enough to notice the shift.

If they had, they would've done more than simply love him without judgment. They would've insisted he get professional help, to see someone to ease the pain of the trauma.

He wouldn't have had to carry this burden and cope with it by himself for so many years. He wouldn't have turned to killing those who wronged him or others as a first resort.

The ones he chose to kill were guilty, my whole being tells me so. What the justice system had failed to do, Vaughn had taken care of.

I believe it wholeheartedly now. My parents trusted him enough to name him as my godfather, to allow him to be in our home even when they weren't there. They wouldn't have left me alone with a soulless man.

But it's more than that. I saw him. I still *see* him.

And I love him. Exactly the way he is. I wouldn't change a thing about him.

Hell, I'm turned on just thinking about him getting his hands dirty when he avenges me, and I had a relatively incredible, trauma-free childhood.

Killing is not okay, not when the issue can be resolved by going to the police, I'm aware of that. But damn, he's so sexy when he's mad.

I wouldn't want him any less different than he is today.

Now—after years of using his hands to relieve what's on his heart—he actually enjoys taking down the bad guys.

He hasn't always been like this, though, I'm sure of it.

Vaughn was born with a good heart and stayed inherently good regardless of his difficult, painful history. Regardless of the trail of corpses he left behind him, he's a decent human being.

He's not a bad person. He just went through a lot.

The early stages of his life, the defining moments of them, had been nothing but one blow after the other.

He chooses to act like he doesn't care. Maybe he doesn't.

But there's no denying the effect it had on him.

Vaughn had been hurt. He's inflicted hurt. He still does to this day.

Anyone else would've collapsed under the weight of it. Might've lost it altogether.

Not Vaughn, though.

I'm in awe that despite everything, he more than survived. He *thrived*.

And my admiration for him grows tenfold at this realization. My love too.

I crave with my whole being to wrap my arms around him and hug him. Except I can't. I'm aware Vaughn wouldn't let me.

Instead, as time stands still, I sit here and stare into his black-as-a-starless-sky eyes.

He's practically untouchable, what I now know is a result of his history. Heartless, cold, impenetrable. He's a loving person as well, I see it in him.

He's nothing like the empty and evil Lincoln.

More sounds of movement reach us from the window area.

"Nod if you understand me," his masked face urges me while his thumb and index finger squeeze my chin. "They have to go, and I will do it."

The fire in him burns through me. I'm aroused by the idea of Vaughn avenging me. I know who he is, and I'm aroused nonetheless.

I'm not kept in the dark anymore about who I am and what's going on.

Then why can't I let him kill them wholeheartedly?

Hint: Less than three days ago, you were sure these people were your friends. Your best friends.

"Elle, please, hold on." Lane's voice filters through the open window first, even though I don't see them coming in.

Vaughn pinches my chin tighter, fixing his eyes on mine through the mask.

I give him the slightest nod.

"Good girl." He presses his masked forehead to mine for an instant.

Then he spins around to meet the two faces of my enemies.

How could they?

"You're gonna die for what you did to Roy and Caroline," Elle half screams, half cries in agony as she stumbles inside.

Her tone and lack of balance indicate she's spent hours either drinking or self-medicating. The mascara she had on last night is dried on her cheeks. Her ash blond hair is a tangled bird's nest.

"Please, don't do it." Lane, who's two steps behind, tries to stop her.

She straightens and I can see her clearly, I understand why. And I'm mad. So mad.

Last week my soul would've hurt for her. I wouldn't have wanted her to cry or be in pain. She has been like a family to me.

Today, I'm infuriated by her. By the view of her wielding a kitchen knife and knowing this isn't the first time she considered killing me.

Now I get why I've kept trying to dissuade Vaughn. I care about his soul being ruined for me.

He might not admit to it. Yet I can't shake the feeling that it does affect him somehow. He'd do it for me without hesitation.

Doesn't matter. I don't want to be the reason another scar is added to his bruised heart.

I don't get a chance to say any of it when Vaughn reacts. His predatory instincts kick in, and he creates a barrier between Elle and me.

"Sorry to burst your bubble, Miss Warren." He stalks toward her, moving fast to grab her wrist. He twists it so the knife she held is knocked out of her hand. "It's not happening. No one touches Darlene."

Lane stands there, as shocked as he was before when Lincoln assaulted me. He doesn't react to her scream when Vaughn kicks her left ankle with his right one, tackling her to the ground where she drops like a ragdoll.

Elle's broken cry echoes in the room, bouncing on the wooden walls. Her partly opened broken eyes reflect the agony she's in.

I feel less for her than I did before.

"No one looks at her funny." Vaughn connects his boot with her in the stomach, sending her curling into a tiny ball. "No one, not ever, so much as considers *killing* her."

"Leave Elle alone." Lane's pleading voice changes into a demanding one.

He steps forward, rising to his full height to face Vaughn. He lifts two angry fists, shaking. "Leave all of us alone, you deranged asshole."

There's no explanation for this sudden burst of confidence. On second thought, there is. He knows what the four of us in the room already know—once Elle is gone, he'll be next.

"Deranged?" Vaughn points at himself. "Me?"

Though his mask hides Vaughn's beautiful face, I can imagine how his lip curls in a sneer. Can picture the twinkle of cruel amusement lighting his eyes.

His derisive tone and the new information I learned about him are all I need to deduce that.

"Yeah, you, you sick fuck." Lane—who I was stupid enough to think wanted me for me—stays firmly in place.

Being the size of a swim team member, Lane shouldn't be afraid of Vaughn.

But oh, boy, he sure does. His efforts to conceal it aren't working as his eyes keep blinking and a slight tremor courses through him.

"Well, then." Vaughn stands there, tall and intimidating. He stretches out the conversation, and I have a sneaking suspicion that he's entertained by watching Lane's terror. "Since you say so, you must be right."

"Doing what you've done to our friends..." A stronger tremor shakes Lane's body. He clenches and unclenches his fists, probably to hide what a chicken-shit he is. "You're deranged. Unhinged, fucking homicidal masked man. Whatever sick name there is in the book for a raging lunatic, you're it."

Vaughn steps closer to Lane until only Elle separates them. The clenched fist with which Vaughn grips his knife is marked by traces of my hymen's blood, his knuckles covered with a red-brown liquid.

He's so beautifully creepy.

Lane's eyes scan Vaughn's body, landing on the blood on his hand. To my delight, he shivers again.

And I hurry to throw on my T-shirt and leggings.

"On any other day"—Vaughn flips the knife in his hand, causing Lane to jump back toward the wall—"I might've agreed with your assessment. I do, however, have a reason to kill you. You were about to do the same to Darlene."

"We weren't." The wall behind him makes a thudding noise as Lane's back hits it. "I don't know where you got it from, but we weren't. Elle was only screaming like that because *you* killed *our* friends, not the other way around."

"Really? You want a second to reconsider, perhaps?"

The second Vaughn's foot rises to step over Elle's body, she lashes her hand up and wraps it around his ankle. "You bastard!"

"Vaughn!" I yell. The need to protect Vaughn overrides my submissiveness to him, and I leap out of the bed and run toward the three at the other side of the room.

Vaughn kicks Elle's hand away, though she doesn't let go. Her grip tightens and although he doesn't lose his balance, his attention is definitely averted.

It's fixed on not one but two people now. Her and me.

"Back to the bed, little raven." My protector, godfather, and lover's voice is firm, despite his foot being held up off the floor. "Stay where I told you to."

I won't go back there. I tell Vaughn, "Okay," so he'll focus on Elle again.

I also do it so Lane doesn't realize I'm watching him.

The idiot pushes himself off the wall ever so slowly. I can see he's planning to strike Vaughn who's occupied with freeing his ankle from Elle.

And just as Vaughn doesn't notice his attacker, neither does Lane.

Moving in stealth mode, I unplug the night lamp on the bedside table, grabbing it firmly. The lamp's body is made of wood to complement the cabin's atmosphere, and while I don't give a fuck about the décor anymore, I do care about it being a great fucking weapon.

I might protest at the idea of Vaughn risking what's left of his soul to protect me. But when it comes to helping him, I don't care about what'll happen to me.

Fuck my soul. His life is what matters.

I slide behind Vaughn, then skip to the side. No one looks in my direction; the three of them are wrapped up in the scenario unfolding before us.

I'm filled to the brim with my sense of mission, and I raise the lamp.

"Fuck you, asshole," I grit out and throw the lamp at my mark's head.

My quick action and Lane's distraction work in my favor. The clash against his forehead procures a loud, thunderous *boom*. An even more deafening noise thunders as the lamp clashes on the floor beneath Lane next to Elle.

All eyes are turned to the source of the noise, staring up at Lane's bleeding temple.

"Darlene, back to bed!" Vaughn roars, breaking the silence.

His final kick manages to extract his ankle from Elle's furious grip.

He steps back to glower at me.

"You motherfucking bitch," Lane seethes.

The hatred in Lane's voice causes my attention to flick from Vaughn to him.

Lane's long fingers trace the path of the sticky liquid. His eyes slide up to meet mine. Anger, hatred, and disgust reflect in them. Gone is the boy who bent over backwards to charm me.

"You're on that man's side, huh? You're more disgusting than I thought." Lane spits on the floor.

Elle keeps wailing in pain after Vaughn crushes her palm beneath his boot.

"Can't believe I agreed to fuck you, you twisted bitch."

"You're the bitch." I hurl a finger at him. "Trying to humiliate someone, then…then…" The word claws at my throat, begging to get out.

It's one thing to hear the truth from Vaughn. To digest it in a safe environment with him alone.

This is different. The look in Lane's eyes makes it real. They wouldn't have hesitated to kill me for their own selfish, sick reasons.

I won't cry. Won't weep for their lies, deceit, and cruel intentions.

I will not shed a fucking tear for what an idiot they wanted to make out of me.

I *know* I'm not one.

My only so-called fault is being a good person. My parents' daughter.

I've been raised to believe those who claimed they loved me.

That's exactly what I did with Caroline and Elle. I trusted Lane too. After all, my *friends* were the ones who tried to set us up.

This whole fiasco started because I dared to love them. I don't regret it for a minute. Mom and Dad's light will forever reside alongside my darkness.

I won't ever give up on it. Won't ever apologize for it.

My voice echoes the fury I harbor. "…Then kill her. Fuck you for planning to kill me."

"I-I—" Lane stammers. My words hit him hard, the courage leaving him just as fast as it came.

He backs away to the wall again.

"Darlene!" Vaughn yells, lowering himself on all fours on top of Elle now since Lane is no longer a threat, "I love you more than anything, but go back to sit on the bloody bed."

He's protecting me. Some men are assholes and controlling. Vaughn loves me. He cares about keeping me safe.

My gaze follows him. I watch how Vaughn fists Elle's long, wavy hair in his palm.

Jealousy races through my body when he presses the blade of his knife to the sensitive flesh of her throat.

I crave to be the one he forces down, the one he digs little cuts into.

I long for his knife to nick my skin, for the black Xs on his mask to be the last thing I see before my body drowns in another mind-blowing orgasm.

Only me.

I'm better than this, I remind myself. *We are better than this.*

He's not down there loving *her*. He's slashing her throat because of his fierce love for *me*.

Vaughn doesn't get off on it. He comes to my defense by slicing her open and ripping the life out of her one inch at a time to protect me.

Eventually, she stops gurgling and lies there dead.

Vaughn did it. For me.

There's no room for envy between us, only for love. As twisted as it might be.

So, I listen to him.

Vaughn's masked face turns back to watch me walking back to sit on the edge of the bed.

"Good girl." He lifts his arm to fend off Lane's miserable punch that he senses without even seeing it.

Assured that Vaughn is okay, I allow the praise he lavished on me to caress my skin and my frail nerves like a soothing balm. My scowl smooths over; the lines in the corners of my eyes flatten.

"Do it." A smile tugs on my lips.

My fears for Vaughn's soul disappear as I eye my avenging angel. He stands up with blood dripping down his strong hands. His muscles pulsate beneath his clothes.

I trust him to know what he's doing. He'll be okay for me. For us. For the family we'll create together.

"Kill him, Daddy."

His low growl of approval accompanies the creaks in the floorboards as he spins toward Lane. He pounces on the younger man, punching him in the gut. The helpless little boy tumbles down like Elle before him, slumping against the wall and to the floor.

Vaughn is quick to follow, positioning himself on top of the guy who wanted to steal my virginity and kill me.

Then he flips him on his stomach, wrangling his sweats and briefs down to his knees.

"Please, God, no," Lane cries out. His hands reach to his ass, but Vaughn restrains him by pinning them to Lane's back.

Nothing will protect him against Vaughn's rage.

And I sit there enthralled, waiting to see what he does next.

"God won't help you, you miserable scum." Vaughn's sexy Brit accent intensifies, turning the scene hotter for me to watch. "Not from me."

Vaughn twists his body to grab dead Elle's ankle. He drags her over to them, aligning her manicured toe to Lane's butthole.

"No, no, no." Lane keeps squirming.

My grin widens and I practically clap with excitement. The full weight of what they planned on doing to me finally settles in, it's like a switch flipped inside me.

I don't care if Vaughn hurts them.

I *want* him to hurt them. To torture them.

To make them suffer.

Lane's cries pierce through the air when Vaughn forcefully shoves Elle's toe inside him. Again. And again. And again.

"Yes!" I yell, watching Lane's tears soak the bloodied floor.

"Oh, you're in pain?" My savior sounds as entertained as I am. "Let me help you with that."

Vaughn leaves Elle's toe inside Lane and grabs the knife.

What is he going to—?

My train of thought gets interrupted. Fucking obliterated.

Because it's then that Daddy slices the top of Lane's rim, opening him up wider. In his desperation, Lane thrashes his body, smashing his head into the floor.

His forehead bleeds more than before. Though not as bad as his behind, Vaughn continues to violate mercilessly.

With *two* of Elle's toes now.

Squish, squish, squish.

"I wish I could've extended our playtime." Vaughn disposes of Elle's body like yesterday's trash and flips Lane on his back. "But Darlene and I are on a tight schedule. You have to go."

"No!" Lane yells one final time.

"Please tell Lucifer I send my regards."

Vaughn grabs Lane's wrists using one hand and presses them above him to the floor, then sinks his knife all the way down Lane's left eye.

The boy's agonized shrieks and twitching body do nothing to free him from Vaughn, who swivels the blade in the boy's eye socket.

Even when he pulls the knife out of Lane, it's not out of the kindness of his heart. He does it to remove an impaled eyeball and gray brain matter.

"Other side," Vaughn warns, amusement painting his tone.

He stabs him again in his right eye, repeating the same maneuver to remove it from Lane's head.

Lane begins to convulse and vomit. He's still showing signs of life, even when it's pretty obvious that this is the end of the road for him.

Finally.

Vaughn understands Lane has mere seconds left, too.

He wipes his blade clean on Lane's shirt, then smooths his own hands on his jeans. All done, he stands up, leaving Lane there to suffer. To choke and gurgle and vomit until he quiets and dies.

When Vaughn stretches his hand to me, I don't hesitate to take it.

Throughout my short life, I've witnessed the ugly and beautiful sides of our world. The happy and sad. So much has happened to me in my—almost—twenty-one years.

Never this. I haven't once been subjected to something so ethereal and magical as Vaughn is wearing his mask with blood covering his hands, wrists, and forearms.

"I love you." He drags me to him, gazing down at me through the tiny slits in his mask. "I worship you, my little raven. I'm bloody proud of you for today, for everything that you are. You're mine now, and I'll teach you everything there is to know about survival. Not like you'll need it. For as long as I'm alive, no one will ever come near you again."

"I love you, too, my dark king." I squeeze his fingers with mine. I know none of the sweet words he says comes easy for him, and I want to show him just how much I appreciate it. "Thank you for your trust in me. I can't wait to go through this lifetime and a million others with you."

"We have one more task before we leave. Before I tell you everything about who you are and why these bastards were after you." His head tilts, his other hand cradling the side of my face. "It'll be your turn to take your revenge. You up for it?"

"Whatever you say." My smile widens, and my heart swells in my chest. "Anything at all, Daddy."

CHAPTER THIRTY-ONE

Vaughn

"LINCOLN," MY LITTLE raven says from the entrance to my tent looking in. "What are you doing here?"

She's playing coy, being saccharine sweet as she stands there, shifting on her feet. It's a pretense, but she's faking it so well, I might've fallen for it.

Except I was the one who helped her practice it on the short walk over.

The shuffling noises of stuff being moved around the tent stop.

A second later, I hear Lincoln's menacing voice. "How did you get away?"

I don't give two shits that he's been rummaging through my stuff. There's nothing there to help him, not even my *work* tools.

He can have access to my knives, other blades, and ropes. He can touch and look at them however he chooses.

For all I care, he can raise one at Darlene.

His fate is sealed either way. Darlene and I arrived here prepared for any possible scenario. With every step we took over here, past gravel paths and trees, we planned. I taught her how to cover every possible angle, to be ready for anything.

Lincoln Hopkins isn't getting out of the woods. Isn't going back to his old life. By the end of the day, he'll be nothing but a sack of bones, or less.

Depending on our mood.

I still haven't told her exactly *why* this is happening. I'm saving it as a reward for her once we make it to the finish line.

Darlene doesn't need proof anymore, though. She fully trusts me at this point, and her bloodthirst for those who wronged her grows ever strong.

Right in front of me, she blooms and evolves into the woman she was destined to be. My dark queen has the light of her parents and my darkness to envelop her.

No one will ever be able to play her again.

"Lane finally agreed to hear me out."

From where I stand, I see her profile thanks to the moonlight filtering between the treetops and my flashlight that Lincoln has aimed at her.

She twists a lock of her hair around her finger in another timid gesture. "He could tell I'm innocent, that I didn't have anything to do with this, so he let me go."

"Did he really?" Lincoln asks from inside the tent.

His voice is as cold and pissed off as ever. He falls for her act, the idiot. What can I expect from a boy who only knows her for her virginity and hidden wealth? Nothing.

"Well, I don't." His anger rises. "He didn't come here to run it by me, and I sure as shit don't allow it."

In another lifetime, I would've respected Lincoln for staying committed to his murderous plan. However, this isn't the case. Mr. Hopkins only earns more of my hate for how he treats Darlene.

And to think that he would've succeeded had I not been stalking Darlene...

My jaw clenches and my hands ball into fists. It takes every bit of my willpower to stay where I am and let her fool him until it's my turn to step in.

My vengeful inclination to leap forward and end this fucker will have to wait.

"Lincoln, you see, there's no need to tie me up again." I'm amazed at her ability to keep her composure and stick to the role of the naïve and somewhat dumb girl she wants him to believe she is. "Lane also said he found the person who killed Roy and Caroline."

"So what? I'm in the fucker's tent and you're still guilty in my eyes. We're not done with you." Authority seeps into Lincoln's tone. "Turn around and start walking back. You need to be restrained."

I imagine he's standing upright, flexing his muscles at her. Doing the whole, *I'm better and stronger than you* charade, thinking Darlene is alone out here, that he can scare her into compliance.

What a useless asshole. My Darlene is wide awake, fiercer than ever, and ready to strike.

She outsmarted the ruthless rich kid. Whatever he does, whatever course of action he takes, he's a walking dead man.

"But,"—she gestures to the contents of the tent, probably enjoying the idea of fucking with Lincoln as she prolongs the conversation—"as you said, there's nothing here saying that I did it. We can…" Darlene licks her bottom lip, huffing and pouting like a clueless kid. "Go get Lane and Elle and run into town before he gets us? Please, Lincoln, I don't want to die."

"No."

Suddenly, the tent rustles and he gets out.

His two filthy hands reach out for Darlene, grasping her hair and her throat. In his jeans pocket, Lincoln has *my* Wartenberg wheel.

My gaze lingers on my stolen weapon and its glinting teeth for a second.

Then my eyes dart up to his filthy hands grabbing Darlene. I seethe as white-hot rage pummels through me. I almost lose it with the need to launch forward, bite off his ear, and snap his neck like a twig.

He's testing my patience and the vow I made to Darlene.

I hate it. Hate seeing her finger moving left and right and telling me "No."

But I won't break my promise to her.

Among other things we discussed, I promised Darlene I'd let her keep her independence to a certain degree. Unless there's a real threat on her life, which I'm beginning to suspect there will be soon, I'm to stay put.

Much like everything else I do, I agreed to do it for her. She argued that it'd be productive for her to learn how to unveil someone's true character for herself, and I agreed with her.

Still fucking hate being sidelined when he's touching her like that.

"No?" she says while fighting for air.

My stone-cold heart wrenches harder at the sight. She soothes the pain quickly though when she clasps her hand around the scissors I gave her. The ones she's stuffed into the back of her leggings.

"Please, Lincoln. You have to believe me. I didn't do this."

Lincoln prowls forward with her in his hold. Fallen leaves and twigs crunch beneath their boots. Their breaths are all I hear.

Darlene keeps up the appearance of a hapless victim, allowing him to push her around. Her chin quivers. Her lips part.

I make a mental note to make good use of those later. Preferably around my throbbing cock.

"Maybe you did, maybe you didn't." His blond hair remains perfectly styled, his clothes are wrinkle-free.

He may be scared and furious on the inside, but once again Lincoln proves nothing will seep out of his impenetrable façade.

"I don't care either way. We're not finished with you."

"You mentioned that," she peeps as her back slams into a tree trunk. Her armed hand bears the brunt of the hit as well.

I see red, digging my fingernails into my thigh to stop myself from unleashing my pent-up wrath.

"So, the silly girl listens." His lips hike up into a rare, unhinged-looking grin.

The blood that rushes in my veins gushes and roars. I can't fucking wait for the second we eviscerate his life for good.

I'm so high-strung, so pissed off. I could explode any second now.

"Not done, as in you're going to hurt me?" Her fingers signal me once more to wait, knowing I'm seething back here. "Why?"

She's lucky I respect her just as much as I love her.

Otherwise, this lowlife degenerate who has the audacity to talk to her like that would've already been on his knees. He would've been begging for death to come.

Soon.

Soon my hands, my boots, and my tools will be all over him.

For now, I'll let her have her win. I'm letting her prove to herself that she's the invincible queen.

"What did I ever do to you?"

"I might as well tell you since I'm going to kill you anyway." He chuckles, dark and low.

And that's my cue. His threat sounds too real for my liking. I'm sure he won't kill her, since it'd ruin his plans, but he *is* about to hurt her.

Besides, it's high time I joined the party.

Soundlessly, I sneak out of my hiding spot and step behind the trees, positioning myself at a closer vantage point. From here it's easier to notice the smugness surrounding Lincoln in a poisonous halo, the stench of entitlement reeking out of him.

It's nauseating. Thank fuck all of it is about to end.

"Your dad—" he starts.

The mention of her father makes Darlene's eyes twitch. Lincoln is blind to it, not having spent years upon years studying her mannerisms like I have.

I see the pain she overcomes and admire her resilience so fucking much.

"—he lied to you." Lincoln lowers his face closer to Darlene's.

I take a step closer to his back, listening to lie number one. Eric didn't *lie* to her, not in the sense Lincoln means it. He hadn't purposefully intended to trick or hurt her.

My best friend adored his daughter. He wanted her to be better than the kids we went to school with, happier than the people he fraternized with his entire life. He wished for her to see what the world has to offer beyond the material shit money could buy.

By not telling her about their wealth, Eric and Helena gave her something way more important than brands. They created a warm, loving family for her.

Except Lincoln can't see it. On the dozens of days I'd followed him, I'd witnessed his interactions with his dad. They weren't pretty.

The older Hopkins is a great lawyer and crappy father. He hangs money over his child's head as a means to bully and control him.

Lincoln is the way he is because of his dad. He'll never be able to understand how Eric didn't withhold money from her until her twenty-first birthday as a form of punishment—he did it *because* he loved her.

Too fucking bad.

He shouldn't have chosen to kill her instead of actually working for his own goddamn wealth. Lincoln Hopkins brought it all on himself.

No one needs this sadistic trash walking the earth.

"He wasn't a small-time lawyer. He wasn't poor. Truth is, in a few hours, you'll be rich enough to buy out *my* old man," Lincoln growls, his jealousy flowing from him in waves. "Twice. Three times, even."

Though Darlene already heard bits of it before, it doesn't diminish the shocked look on her face. Her eyes glisten from learning that Lincoln knew what her dad hid from her.

My muscles strain, but not to spring forward and murder Lincoln. I'm encompassed by a strange emotion. By the desire to engulf Darlene in a hug, to comfort her, and to wipe out the pain emanating from her pores to mine.

This isn't just the protective instinct I've always had toward her. What I'm experiencing is on a deeper level.

This is warmth. This is kindness.

This is another type of love that I've never felt for any other human on this planet but her.

"H–how?" Darlene mumbles. Discovering her parents led a secret life is beginning to take its toll on her. "He went to the same office for years, owned the same car… I received a scholarship for my education. What. Money?"

Lincoln cocks his head. "Jesus fuck, you really are a moron, aren't you?"

Calm down, she signals with her hand again. Darlene must be reading my mind, has to realize I'm this close to snapping.

She's right, too. It won't be long before I do, and I have to alert her of that fact.

I slip out of my new, closer hiding place, careful not to crunch any dry leaf as I do. Several feet from where she and Lincoln stand, I raise my hand—the one holding the knife— spinning my wrist in a circular *Move it* motion.

There'll be spoiling and loving and all the corny shit my twisted guts ache to give her. Later. Now, she needs to do as I say.

Darlene acknowledges me by blinking once. She ignores Lincoln's insult, getting to the point by asking him in a flat, businesslike tone, "Just tell me what is it about my dad's secret life that makes you want to hurt me."

"Fine. You don't know who your own dad was, moron. Do you know mine?" He doesn't sound bothered by her change of tone. In fact, he lowers his to a whisper.

Little boy is still scared of Daddy, even here, hundreds of miles from home. "Know what he does for a living?"

"He's an estate lawyer," she says when he loosens his grip on her throat a little.

"Ding, ding, ding, silly Pierce girl," Lincoln mocks her for the millionth time.

It fails to insult her anymore. I see it in her eyes.

"Guess who was his favorite client? His *biggest* client?"

Her mouth gapes, her eyes a pool of unanswered questions. "My dad?"

"Correct again. He was the owner of an international law firm whose name he changed to Doran & Platt Law. It used to be only named Dowling—your grandpa's first name—up until…" He lowers his chin, beckoning her to complete the sentence.

"I was born, and my grandparents passed away. When he inherited everything." Darlene's throat bobs as she swallows.

Such a smart little raven she is. A sudden surge of regret floods me for not being the one to tell her about her history. I'm aware of the necessity of the process to go the way it has, especially since I insisted on these steps to be taken.

Except so much has changed over the last three days. The murderous side of me is ever strong, but for her…for her, I'm worried I might've grown a heart.

"True," Lincoln spits out. "What else do you see? Or do I have to spell it out for you?"

Darlene's eyes skate toward mine briefly. "He changed the name to my initials?"

335

"Unbelievable, you managed to dig into that tiny head of yours and connect the dots."

He has no idea how wrong he is about her. His jealousy curtains him from seeing how brilliant she is, how fortunate he is to breathe the same air as she does.

Too bad he won't live to go to a therapist to sort out his issues.

"Anyway," he continues. "Yes. He did. My dad handled his inheritance where he left *everything* to a worthless little kid. You don't deserve any of it. You haven't suffered a day in your life. And it's not like you would have a clue on what to do with it either."

I would've waited for him to elaborate. Would've let him continue unraveling his plans so Darlene would know without a shred of a doubt that I hadn't lied to her.

Then the scumbag went and ruined everything.

"Too bad I can't have my face or any part of me on that porn tape you're going to do with Lane." Lincoln dips his mouth to her jaw while pressing himself to her. "See, if anyone ever found it, my dad would've realized I did it because of the will. But just so you know, I would've fucked you. To be honest, I've been fed up with Caroline's boring-ass hole for a while now."

Sorry, little raven. I can't hold back anymore.

"Tough luck, fucker." Fueled by my rage, I'm behind him in a split second.

He doesn't breathe another word before I choke him with one hand and slice his face from his temple to his jaw with the other. "Since you'll be seeing a lot of Caroline real fucking soon. In hell."

CHAPTER THIRTY-TWO

Darlene

VAUGHN'S PATIENCE HAS been ripped to shreds by the time he jumps Lincoln.

The way he's looked as he lurked behind Lincoln, I'd say he's been running low for the past ten minutes. Maybe even longer.

Frankly, I'm all out of it too. Vaughn, my deceased parents, the boy who's been adamant on humiliating and killing me. The entire goddamn world has stolen my patience from under me.

This still isn't about the money for me. I'm not frustrated over that.

Fuck the money, fuck the lack of it. Fuck the luxury I so-called missed.

I wouldn't have traded my past for *anything*.

Mom and Dad gave me the most important thing a child could ever wish for: a loving family, an abundance of hugs, happy memories and a ton of smiles.

And Vaughn is one of the biggest gifts they ever gave me. He's—almost—always been the one constant in my life. A caring uncle figure, a devoted watchman, and now, a lover.

So, no, I'm not angry about the money. It means nothing to me. Especially when I see what a miserable existence Lincoln has had when he had plenty of it.

It's the lies. The more I stew in it, the more it bothers me.

My family and Vaughn hadn't just hidden something as miniscule as money or my relatives. Evidently, they lied about virtually everything, every day for years.

My parents didn't even give me the courtesy of leaving me a note in their will, the one the fake lawyer read to me.

They told me time and again how proud they were of me. How they trusted my decision-making process, my values, my opinions. Yet they didn't trust me with the truth.

Vaughn respected them and stuck to the lie for another three fucking years.

What the hell am I supposed to do now? Who do I trust, if anyone?

"Get out of your head, little raven," Vaughn grits out.

His jaw is set tight, the veins on his forearms pumping in the efforts to subdue Lincoln who's twisting and turning in his arms.

"Being born into money, into luxury, it has a way of messing with a lot of people's heads. It wasn't *you* Eric and Helena didn't trust. Deep down, you know better than that."

I'm blown away by how he reads my entire train of thought again. He's right. And I can't be angry, not at the three of them and their good intentions.

It's still so much to process, though.

If only I could have another second to myself, to regroup...

"Look at me." Vaughn and his tough kind of love don't allow me one. "You had been loved. You *are* loved. Don't let this lowlife make you second-guess it."

My Vaughn digs his fingers deeper into Lincoln's throat. The asshole chokes, spitting blood and saliva on my face. I wipe it off with the back of my palm, then cast my eyes behind him to Vaughn.

His mask conceals his dark and majestic features. I see him, nonetheless. Past the black X marks, I gaze into his soul. His beautiful fathomless darkness and endless love for me shines through it.

Calm washes over me, clearing my head from the negative shit Lincoln planted there.

"I love you, too." I smile at Vaughn. "Thank you for reminding me who I am."

"Psychos." Lincoln's strangled voice is challenging me, his last dire attempt to come between Vaughn and me. "Fucking bat-shit lunatics. You're gonna die for this, you know that? My dad will find out what you did and—"

Vaughn doesn't reply verbally. In a sharp movement, he swipes his hand up and slices Lincoln's ear right off his head.

Thick blood spurts out of where his ear once was, dripping down his throat and painting Vaughn's palm, wrist, and forearm in another layer of red.

Lincoln's screams break from his mouth a second later, playing catch up with the shock his body went through. The pain turns on a switch in him, turning even *his* emotionless soul into a mess of feelings.

However…none of what's happening to him is enough to tear my eyes away from Vaughn's.

"Baby." Vaughn's calling is both authoritative and soft. "No one could promise them you wouldn't have been the same woman you are today. When Eric—"

"Leave me the fuck alone," Lincoln seethes, breathing hard to calm himself as though regaining composure would help him regain control over the situation. "You're deluding yourselves if you think either of you will survive what you're doing to me."

"Jesus fucking Christ," Vaughn growls. "And here I thought you weren't a bore like the rest of them. Guess I got that one wrong."

"Fu—"

"Oh, shut the hell up."

My all-powerful godfather releases his hold on Lincoln, though in no way does he let him go. He hits Lincoln where his ear used to be, the pain of it sending Lincoln to topple to the ground.

Adrenaline and excitement flood me from the force Vaughn exudes. He moves to stand over my offender, his boot pressing to Lincoln's struggling form while blood keeps pouring out the side of his head making a crimson puddle in the sand.

"As I was saying." Vaughn leans over to cup my cheek with his clean hand, drawing me to him.

"Yes?" I bat my eyelashes, feeling like a high schooler all over again when I stare up into his mask. He's beautiful, with or without it.

"Eric and Helena knew that one day you'd have everything you ever wanted, material and otherwise. They never wanted to keep it from you."

Unlike what happened back in the cabin, this time Vaughn anticipates Lincoln's attempt to grab his ankle. He kicks his hand off, causing Lincoln to curse in pain.

"They wanted to wait until you're twenty-one and out of college, old enough to tell right from wrong and away from bad influences. Like this trash beneath me or the kids your dad and I went to school with who judged me and treated me like shit for being different."

"But…" My eyebrows pull together, my brain fighting to understand their motives now that Vaughn is willing to be an open book and give me my answers. "Did I do anything wrong? Over the years? I mean, Dad loved me. The three of you did. I even remember you nodding once when they said they were proud of the girl I'd become."

Vaughn's head tilts, his eyes flashing in what could be interpreted as compassion. "It wasn't a lie. We all loved you. *I* love you."

"Fuck, no wonder you're such an idiot," Lincoln grunts since one part of his lip is mashed against the ground. "With parents and a godfather like that…"

This time it's not Vaughn who strikes him.

I do.

I bend down, fishing my scissors from the back of my waistband to shove them straight in the middle of Lincoln's shoulders. I feel the blades pushing past his bones, the heavy-duty scissors bisecting skin and flesh.

He screams again, twitching and flailing. Dirt and dust rise around him.

I leave the scissors buried in his back.

"Don't you ever talk about my parents." I spit on his exposed profile. "They had a conscience. Good hearts. And you're a miserable piece of shit who has *nothing*."

CHAPTER THIRTY-THREE
Darlene

"GOOD GIRL." VAUGHN grips my bicep, hoisting me up. While I was busy getting into Lincoln's face, he wiped his fingers clean and now he runs them up my shoulder, dipping them into my mouth. "Suck them, lick them like you would my tongue."

There has to be some kind of mental flaw in me to be turned on after doing what I did, with the scent of copper whipping in the breeze and into my nose. But to be honest, it's the most right I ever felt in my life.

I'm high on Vaughn's praise, aroused by his coarse fingers dragging across my tongue, and my hormones shoot through the roof as my vengeance is being served.

"That's it," he groans louder as I close my lips around him, lapping my tongue on the skin that tastes so much of him with everything I have in me. "That's my good girl.

Take them, baby, and I'll tell you everything you need to know. Daddy will bring you your closure."

While I keep sucking him down my throat, coating Vaughn's fingers with saliva and desire, he does what he promised. Tells me the truth. I see the honesty in his eyes first, then I hear it in his words.

"We were all proud of you. Whether we—more likely, I—said it or not." His thumb hooks under my chin, forcing me to stop the bobbing motion of my head. "You have to remember that."

"Dad,"—I mumble, then wrap my fingers around his, pushing them slightly out of my mouth so I can ask another question that's been bothering me—"Dad approved of you."

"I told you, we navigated through my darkness together. He helped me navigate through it, and he knew I would never hurt any of you. On the contrary, he made me your godfather knowing there was no one out there who loved you so fiercely from when you were in your mother's womb."

He dips his head lower, and I get a deeper glimpse into his beautiful soul. "I couldn't escape my past. Couldn't unsee my birth parents being slaughtered or change the trajectory of my life. *You*, you were our salvation. All of ours. I would've never put you in danger. That's also why I stayed away. I didn't trust my darkness not to ruin you until I couldn't bear another moment without you."

I'm rendered immobile as he grazes his damp fingers along my jaw. My heart gallops wildly in my chest when he dumps the knife to have his bloodied palm cradle the other side of my face.

"We couldn't risk tainting you, you see?" Vaughn's rare show of compassion shines through behind his mask. "So Eric, the best fucking person I've met, he denounced his wealth, the servants, the penthouse and vacation homes, all of that, for you. I…"

My gaze follows Vaughn's as he angles his head to look at Lincoln who's been silent for too long. He doesn't move so maybe he fainted. Maybe he's dead. If he isn't, eventually he will be. Then Vaughn will give me another one of his lessons on how to dispose of the evidence. Later.

Once I unveil the truth.

"You're my sponsor, aren't you?" I ask without a shred of accusation. More of an epiphany. "In college. You pay for my tuition. For my apartment. You followed up with Mom and Dad's wishes, right?"

"Always been so bloody clever, my little raven. Now for the final piece of the puzzle. Them." Vaughn moves back, kicking Lincoln's limp body. "Your parents put in a lot of effort to hide their identity, to go undercover for your sake. Then this one snooped through his daddy's files. I did the same and discovered his father had cut him out from his will. I'm assuming Lincoln knew about that too, because guess what he did with that information?"

"*Made* Caroline be my friend?" My head shakes on its own in disbelief. Vaughn firms his grip to force me to hear him out. "But that's impossible. He wasn't dating her when she and I started being friends."

"An asshole like him, he has no issues with manipulating whomever he chooses." The fire in Vaughn's black eyes could burn the entire world. "I read his texts from when you'd entered college. After he recognized you, he went to Caroline who was practically his groupie. He promised her a relationship and your money if she helped him trick you. They befriended you until the time was right, until you were about to turn twenty-one."

My godfather, the man who's hellbent on protecting me by any means, skips over Lincoln to press his body to mine. He envelops me in his arms, driving his hands into my hair, burrowing them into my scalp.

"You had no way of figuring it out." His masked forehead presses to my bare one. "They played nice until today. But I didn't trust anyone in your vicinity. Eventually, I hacked their phones and found the incriminating messages about threatening to humiliate you with the sex tape, have you sign off your inheritance, then kill you so you'd never try and claim it back ever again. It was too late—*I* was too late—and I'm bloody sorry for that. There'll be no more of that, though, love. It's done."

"It's over?" I blink, befuddled yet so fucking ready to start my new life. Newfound energy and the desire for life wash over me until they're everywhere in my body. "I get to live in peace?"

"No one's coming for you." Vaughn trails one hand down my spine, pinning my stomach harder to his erection that I want more desperately than I want air. "No one but me, darling."

I grind myself against his cock, telling him by using my body how on board I am with it.

"And I'm not waiting anymore." He tugs on my hair, pushing himself into me while I gasp. "Not another second. Daddy's coming for you right fucking now."

CHAPTER THIRTY-FOUR

Vaughn

VARIOUS TYPES OF scenarios arouse different people in many ways.

Some may get turned on by the opera, some by a good meal, others by being spanked. Everyone has their own unique buttons that when pressed, they get horny, feral, insanely ravenous, or all of the above.

My kink? What takes me from zero to sixty in less than a second and makes me so hard I can't even think straight and throws any semblance of inhibitions I might still have out the fucking window?

It isn't what. It's *who*. Nothing has ever delivered me to these heights other than simply looking at Darlene when she started growing up, turning from the girl I loved to the woman I lusted after. The sexiest human to exist on this godforsaken planet who managed to thaw my impenetrable heart just by being herself.

Before my love for Darlene evolved into something more sinister, getting myself off was more of a necessity, a means to an end. The resentment and desire to kill I had bottled up inside would demand an orgasm just as violent, just as primal as my urges if they went unattended for a while.

Thing is, Lincoln's dead body beneath me doesn't satiate the fire burning inside me. I'm set ablaze, the pores on my skin bursting with the need to claim my little raven who helped me slaughter the bastard.

I had to hold off on eating her alive until I finished revealing the truth about her history. Doing it cost me my damn near sanity, but I did it for her.

There are no more secrets between us.

I'm done waiting.

I'm taking her.

"Yes, please," Darlene whispers, her plump lips wet with her spit, her eyes as lit up as my soul. "Fuck me, Daddy. I need to have you everywhere. I need you to make it hurt. Please."

Fuck.

"So fucking hard for you and your twisted mind." Applying pressure on her hair, I lower her to the ground, my knees bending too until we both land on the harsh terrain.

She lets me arrange her like a doll so she's lying down and spread eagled. Her gaze follows my movements as I press two fingers to the apex of her thighs over her leggings. "Executing this cunt got you hot and dripping for me, little raven?"

Her whimper is all I get. But I'm after making her body subdued and docile for me, not her voice.

"Words." Her old T-shirt tears easily by the sheer force of my hands, straight down the middle. I hover over her, yanking at the cups of her bra, exposing her round, large breasts to me, and grip the left one without a shred of mercy. "Say it. I want to hear it. Need to hear you telling me what I do to you."

"Yes, Daddy, it turned me on." Darlene bites her lip, her heavy tits rising and falling with each aroused breath. "My panties are so wet. I've never needed anything in my life like I need you inside me."

She's not the only one. I'm a heartbeat away from tearing off my mask and latching on her breasts, stomach, sweet fucking pussy. I want to eat her out until she screams, to watch her crying when she can't take another orgasm, and then push her gorgeous body to the ground and make her come again and again.

Until she bloody begs for my dick.

But I'll have to bring her to tears in another way. My goddaughter told me on our walk here that she loves the mask, and it's blatantly visible that watching me wear it is everything she needs.

And I'm more than willing to give it to her.

"That's it." I press my fingers to her tongue. "Spit on me."

My little raven soaks my fingers, and I mimic what my tongue, lips, and teeth would do to her nipple. They turn harder and redder under my attention as I rub my thumb on

351

one tit, then switch to the other, stroking, flicking, pinching while I grind myself on her.

Layers of clothes separate us, but I'm such a horny fuck that it feels as though I'm deep inside her. What really does it for me, though, is knowing how needy she is and yet she doesn't touch me, being my perfect submissive girl.

"You're so good, baby." My thrusts are almost enough to tear her leggings off. "My good little girl."

"I am?" Her lips part and quick, desperate breaths fall from them.

"Yes, love." I leave her breasts, admiring the marks I left on her skin. "It might be *your* birthday tomorrow, but you and that greedy little cunt are *my* gift. Every second of every day."

I rake my hands down her soft curves. My fingers bite into her flesh, marking her some more before I back away and sit on my knees.

Her eyes sink into my soul, wide with fear that I'm stopping this.

She thinks I'm gonna leave her.

Not fucking likely. Never again.

"You belong to me." In deft movements, I rid Darlene of her boots and socks. "You're mine to debase,"—while ignoring how dead he looks, I grab the Wartenberg wheel out of Lincoln's pocket, rolling the sharp, metal teeth along her sole—"mine to torture."

I increase the pressure, watching her skin whiten where my device touches. Her head flies back, the sudden sensations making her thighs clench.

My dick jerks in a reaction to her, pressing hard against my jeans. She thrives on the pain I inflict on her, and it sets me off every fucking time.

"Mine to fuck however and *when*ever I please."

I don't bother suppressing the low growl emanating from my chest when I lift her foot off the ground to taste her. I'm salivating for her, raising my mask to expose my mouth then suck and bite on her toe.

She screams, the surprise and brutality of my action turning out to be too much on her already overloaded senses. Yet she doesn't kick me away, doesn't tell me to stop.

My feral woman.

"Sensitive, darling?" My question, in its essence, may be soft. My voice is anything but. I sound cold and detached, then bite her a second time.

Knowing I want her to speak up, my Darlene doesn't waste another breath before saying, "Yes."

"You still want Daddy to do whatever he wants to you, don't you?" Her pants are in my way, so I lower her foot to the ground and lay my torture device on her bare belly, then curl my fingers around the waistband of her leggings. "To screw the pain out of you, the one you have because you're such a horny girl?"

"Yes, Daddy." She arches her back, her butt lifting in the air in her plea for me to remove her clothes, to defile my filthy queen. "Ruin me. Abuse me. I'm yours."

Precum leaks from my cock as her words lace into my soul. I obey her silent plea, tugging off her leggings and underwear in a violent motion.

As if I'm not already drunk on looking at her swollen, slick lips, knowing the dark caverns of her mind match mine, I can smell her better too.

My control gets overrun by the musky perfume of her arousal. I'm done teasing her. Done pacing myself. Her desire fuels mine to the extreme, threatening to split me from the inside unless I do something about it.

"Since you've been such a good girl,"—I yank my mask off the lower part of my face again, high enough to expose my mouth— "such an obedient puppet and the sexiest violent little thing, you're going to get your reward."

I bend at the waist, pulling her thighs apart. My fingers spread her swollen lips, clearing the soft hair to look at her pussy.

"You're gorgeous." I let out a breath on her red and tight clit, on the lips that are drenched with our cum.

"Touch me," she moans; her words are mere groans.

I need as much as she does, swirling my tongue around it, rocking my cock on the ground as she screams when my teeth chafe her puffy skin.

"Oh, my love." Her arousal drips down my chin after I've licked and nipped her sensitive skin over and over again. I fix my mask back on and rise to my knees. "This is nothing yet. We're just getting started."

Darlene's eyes are black oceans of curiosity, lust, and something else. Something similar to what I see in the mirror on a daily basis, a profound sense of depravity only a dark soul can recognize in another.

It's been inside her, triggered by the events of the weekend.

I can't say I'm the least bit sorry about it.

"All those years you've been exploring the cruel side of humanity…" I whip off my T-shirt above and over my mask, throw it to the ground, then stand up. "All these dark urges you had in you…"

"You had cameras set up in my apartment, right?" Darlene doesn't sound surprised. In fact, she sounds pleased.

"Legs open wide." I nod as I drop my jeans and boxer briefs, letting my cock hang heavy for her to understand how hard she makes me.

I fist myself, stroking hard and painfully. "See what you're doing to me? You're going to get every inch of it, raven."

Her knees drop to the sides immediately, exposing more of her.

Darlene's obedience gets her the answer she wants.

"Yes." I lower myself to sit between her thighs, another drop of precum wetting the throbbing head of my dick. "I stalked you, had cameras recording you twenty-four seven."

My gaze fixes on hers while I pick up the wheel from her stomach while I keep fisting myself. "I rubbed my painful erection exactly like this when you touched yourself. When you discovered things about yourself, about how pain made you come hard, and when you came for Daddy, I was right there with you."

Her moan and lustful gaze tell me just how much she loved it.

With my dick sinking into her, I feel the need to repeat these words, "I'm not sorry I invaded your privacy."

I thrust so deep I'm practically in her womb. "Not sorry for needing you, for loving you, for protecting you. Never will be. So don't expect an apology from me."

"Don't"—her groan is throaty and insanely visceral, and I fuck the need out of her harder—"don't need an apology. I've always wanted you there. Needed you, all of you."

"Good." The metal of the wheel's handle digs into my skin the more raw and rugged my thrusts become. "You have me. You have me for the rest of your life. Forever."

Wielding the torture device between us, I press the spiky wheel to her clit, rolling it to the rhythm of my hips while I pound into her.

Her moans from before transform into cries of pain and pleasure, into screams as her pussy milks me tighter and more juices soak my cock.

"You know what made me come the hardest?" I keep rutting into her, thriving on her squirms and groans of torment. "That had my semen spraying up to my chest?"

"W-what?" she asks, as much as her breathless panting allows her.

My lips are hidden from her, although I'm pretty sure my sinister smirk permeates through my voice.

"Your tears," I grunt out, rutting into her and bottoming out each time. "But they were for your parents before. Now I need you to cry for me, cry for your Daddy."

"I love you," she mouths, then she sucks in the air she seems to have been desperate for. "I need more."

A split second is what I need to get what she means. I draw out of her, every inch of my cock dragging along her sopping, tight walls while I increase the pressure of my wheel and continue to roll it up and down her clit.

Once I'm out and aiming my cock lower, her pucker squeezes, realizing I'm about to give her what she asked for.

"Relax." I prod the crown of my dick to the little hole that my fingers remember claiming. "Let me in."

"I…"

I gather dampness from her pussy, massaging two fingers on her tight rim. "When I tell you something, anything, you either say *Yes, Daddy*, and obey, *Please*, or *Enough*. No other options."

She gives in to my ministrations, letting me lube her sweet ass using her own arousal.

"That's it. That's my girl," I goad her.

When she's wet enough from the inside, I remove my fingers and shove the head of my cock inside.

"Daddy!"

"Fuck, you're tight." I grit out, pressing my free hand on her sternum, feeling her rapid heartbeat beneath me. "Tight and *mine*."

"Yes, always yours." A bright pearl of wet salt twinkles in the corner of her eye. Then her other one.

She's crying for me.

"Beautiful."

Her tears will forever be mine. Like every part of her will.

"Now take it." I drive every inch of me into her ass, gliding in and out, groaning like a hungry animal as she milks me into her. "Just like that, take everything I give you."

Darlene's thighs clench harder than before, her breaths are more clipped, and her eyes are clouded beyond the tears that well and roll down her cheeks.

She's close, and it's time she gets to have her release.

I throw the wheel to the side, pinching the hyper-sensitized clit and massaging it in intervals. "Come for me. Come *with* me, my depraved little raven."

The word "Yes" plays on her lips before her orgasm sweeps it out of her in a choked breath. She screams up to the skies above her, then looks at me. The orgasm still ripples through my little raven, and that's when I rip my mask off.

My lips steal the sounds of pleasure from her, my cock driving faster and harder than before. She gives me her tongue, her air, her essence. I'm taken over by how honest, pure, and dirty she is, wrapped up into one perfect gift.

My gift.

"Fuck," I breathe into her mouth the moment I come inside her ass, filling her with my semen. My kisses turn from punishing to caring, caressing, my tongue lapping against her tears. "Fuck, my love, you feel so good."

"I love you." She cups my cheeks, her tender palms a contrast to the rugged man that I am.

"I love you, too." The admission isn't that difficult to articulate anymore. "I'll always love you."

As dark as she is, she's also that bright light that I need in my life. I kiss her again, pulling out and rolling on my back to cradle her in my arms, entwining her legs between mine.

"It's your birthday in a few hours."

"It is." She hums as I kiss the top of her head and stroke leaves out of her hair.

"What do you want me to get you?" I rub up and down her arm, stroking her breasts and stomach, then coming back up to cradle her cheek in my palm. "Anything you want, darling, it's yours."

"I have everything I need right here." Darlene's grip on my torso fastens, and Jesus, do her words make me love her even more. "You're everything I'll ever need, Vaughn."

I press my lips to her forehead. "You already have me. For an eternity. I'm never leaving you again, my love, never again."

EPILOGUE
Darlene

"ALL SET, DARLING?" Vaughn, my godfather, my dad's best friend, and now my husband calls me from the living room.

Almost a year has passed since he finally came to get me, and I've already learned so much about him.

Like how he prefers to own his British accent when he's free to be himself around me.

How it turns him on to wear the mask when he violates any of my holes.

How fiercely handsome he looks when he puts it on for his night-time job.

What a cinnamon roll he turns to every now and then when he kisses the top of my head and tells me I'm his good little girl. Daddy Vaughn loves it when I go to work with him to take down one of the bad guys.

That is, until I started to show.

Anyway, stuff like that.

With every discovery I make, every door he opens for me to look through, I love him even more.

He's such a good man. The best there is. There isn't a second that I don't feel as loved as I love him, not a minute goes by without him showing me how much he cares.

Through his hugs, the tiny nicks he marks me with, his fierce sucking of my clit until I'm blown to pieces by my fifth orgasm of the day. Through the black petunias he delivers from God-knows-where every weekend and the black diamond engagement ring he put on my finger.

He's tender on my sad days, when my tears suddenly don't belong to him. He encourages me to think about Mom and Dad, to mourn them, and once I'm better, he strips me of my clothes and spanks me senseless to remind me who my real Daddy is until I come on his lap.

I'm the luckiest woman alive. The luckiest one to ever exist.

"I'll be out in a second," I call back from our walk-in closet, pulling on the black maternity dress I bought last week.

Vaughn set me up with a brand-new wardrobe once the single blue line on the test turned to two, but very quickly we discovered we had to add bigger sizes to it. Because this isn't one baby we're expecting; it's three.

I guess my womb took my husband's adamant breeding attempts as seriously as he did. Not that I'm complaining. The two little Vaughn's and one little me in my stomach are the best possible blessing I could've asked for along with the love of my life and graduating from college.

I'm not rushing to go to grad school, though. Law school can wait.

I'll get to it, someday, then Vaughn and I will take over Dad's old empire. Until then, growing and birthing the little ones in my belly take precedence over everything.

Honestly, I can't wait to have them here. To see Vaughn become a father and not just a Daddy. To have a family of our own.

We already discussed how we plan to raise them. They'll be brought up to have the same values my mother and father passed on to me, but with an added evil twist. After all, they can't be the Grimm children unless they're badass, unrelenting monsters like their dad and now their mom.

They'll be just the right amount of nice, not too much and not too little. None of them and or the rest of our future children will ever be subjected to the cruelty both Vaughn and I had in our lifetime without fighting back.

"They'll kill if they must," he told me.

I nodded while rubbing my swollen belly. "They'll do anything they have to. And we'll support them every step of the way."

Vaughn's smirk curved his lips in a sinister way before he ripped my shirt off and took my full breast in his lips, then looked up at me before he ravaged my body. "Always, little raven. Always."

But before we even considered what we'd teach our children, we had to wrap up some unfinished business of our own.

My bank account. My dad's business. To claim what's rightfully mine or more like *ours* now.

We didn't really need the money. Vaughn's wealth could provide for us, our children, and our grandchildren, easily.

It's the principle that counts.

A bunch of assholes tried to murder me for the only thing I had left of my family, and fuck if that didn't make me pissed off and irrationally territorial.

Vaughn too.

Which was why we headed to Richard Hopkins's law offices right after we did a proper cleanup of the carnage in the woods and our shotgun wedding at city hall.

Granted, it wasn't as fast as I would've liked it to be. It took us over two days to dunk the five bodies of the traitors in acid until they were beyond recognition and then bleach Lincoln's family's cabin clean. Then there was the short ceremony and the day I needed to recover because I was so fucking emotional.

But eventually, we got there.

We showed up at the law firm my dad hired years ago wearing our shiny wedding bands, demanding Lincoln's dad hand over the documents I had to sign to get my inheritance.

"Where's Lincoln?" his father asked. His dark gray suit was crumpled, his full salt-and-pepper hair pulled up like he ran his hand through it one too many times.

He didn't seem like the obnoxious, entitled man Lincoln described him to be or the man whom Vaughn had stalked. He looked genuinely concerned for his son, the redness in his eyes speaking volumes of the sleepless nights he must've had.

"I don't know, sir." I grinned, giving him an equally innocent act to the one I gave his son right before we ended him. "They were all still there when I left Saturday night. See, I wasn't feeling well, and my husband had to come pick me up."

"Don't fucking lie to me." He prowled around his desk toward me, only to have Vaughn's palm flatten against his chest.

My husband in his black three-piece suit stepped between us and tsked. "I wouldn't if I were you."

"My son disappeared, and she knows something!" Richmond's spit only served to add to his maniacal outlook. "Where is he?"

Vaughn wiped his cheeks with the back of his hand but otherwise didn't so much as wink. "Your son is none of our concern. That's the police's job to find him."

"Fuck them. I already hired a private detective." His accusatory eyes darted between Vaughn and me. "You…the both of you did something to them. I'll find out. You wait and see."

Richmond Hopkins wasn't stupid. He knew his son. He knew who I was. He probably figured out Lincoln tried to do something he shouldn't have, which he did, and got punished for it. Which he also did.

But without any proof, all he had was his hunch.

"Perfect then." Vaughn nodded, his dark gaze enough to frighten the biggest of men, and Richmond, who backed off to the other side of the office, was no different. *"Send your dogs, let's see what they find. Until then, do your bloody job. The inheritance papers. Move it."*

"Darling?" My husband pokes his head into the small space, tearing me out of my daydreams.

"Everything okay?" One of his hands rises to thread his fingers in my hair, the other one to rub my belly. "Or do you need a spanking to make you feel better?"

"Ha." I blush, then I remember we'll have time for that where we're going.

"So…?"

"I just…" I bow my chin to my chest, playing with the fabric of my dress. I look at my breasts that feel like they tripled their size overnight. "I want to hug them already. Is that weird? To love something so much before you've even seen it?"

"Not at all." Vaughn's fingers tug on my hair, forcing me to tilt my head up. "That's how I felt about you."

"Oh." My eyes tear up.

"And it's exactly how I feel about our kids." He leans down to kiss my lips, biting the bottom one and sending shivers down my spine. "They'll be perfect. Just like their mom. Now come on, we have a long flight ahead of us, and I'm desperate to take that dress off you in our new home."

"Okay, Daddy."

My lips hike up thinking about our move to Spain. It's a stopover until I give birth and then maybe after another pregnancy. Once we have our babies, we'll start our way-overdue revenge trip to London to avenge Vaughn's family by taking down the Fletchers one by one.

"Good girl." His black eyes consume me, the heat in them making me clench my thighs with an everlasting need. "My perfect little raven. Now, let's move. We've got a whole new life waiting for us."

"Forever."

"Yes, my love. Forever."

The end.

Eva Marks

About the Author
Writing edgy spicy novellas, addicted to HEAs, and an avid plant lady.

Stay in Touch!
Newsletter for new releases: https://bit.ly/3c3K2nt
Instagram: https://bit.ly/3QQ3Nh4
TikTok: www.tiktok.com/@evamarkswrites
Facebook Group: https://bit.ly/3LnFpln
Website: https://www.evamarkswrites.com

Obsession

More Books from Eva Marks

Blue Series
Little Beginning, book #0.5
Little Blue, book #1
Little Halloween, book #2
Little Valentine, book #3

Adult Games Series
Toy Shop, book #1
A New Year's Toy, book #2

Standalones
Primal
Dad Can't Know
I'll Be Watching You
Obsession
Stalked – Coming December 7, 2023

Obsession: A Dark Stalker Romance
Coming December 7, 2023. Pre-orders are live on
Amazon

She owns me—heart, body, and soul. It's only
fair that I own her, too.
And I will. Soon…

I have one rule I've never broken in all my years
as a doctor.
I don't sleep with patients. Never even wanted to.
Until I laid my eyes on *her*.
Prue Bishop is everything I'm not. Sweet and
innocent. The sunshine to my darkness.
And yet in the short while we've known each
other, she's changed me from being a good person to
what you might call *morally gray.*
See, I can't help but stalk her when we're not
together…
And visit her at night.
If she had any idea what I do while she's asleep,
she'd probably never forgive me.
I can't stop myself. Not when it comes to her.
It's a good thing that I'm there, though.
Because I'm not the only one who's watching her.
But I am the only one to save her.

Don't forget to lock your door…

Printed in Great Britain
by Amazon

29739603R10208